DEATH SENTENCES

Death

Sentences

KAWAMATA CHIAKI

TRANSLATED BY **THOMAS LÁMARRE**
AND **KAZUKO Y. BEHRENS**
FOREWORD BY **TAKAYUKI TATSUMI**

UNIVERSITY OF MINNESOTA PRESS
MINNEAPOLIS • LONDON

Originally published in Japanese by Chuo-Koronsha Publishers as *Genshi-gari*. Copyright 1984 by Kawamata Chiaki.

English translation, Foreword, and Afterword copyright 2012 by the Regents of the University of Minnesota

Published by the University of Minnesota Press
111 Third Avenue South, Suite 290
Minneapolis, MN 55401-2520
http://www.upress.umn.edu

Produced by Wilsted & Taylor Publishing Services

Library of Congress Cataloging-in-Publication Data
Kawamata Chiaki, 1948–
[Genshi-gari. English]
Death sentences / Kawamata Chiaki ; translated by Thomas
Lamarre and Kazuko Y. Behrens ; foreword by Takayuki Tatsumi.
ISBN 978-0-8166-5454-3 (hc : acid-free paper)
ISBN 978-0-8166-5455-0 (pb : acid-free paper)
I. Lamarre, Thomas, 1959–. II. Behrens, Kazuko Y. III. Title.
PL855.A863G4613 2012
895.6'36—dc23   2011047602

Printed in the United States of America on acid-free paper

The University of Minnesota is an
equal-opportunity educator and employer.

19 18 17 16 15 14 13 12   10 9 8 7 6 5 4 3 2 1

WILLIAM F. SIBLEY

IN MEMORIAM

CONTENTS

From Surrealism to Postmodernism

Takayuki Tatsumi

In 1984, George Orwell's symbolic year, Kawamata Chiaki (born in 1948) published his ambitious novel *Genshi-gari*. Here translated as *Death Sentences,* the Japanese title literally means "hunting the magic poems" or "in pursuit of the magic poems." Kawamata was one of the most talented of the second generation of Japanese science fiction authors to debut in the 1970s, and *Genshi-gari* attracted a wide audience and received good reviews, winning the fifth Japan SF Grand Prize, the Japanese equivalent of the west's Nebula Award, established in 1980 by Science Fiction and Fantasy Writers of Japan. In order to complete this masterpiece the author had patiently developed its plot for more than three years. This novel actually grew out of a single mysterious image of André Breton waiting for a young poetic genius at a café in Montmartre on February 2, 1948, an image that had already served as the opening scene of Kawamata's archetypal short story "Yubi no Fuyu" (Finger winter), published in the December 1977 issue of the science fiction monthly *Kiso-Tengai.*

Of course, Breton is the literary historical figure who inaugurated the surrealist movement in Paris with "The Surrealist Manifesto" he published in 1924. Without this guru of surrealism, we could never have attained the perspective that allows us to trace a magic artistic genealogy from Hieronymus Bosch, Pieter Brueghel, and Albrecht Dürer down to Marcel Duchamp, Giorgio De Chirico, André Masson, and Salvador

Dalí. Developing and even repurposing Sigmund Freud's psychoanalytical theory, Breton's surrealist poetics renovated the conventional view of reality and created a new framework of reality peculiar to the twentieth century. Therefore, the primal scene in chapter 2 of Breton waiting for a young Asian French poet in Paris is intriguing, for it naturally induces us to expect that something wonderful will happen. And indeed, glancing at the manuscript of the poet Who May (whose name sounds like a pun on the Japanese term *fumei,* meaning "anonymous"), Breton has to acknowledge his special talent and the supernatural wonder of the poem. What Who May composes, however, cannot help but seduce whoever reads it into another world, depriving the reader of his or her life. Who May's poetry is at once alluring and fatal. His poems "Another World," "Mirror," and "The Gold of Time" haunt the reader like drugs and make victims of a number of Dadaists and surrealists and their literary and cultural descendants: Arshile Gorky, Paul Éluard, Francis Picabia, André Breton, Marcel Duchamp, and even Philip K. Dick. Who May's poems attract and murder so many addicts that a poeticaholic crackdown takes place around the globe. This is the beginning of the magic poem plague that will afflict human beings until the twenty-second century. The imperative: throw away Who May's poem before you read it. Nonetheless, Who May's poetry continues to be copied and perused by fans. Finally, André Breton's suitcase, which secretly contains Who May's manuscripts, is purchased by the Seito Department Store, which attempts to mount an exhibition of surrealism with a detailed catalog to be edited by Kirin Publishers, whose name evokes not only the mythic Kirin but also Salvador Dalí's famous surrealist painting *Burning Giraffe.* This is only the beginning of a magic poetic plague on a global scale, more horrific than anything inflicted by historical weapons of mass destruction.

Fans of science fiction may be puzzled to see Philip K. Dick included in the list of Who May's possible victims. Although Dick endured great mental and financial hardship during his lifetime, since his death in 1982 (the same year that saw the completion of Ridley Scott's film *Blade Runner* based on Dick's 1968 novel *Do Androids Dream of Electric Sheep?*) Dick has become known as one of the United States' major science fiction writers and now is among the American literary historical figures canonized in the Library of America series upon the publication of a three-book boxed set, *The Philip K. Dick Collection,* with an endorsement by Fredric Jameson referring to Dick as "the Shakespeare of science fiction." Nevertheless, it might be hard for a general audience to identify him as one of the postsurrealists. Therefore, at first glance this list of Who May's victims may look absurd. And yet, readers familiar with the New Wave movement (which promoted *speculative fiction* instead of *science fiction*) will recall that British writer J. G. Ballard's New Wave manifesto "Which Way to Inner Space?" (1962) was deeply influenced by surrealist poetics. While modernism as such was alive and well in the first half of the twentieth century, Ballard and other proponents of the New Wave movement headed for inner space in the 1960s instead of the outer space explored by conventional hard-core science fiction, and they revolutionized the conventional idea of science fiction by resurrecting the spirit of modernism, especially surrealism. This is how Dick's works, which had been the products of inner space from the beginning, came to be appreciated alongside the works of other American speculative writers such as Thomas Disch and Samuel Delany. This viewpoint permits us to reconsider Dick as another descendant of the surrealist tradition.

What I would like to stress here is that many years before writing *Death Sentences* in 1984, as early as the 1970s, Kawamata had already taken for granted the intersection between surrealism and New Wave speculative fiction. What is more, in his introduction to the reprinted Japanese edition of Dick's highly surrealistic novel *Martian Time-Slip,* Kawamata confesses: "If someone like Mephistopheles showed up and proposed to endow me with the same genius as my literary heroes, I wouldn't hesitate to claim Philip K. Dick's talent and to start to write *Martian Time-Slip* by myself."[1] Originally published in 1964, *Martian Time-Slip* was very quickly translated into Japanese in 1966 and amazed us with its dense representation of the surrealistic inner space of a schizophrenic, autistic, and precognitive boy, Manfred Steiner, who has the supernatural ability to travel through time. So there is no doubt that Kawamata's first encounter with the translation of the novel determined and developed his taste in science fiction. In fact, before making his debut as a fiction writer, Kawamata published his translation of Dick's short story "Small Town" in the October 1971 issue of *Hayakawa's SF Magazine*. Here I find it useful to compare two key passages from *Martian Time-Slip* and *Death Sentences*. First, let me remind readers of the alluring spell haunting the inner space of human beings in *Martian Time-Slip*:

> A voice in his mind said, Gubble gubble gubble, I am gubble gubble gubble gubble.
>
> Stop, he said to it.
>
> Gubble, gubble, gubble, gubble, it answered.
>
> Dust fell on him from the walls. The room creaked with age and dust, rotting around him. Gubble, gubble, gubble, the room said. The Gubbler is here to gubble gubble you and make you into gubbish.
>
> Getting unsteadily to his feet he managed to walk, step by step, over to Arnie's amplifier and tape recorder. . . .
>
> The door to the kitchen opened a crack, and an eye watched him; he could not tell whose it was.
>
> I have to get out of here, Jack Bohlen said to himself. Or fight it off; I have to break this, throw it away from me or be eaten.
>
> It is eating me up.[2]

Next, let me trace the way Kawamata Chiaki re-created Dick's surrealist inner space within his "another world," which is so surrealistic that in the novel it becomes the obsession of hardcore surrealists and their descendants, including Dick himself. The following scene reveals how Who May's magic poem excites and even infuriates André Breton:

A fish. Dobaded. Its eyeball sliced down the middle. Sections quivering. Images reflected on the split lens are stained with blood. Dobaded. The city of people mirrored there is dyed madder red. Reversal of pressure, dobaded, and there you go! It's taking you there. . . .

There was no room for doubt.

Breton had experienced it. At the command of these verses, he had been transported to the world that Who May had named "Another World" and then had returned. . . .

Breton held his eyes shut tight.

(Is this thing poetry?! Dobaded! No, it isn't like poetry. It is a spell! It is a sort of . . . hypnotism! It is like the use of words in hypnotism.) . . .

(*He must have made a deal. That's how it was decided. At midnight he had carved summoning spells on the floor and summoned the devil. And in exchange for the secret of words, he sold his soul to the devil.*)

As such thoughts crossed his mind, Breton grew angrier still, at his own foolishness.

(. . . in any case, dobaded . . . shit!)[3]

While the incantation "Gubble" seems to invade the Martian mindscape in *Martian Time-Slip,* in *Death Sentences* the spell "Dobaded" dominates whoever reads the magic poem and transports them literally into another world. Yes, what Kawamata learned from Dick and wanted to expand on is the performative and even science fictional aspect of language itself. Furthermore, if you take notice of Breton's response to Who May's poem, "And in exchange for the secret of words, he sold his soul to the devil," you will naturally recall Kawamata's own obsession with Dick's novel and his mention of Mephistopheles. Therefore, it might be said that Kawamata composed *Death Sentences* as his own version of *Martian Time-Slip.*

This background will make it easier to understand the scene in which David Hare, editor of the surrealist journal *VVV* (Triple V) that Breton and his fellow surrealists published in New

York, gives Breton his candid opinion of Who May's work. Though Who May's poem cannot help but conjure up Breton's own "Soluble Fish" (1924), published almost simultaneously with "The Surrealist Manifesto," Breton has no idea how to evaluate Who May's work, and Hare tells him, "I would wait another fifteen years and bring it out in a science fiction magazine." Note that they discuss the magic poem in New York City in 1943. J. G. Ballard, the guru of New Wave speculative fiction, made his debut with a short story "Prima Belladonna" in 1956, very close to Hare's "fifteen years" later. So Breton finds it hard to distinguish between surrealism and Who May's poetics, whereas Hare very easily defines the poem as different from Breton's hard-core surrealism. This heated controversy makes the novel *Death Sentences* a kind of meta–science fiction, science fiction that holds within itself a critical commentary on its own generic framework.

Kawamata Chiaki; or, The Making of a Speculative Fiction Writer

At this point, let me take the opportunity to sum up the author's biographical data. On December 4, 1948 (the very year André Breton was waiting for Who May in Paris), Kawamata Chiaki was born in Otaru on Hokkaidō, the northernmost of Japan's four main islands. Hokkaidō was the vast homeland of the Ainu race but was incorporated into modern Japan after the Meiji Restoration in 1968 and separated into four prefectures. If science fiction is the result of a certain kind of frontier spirit (of the kind seen in the postrevolutionary United States), it is not very difficult to set up an analogy between America as a New World and Hokkaidō as another New World. Therefore, I do not think it is a coincidence that Hokkaidō has nurtured quite a few science fiction writers, such as Arakami Yoshio, Kojima Fuyuki, Tachihara Tōya, and Enjo Toh. In 1966, as a student at Otaru Oyo High School, Kawamata published a short story "Fuyu ga kaette kita" (Winter has come back) in the first issue of the fanzine *Asteroid* (later renamed *Planetoid*). The story was quickly reprinted in issue 104 of *Ūchūjin,* the oldest and the most authentic fanzine in Japan, edited by one of the founding fathers of Japanese science fiction, Shibano Takumi (1926–2010). This means that even as a high school kid, Kawamata was already famous for being a BNF (Big Name Fan) in Japanese science fiction fandom. After entering Keio University in Tokyo in 1968, Kawamata wrote his BA thesis on Shimao Toshio (1917–1986), one of the most surrealistic among Japan's mainstream writers. (Shimao's 1960 short story collection *The Sting of Death,* which features his mentally ill wife as the heroine, was made into a movie directed by Oguri Kōhei in 1990, a film that won the FIPRESCI Prize and the Grand Prize of the Jury at the 1990 Cannes Film Festival.)

We should also note that Kawamata's alma mater, Keio University, from the early twentieth century had functioned as a literary incubator for Japanese surrealist poets such as Nishiwaki Junzaburō, Satō Saku, Yoshimasu Gōzō, and Asabuki Ryōji, most of whom taught at Keio as scholar-critics. Especially important was Nishiwaki Junzaburō, a one-time finalist for the Nobel Prize in Literature, who studied in England between 1922 and 1925. (In the year 1922, T. S. Eliot's published his modernist masterpiece "The Waste Land," and 1925 was one year after André Breton's "The Surrealist Manifesto.") Nishiwaki so fully imbibed the transatlantic modernist atmosphere that on coming back home he got a professorship in the Faculty of Letters at Keio University and started playing the role of surrealism's ideologue by popularizing transatlantic modernist poetics. One of his early books on literary theory, *Chōgenjitsushugi shiron* (Surrealist poetics, 1929), is filled with illuminating remarks like the following:

> Presently in France there is a movement called *surréalisme.* This rather inclusive name subsumes members of what used to be called cubism or dada, who are now content to be under this name. . . . In December 1924, a magazine called *La Révolution surréaliste* appeared in Paris. In its introduction, the editor urged us to use dreams as the material for poetry. . . . It is as an inevi-

table development from Baudelaire that surrealism has become a prevalent mode of art in recent years. In the final analysis, surrealism and supernaturalism are the same and share a classical tradition of art.[4]

Given that most of the early surrealist poets in Japan could be called Nishiwaki's descendants, it was very natural for Kawamata to establish his own theory and style of speculative fiction by imbibing the surrealist tradition of his alma mater.

What matters most for Kawamata is that the early 1970s, when he was studying at Keio University, saw the beginning of the golden age of science fiction in Japan. In 1970, when the World Expo took place in Osaka, an International Science Fiction Symposium was convened by Komatsu Sakyō, the dean of Japanese science fiction, and other first-generation members of Science Fiction and Fantasy Writers of Japan, with British writers Arthur C. Clarke and Brian Aldiss in attendance, along with American writer Frederik Pohl, Canadian writer Judith Merril, and Vasili Zakharchenko and Eremei Parnov from the Soviet Union. It is noteworthy that Judith Merril returned to Japan again in March 1972 and lived for half a year in Higashi-Koganei, a suburb in western Tokyo now well known as the hometown of anime guru Miyazaki Hayao's Studio Ghibli since 1992. In this way Merril influenced Japanese writers by preaching the possibilities of science fiction as speculative fiction, as represented by the New Wave experiments of J. G. Ballard and other writers who were then on the rise. Moreover, Merril contributed much to the direction of Japanese science fiction by holding discussions with translators such as Itō Norio and Asakura Hisashi and promoting the translation of Japanese science fiction into English. In his memorial to Merril, "Higashi-Koganei no ōgon hibi" ("Golden Days in Higashi-Koganei," 1997), Asakura Hisashi recollects how this superb mentor elevated his professional life during these six months in 1972. The translation project Merril had begun was not completed during her lifetime, but friends Gene Van Troyer and Grania Davis spent thirty-five years compiling a Japanese science fiction anthology called *Speculative Japan: Outstanding Tales of Japanese Science Fiction and Fantasy*.[5] The publication of this volume coincided with the first World Science Fiction Convention held in Asia, Nippon 2007 (nicknamed "Nipponcon" in the United States), which took place at Pacifico Yokohama.

After the genre of Japanese science fiction was formally started with the first fanzine *Uchūjin* (from 1957) and the first successful commercial monthly *Hayakawa's SF Magazine* (from 1959), the first generation of writers and translators very quickly and concisely simulated, within the decade of the 1960s, the half-century history of Anglo-American science fiction since the 1920s. This first generation of writers born in the 1920s and '30s—including the so-called "Big Three," Hoshi Shin'ichi, Komatsu Sakyō, and Tsutsui Yasutaka—succeeded in establishing not only the genre but also the market for Japanese science fiction. The second-generation writers, most of them baby boomers, made their debuts in the 1970s: Hori Akira, Kajio Shinji, Yokota Jun'ya, Tanaka Kōji, Yamada Masaki, Yamao Yūko, Hagio Moto, and Kawamata. While the first-generation writers found it necessary to imitate and innovate upon Anglo-American hard-core science fiction, the second-generation writers inherited their precursors' heritage and also imbibed the essence of the British New Wave movement, which had been paving the way from outer space back to inner space since the late 1960s, with Ballard, Dick, and Stanislaw Lem as its new idols. In 1970, Yamano Kōichi, one of the most speculative writers of the first generation, inaugurated the new magazine *NW-SF*, which started attracting new talent among speculative fiction writers, including Kawamata.

As a student at Keio University, Kawamata made his debut in 1971 as a science fiction critic with an essay titled "Baraado wa doko e iku ka" (Which direction is Ballard headed?), published in volume 3 of *NW-SF*. After graduation, he began working for the advertising agency Hakuhōdō and published his own New Wave manifesto, "Ashita wa dotchi da" (Which way to tomorrow?) in the April 1972 issue of *Hayakawa's SF Magazine*. He completed his long and influential essay "Yume no kotoba,

kotoba no yume" (Dream words, word dreams) in 1975 and published it in book form in 1981.[6]

The originality of Kawamata's view of science fiction lies in his emphasis not on out-of-control technology but on "out-of-control sensitivity." His manifesto references everything from literature (Lewis Carroll, William Hope Hodgson, Edgar Rice Burroughs, C. L. Moore, Boris Vian, Ray Bradbury, Ballard, Shimao Toshio, Kurahashi Yumiko) to the icons of rock and roll and J-pop (Rolling Stones, Grand Funk Railroad, Free, Zunō Keisatsu, Yoshida Takurō, and even Asaoka Megumi). After the New Wave movement, science fiction changed from a take-it-or-leave-it format to a new style that could transform itself freely from within. While Japanese science fiction of the previous decade had treated the genre as a prediction of civilization's future, the writers of the 1970s thought of it simply as one of many "cultures" that are arrayed together and interact or negotiate with one another. Kawamata does not distinguish between Edgar Rice Burroughs and William S. Burroughs; what matters to him is the strategy for questioning existing literary discourses and redefining inner space as another world, a world growing out of "nothing" in a utopian sense. While Augustinian Christian theology used to dismiss "nothingness" as a kind of evil deficiency or vacuum, Sir Thomas More's *Utopia* (1516) reevaluated the idea of "nowhere," anticipating the rise of "nonsense" literature that subverts our common sense. As Kawamata states: "I find it unreasonable that SF, the most liberating of literary genres, should also follow nineteenth-century novelistic conventions based on the most immature logic and philosophy. It is not that SF has become diffused, but that it has regained its natural status after a long history of unjust repression."[7] It is noteworthy that in the age of a counterculture that bravely vindicated *nothing, nowhere, nonsense, vacuum,* and even *entropy,* Kawamata's insightful criticism coincided with Tony Tanner's masterful overview of postmodern fiction *City of Words: American Fiction, 1950–70* (1971) and Susan Stewart's strategic intervention into literary history *Nonsense: Aspects of Intertextuality in Folklore and Literature* (1979).[8]

After completing the serial publication of "Yume no kotoba, kotoba no yume" in 1975, Kawamata made his debut as
a fiction writer with a short story "Yume no kamera" (Dream
camera) published in the May 1976 issue of *Kisō-Tengai*. In 1980,
he resigned from Hakuhōdō to be a full-time writer. In 1981,
he received the Seiun Award, the Japanese equivalent of the
Hugo Award, for *Kaseijin senshi* (A prehistory of Martians),
which describes the fate of a tribe of kangaroos mentally up-
lifted and biogenetically transformed to be workers on Mars
that end up becoming independent from human beings.
Kawamata then began to write numerous novels or series in a
variety of genres: hard-core science fiction, fantasy, adventure,
and others. Highly ambitious experiments with a diversity of
literary styles made it possible for him to blend the sensibility
of speculative fiction with the format of entertainment novels.
When *Death Sentences* (his sixteenth novel) won the fifth Japan
SF Grand Prize in 1984, his acceptance speech was very illuminating, for it sharply redefined the novel: "For me *Death Sentences* is clearly a sort of wish-fulfillment novel. If I myself had
been endowed with the poetic genius Who May employed to
invent antigravity words, I would not have found it necessary
to weave this narrative. In this sense, *Death Sentences* could well
be considered a kind of Mad Scientist Fiction."[9] This statement
immediately reminds us of Kawamata's 1980 comment about
"writing *Martian Time-Slip* by myself." Taking a glance at the
steps from Dick to Who May, whose magic poems captivated
not only the original surrealists but also Dick himself, one
may feel convinced that by writing *Death Sentences* Kawamata
attempted to transcend the limit of what Dick had achieved.
Here it is helpful to refer to the report of Toyota Aritsune, chair
of the SF Grand Prize selection committee:

> As regards the idea of the novel, *Death Sentences* is a
> kind of fantasy. . . . The author's storytelling is skill-
> ful. Quite a few surrealist writers and artists including
> André Breton could be compared with science fiction
> writers. Some critics go so far as to say contemporary

science fiction should incorporate into itself the surrealist tradition. Nonetheless, Kawamata Chiaki is not content with this redefinition of the genre. Digesting the surrealist movement as part of his material, he succeeds in completing a brilliant entertainment novel. A wonderful page-turner, *Death Sentences* attracts even those who are not interested in surrealism.[10]

Death Sentences:
Within or without Japan's Postmodernism

I have emphasized that *Death Sentences* is a literary historical novel foregrounding the surrealist movement and reappropriating Philip K. Dick's speculative imagination. However, Kawamata's literary masterpiece can be interpreted in any number of other ways as well. For example, my afterword to the Japanese paperback edition focuses on the analogy between the novel and George Orwell's *1984* (written in 1948 and published in 1949), for *Death Sentences* undoubtedly describes another totalitarian society desperately censoring literary texts, which reflects back on the repression of the surrealists themselves.[11] If one recalls Kawamata's fascination with Ray Bradbury, it is also possible to assume that he came up with the concept for the novel by way of Bradbury's homage to Orwell, *Fahrenheit 451* (published in 1953). However, when I wrote the afterword I was not aware that the Orwellian year 1984 saw the rise of the cyberpunk movement, ignited by William Gibson's *Neuromancer,* published that year. Therefore, today it is also possible to set up an analogy between Who May's another world, Kawamata's version of inner space, and Gibson's cyberspace. What is more, in the wake of the multiple disasters plaguing eastern Japan in March 2011, Who May's magic poems will conjure up the menace not only of fatal drugs but also of nuclear disasters: the original term in Japanese for the "magic poem" (*genshi*) has the same pronunciation as the term for "atom" (*genshi*) and thereby revives the image of the atomic bomb (*genshi bakudan*). Just as the Japanese government continues to attempt to seal nuclear leaks, this novel's agents try to defend against magic poetic leaks.

And yet, after rereading *Death Sentences* more recently, I also feel the need to point out the novel's vivid description of atmosphere during the early years of Pax Japonica, another name for the rise of Japan's postmodernism. As Ezra Vogel predicted in his best-seller *Japan as Number One* (1979), Japan achieved huge economic success in the 1980s and ended up expanding and exploding its bubble economy in 1993.[12] Note how Who May's magic poems are imported into Japan: chapter 3 in *Death Sentences,* "Undiscovered Century," narrates the way a small press called Kirin Publishing gets involved with the Seito department store's huge exhibition *Undiscovered Century: A National Exhibition on the Age of Surrealism.* The exhibition is based on materials recovered from a newly discovered trunk of André Breton's, a trunk that also contains Who May's manuscripts. The whole exhibition is organized by "Hakuden," one of the largest advertising agencies in Japan. All the editors at Kirin Publishing have to do is edit the exhibition catalog. According to Kawamata, his vivid description of the meeting about the exhibition draws from his own experience as a member of Hakuhōdō, the model for Hakuden. We may also note that the entry on Kirin Publishers in the project dossier distributed at the first meeting lists one of their publications as "Yubi no fuyu" (Finger winter), the title of the 1977 Kawamata short story on which *Death Sentences* is based. Therefore, this scene of the first meeting is semiautobiographical and metafictional.

Most important is the novel's characterization of Tsujimi Yūzō, general owner of the Seito Group and connoisseur of fine arts and literature, who proposed the idea of holding this surrealist exhibition. Kawamata claims that this businessman and his department store are imaginary, inspired by the author's involvement with the art exhibitions sponsored by Mitsukoshi, the oldest department store in Japan, during his time at Hakuhōdō. But the location of the Seito department store in Ikebukuro recalls the Seibu department store—then in the avant-garde of Japanese department store chains—and

its ex-owner Tsutsumi Seiji (born in 1927), a mainstream author who has written under the pen name Takashi Tsujii and
whose poems and novels have won numerous literary prizes
such as the Tanizaki Prize and the Yomiuri Prize. When the
novel's character Tsujimi Yūzō introduces himself as a big
fan of Kirin Publishers and explains why he puts "so much
effort into cultural ventures," he cannot help but recall Tsutsumi Seiji, who wanted to foster the cultural independence
of Japanese consumers by selling cultural artifacts in addition
to everyday goods. In short, Tsutsumi Seiji aimed to sell not
only visible and tangible items but also an invisible intellectual atmosphere. His strategy eventually coincided with the
way that books on French structuralist and poststructuralist
thought began to become popular with Japanese consumers,
and it is at this point historically that Japan's postmodernism becomes a cultural phenomenon. As Marilyn Ivy acutely
points out, the early 1980s saw Japan become a postmodern
nation capable of consuming even knowledge or "new knowledge," which is very close to what is termed *theory* in American
literary critical circles: "Japan presents the spectacle of a thoroughly commodified world of knowledge."[13] Ivy recognizes a
parallel between the new academics who turned theory into a
commodity and who mediated between the university and the
masses, and figures like Itoi Shigesato, the star copywriter who
became famous working for PARCO, one of the department
stores run by Tsutsumi Seiji's Seibu Group, and who "medi-
ates between the capitalist and the masses."[14] Of course, given
that the bursting of the bubble economy brought about Japan's
decline in the mid-1990s, the early 1980s postmodernism fos-
tered by Tsutsumi Seiji and his splendid fellows might be re-
garded a shameful episode in contemporary history. However,
Death Sentences was written and acclaimed within this historical
context, skillfully capturing and even keenly criticizing the essence of Japan's late capitalist and postmodernist imagination.

Here it is not my intent to recuperate the zeitgeist of early
1980s Japan but to stress the performative aspect of *Death Sentences* as a text. Although I have considered the magic spell or

speech act of Who May's poems, it is Kawamata's novel that really demonstrates the performative aspect of language, by prophesying and creating the later history of Japan's postmodernism. Tsutsumi Seiji's Seibu department store aroused consumers' interest in Dadaism and surrealism with an exhibition of Arshile Gorky's work in July and August 1963 and a Marcel Duchamp exhibition in September 1981. Therefore, it is highly plausible that Kawamata Chiaki noted the popularity of Duchamp caused by this exhibition and incorporated this genius into his new novel. Nonetheless, while the Seibu Group as led by Tsutsumi enjoyed its heyday between 1975 and 1982, the fatal decline of the economy in 1991 required him to retire and pay Seibu's debts, amounting to ten billion yen (about $100 million). Contemporary cultural historians tend to assume that it was Tsutsumi's post-leftist progressive ideology that functioned as the engine for accelerating Japan's high-growth economy and eventually exploding its late capitalism, which ironically passed the death sentence on Japan's postmodernism.

With this historical context in mind, readers may note that the fate of the Seito department store's exhibition "Undiscovered Century" in Kawamata's narrative unwittingly but miraculously predicts the fate of Japanese postmodernism nurtured by Tsutsumi Seiji's Seibu Group. Indeed, *Death Sentences* is primarily a kind of speech-act novel in the tradition of the linguistic science fiction cultivated by Stanislaw Lem, Samuel Delany, and Ian Watson. And yet this novel not only describes an alternate literary history created by Who May's magic poem but also performs and produces Japan's real contemporary history, much earlier and much more vividly than Haruki Murakami, whose new novel *1Q84* represents another take on *1984*.

I hope you will share my pleasure on your own fabulous trip through Kawamata Chiaki's masterpiece *Death Sentences*.

Bon voyage!

DEATH SENTENCES

THE TRACKER

1

Someone was coming out of the apartment building—the woman.

Sakamoto took the unlit cigarette from his mouth, tossed it on the ground, and stubbed it out with the tip of his shoe.

That was the signal.

With an air of perfect nonchalance, the three detectives entered the building just as she was leaving.

With a brief glance to make sure it was she, Sakamoto began casually walking after her.

Another man, a young detective called Harada, passed Sakamoto, tailing the woman at about fifteen paces.

Harada's role was to distract her.

It didn't much matter if she noticed him or not, he was going to stick to her. Once she caught on to him, he'd make himself scarce.

Basically, Harada's presence served only to draw attention away from the real tail, Sakamoto.

Harada was the decoy.

He'd dressed to call attention to himself.

Leather jacket, leather pants, leather boots. He'd added a splash of color to a greased spike of hair.

He looked really punk.

And it looked pretty good on him.

He swaggered along, hamming it up.

Sakamoto chuckled inwardly.

If Harada overdid it, though, he was going to scare her off.

The woman came to the main street.

As she waited for the light to change, she cast a glance at Harada.

She didn't seem particularly worried, though.

The light turned green.

She crossed the street, paused as if to take her bearings, and turned right.

There was a bus stop just ahead.

If she caught a taxi, Harada's part was over. An unmarked car was waiting ready to pick up Sakamoto and continue the chase.

But, for whatever reason, it looked like she'd opted for the bus.

Checking her watch, she got in line for the bus.

There were three people ahead of her and Harada right behind her.

Sakamoto walked past them to take a closer look at the woman.

Not a doubt.

It was Miura Sachiko.

Heavy makeup masked her features. But even the thick eyeliner couldn't hide the hollow look in her eyes.

Sakamoto bought a pack of Seven Stars at the kiosk right by the bus stop.

Opening the pack, he circled back and got in line behind Harada.

"Uh, 'scuse me . . ."

Mumbling something senseless, he deliberately swung around, knocking her in the back with his elbow.

She ignored him.

Without even turning, she stepped forward a bit and stood there rigidly.

Concealed behind Harada, Sakamoto watched her.

The bus finally came. It was bound for Shibuya.

The sun was still high. It was just past four.

The six passengers filed onto the bus.

The bus was pretty empty. Quite a few seats were left.

Miura Sachiko placed herself in the middle of the bus near the door.

Just across and down from her, in the seat reserved for seniors, Harada plopped himself down, stretching his legs into the aisle.

The other passengers gave him the hairy eyeball.

Sakamoto used the opportunity to move unobtrusively to the rear of the bus.

The bus began moving.

He turned to look out the rear window: a dirty white Corolla was tailing the bus.

The guy in the driver's seat was his partner.

He'd take over if the woman caught on to Sakamoto.

For the moment there didn't seem much to worry about, though.

The woman gazed out the window as if her mind were somewhere else. Clearly, by the looks of her, she was "afflicted." She looked well past the middle stages. If so, she'd be spending about 30 percent of her waking hours in a state of utter delirium, soul adrift. Her sense of reality would be tenuous at best.

You couldn't take chances, though.

In some cases the afflicted gained exceedingly acute perceptual abilities.

Sakamoto, cautious, calmed his mind in case she could sense his concern.

Only about five more stops till the terminus at Shibuya station. As they approached the station, the traffic became congested.

Just then—

Miura Sachiko suddenly stood up. She pressed the buzzer.

From the reserved seats, Harada rolled an eye in her direction.

The bus was approaching the last stop before the terminus.

The bus slowed, pulled in the far lane, and stopped. The door opened.

Harada followed the woman.

Sakamoto also got off, concealing himself behind Harada.

"Hey there."

Harada sauntered out in front of her.

"How about a cup of coffee or something, you and me?"

She did not reply.

She pushed past him and crossed into the intersection.

"Snobby bitch."

Harada gave her an angry look.

Then, with a shrug of indifference, he walked rapidly off, moving with the crowd.

Miura Sachiko paused for a moment on the other side of the intersection. She watched Harada go into the station directly ahead.

Seconds later—

With what looked like a sigh of relief, she relaxed her shoulders.

And then she started walking again.

Sakamoto tailed her.

Since people had not yet begun to leave work, the streets weren't so jammed.

Most of the passersby were students and housewives.

With the crowds rather dense but not congested, tailing was an easy matter.

Miura Sachiko turned left at Shibuya Station, heading toward Miyamasuzaka. She was walking fairly fast now.

She wore a long coat with a purse slung over her shoulder.

Her clothes were nothing remarkable. But she was attractive and shapely enough that you might have pegged her as early twenties.

Actually—

Sakamoto figured her real age to be forty-two. She looked about twenty years younger.

This was one of the characteristic "symptoms" of the afflicted. It was said to be an effect of their state of delirium in which the soul drifted free of the body. But little progress had been made on a detailed account of causes and effects. You weren't supposed to look for explanations. That just slowed things down. The idea was to eradicate it, not figure it out.

In the middle stages, some afflicted would grow physically younger in the blink of an eye, while others would advance horrendously in age.

In any event, the effects varied a great deal from individual to individual. Everything hinged on individual characteristics. But all of the afflicted eventually met with the same end. Researchers referred to the last stage as "salvation."

But whatever you called it, in the end it amounted to a person turning into a complete vegetable. Death was quick to follow.

As if drawn there magnetically, Miura Sachiko entered a coffee shop located halfway up the rise of Miyamasuzaka.

The coffee shop was small with a narrow entrance.

It looked like this was the meeting place.

"All right, see you there at five," she had said on the phone. Sakamoto's team had gathered this much from their wiretap.

About ten minutes left until five.

Sakamoto checked his pace and turned back.

He saw the blinker of the white Corolla as it pulled over. The driver gave him a thumbs-up, and Sakamoto drew a deep breath.

So far things were going smoothly.

The hard part came next. How things turned out depended entirely on Sakamoto's actions.

Sakamoto continued to stroll casually.

Through the coffee shop window he spotted Miura Sachiko out of the corner of his eye.

She was sitting alone.

The waitress had just brought her a glass of water and a hot towel, and she looked up at her to order something.

The shop was pretty much empty.

Except a couple of young slackers glued to a video game, there were no other customers. Neither looked like the guy Sachiko was waiting for.

Sakamoto continued past the shop.

He found a pay phone in front of the building just next door.

He was going to need some information after all.

Sakamoto picked up the receiver coated with car exhaust and dropped a couple of coins in the slot. He started dialing.

The number would connect him with Sachiko's apartment.

After two rings somebody answered.

"Well?" Sakamoto asked.

2

"Not a thing. Clean as a whistle."

It was one of the guys who'd slipped into her apartment as she was leaving.

"Nothing?"

"She must have known we were on to her. Cleaned it inside out, not so much as a speck of dust."

"Hmmm."

"But we did find something kind of interesting in the trash."

"What's that?"

"You know those print kits? The ones you can make post-cards and stuff with?"

"Yeah."

"Well, we found one tossed in with the nonrecyclables."

"Think it's hers?"

"We're looking into it now. But we're pretty sure it is. The landlord saw her taking out quite a pile of trash two nights ago. Apparently, most of it was paper, but the print kit turned up where she'd dumped her trash. She probably thought they'd take it away with the rest, but they can be awfully picky, you know."

"What about the papers?"

"A garbage truck passed yesterday morning. So we've contacted the municipal sanitation crew. Some of our people are already off to the dump."

"Good. Nothing along with the print kit, then?"

"Unfortunately not. But on the surface of the stand—you know, the place where you stick the paper—well, there's a fair amount of ink left on it, and a series of words that look like part of a sentence. The writing is incredibly small and cramped. Anyway, we're not supposed to read it, so we're turning it in as is, as material evidence."

"Do that."

Sakamoto hung up.

A coin dropped into the change slot.

As he fished it out and slipped it into his pants pocket, Sakamoto took a leisurely look out over the darkening city.

The stuff hadn't turned up.

At least we were on the right track.

Maybe our timing was off.

Yet the problem wasn't just one of our timing.

Sensing danger, she would have gotten the stuff out of the house right away. Then she would have hidden it somewhere.

If she was using the print kit, no doubt she made quite a lot of copies.

She wouldn't just toss them in the trash. That would only put her in greater danger. With the new regulations on the use of photocopy machines, which demanded that all copies be numbered and accounted for, people had begun reproducing the stuff manually, copying it by hand or using old-fashioned mimeographs.

As a result, the number of reproductions circulating illicitly had fallen to about one tenth of what it had been with the use of photocopies.

That meant a hike in price.

Reproducing the stuff was a serious offense. Sakamoto and his detectives, as members of a covert deputation of Special Police, had pretty much free rein when it came to dealing out justice.

It was unlikely, then, that after running such a serious risk, she would simply let it go.

Especially not now that she had a buyer.

She had to be hiding it.

She was going to palm it off.

Sakamoto was sure of it.

That's why she'd gone to such great lengths to clean her apartment. Miura Sachiko was planning to fly the coop.

He couldn't let her get away.

Sakamoto pulled his right hand out of his pocket and felt along the left side of his coat. Feeling his piece there, he began to walk.

The Corolla with his partner sat at the edge of the road like a watchdog.

No one had gone in the shop since she had. No one had come out.

After carefully buttoning his coat, Sakamoto opened the door.

The waitress greeted him sullenly as he entered.

"Take any seat that suits you."

Miura Sachiko looked up anxiously.

She quickly looked away.

Ignoring her, Sakamoto went past her and eased into a booth.

A glass of water and a hot towel were plunked down in front of him.

"What'll it be?"

"Hot coffee."

The waitress went in the back.

Sakamoto stretched across to pick up the sports page from the creased newspapers on the seat next to him.

It was yesterday's. Covered with stains.

He folded it so he could read part of it.

The coffee soon arrived. It must have been reheated many times; it looked thick as mud. You don't often see coffee that bad these days.

Without so much as a sip, he knew how it'd taste. That's how coffee had been in the old days, when he was a kid. It didn't occur to him to complain. He didn't care all that much for coffee anyway.

He stirred in lots of cream and sugar and took a sip.

Just then—

The door opened.

A man entered.

Miura Sachiko looked up and nodded at him.

It was him—Sagara.

It looked like this investigation was really on the right track after all.

Sakamoto took a big gulp of the syrupy liquid.

Until about a year ago, Miura Sachiko had worked in an administrative building at one of the city colleges.

Sagara had been Sachiko's boss at the same college. He was assistant director of education.

The two began an affair. Nobody knew exactly when it started.

As a matter of fact, the investigation hadn't really started in earnest till yesterday around three. By four they'd had a tap on her phone.

There hadn't been any real evidence till then. Actually, from the very beginning, there hadn't been much to go on.

It had all been a hunch.

But that's how Sakamoto's team worked.

Whatever it took to get the job done.

Four days ago they'd begun with "whatever it took." Completely by coincidence, one of the team on a stakeout had caught wind of something.

Before long they had a name—Sachi. Initially, though, they didn't know if Sachi was a man or a woman, or even a real person.

Pursuing the source of the rumor turned up the name Miura.

The rest was done on computer. They located the addresses for five persons named Miura Sachiko, which they had printed out only yesterday afternoon.

There was a complete absence of data about one of them.

That's precisely what bothered Sakamoto.

There was something strange about that blank—or so he thought.

Sakamoto concentrated on her.

So it had begun.

First he had had his staff check her records. They did it discreetly, of course.

He himself waited for information from the wiretap.

Confirmation had come at ten last night.

She had received a call at her apartment.

"Hey, it's me."

It was a man. He didn't give his name.

"Everything okay?" Miura Sachiko asked.

"Yeah," he answered.

They'd traced the call back to a pay phone at the college.

"See you there at five, okay?" she said.

"Are you sure everything's all right?"

This time he sounded worried.

"Sure . . . right on track."

"See you then."

That was the end of it.

It was hardly what you'd call a normal conversation.

One of the squad had taken a quick spin to the college.

Since it was the end of the fall term, only a handful of people were still there, grading papers.

Sagara was one of them.

The squad leader waited patiently for them to come out after work, snapped pictures of all six, and returned.

In the meantime, they learned more about Sachiko and Sagara's affair.

She had undergone a divorce in her twenties. She'd remained single since.

After the divorce, Sachiko had found work at the college; it was her alma mater, and she had pulled some strings. Sagara was the one who had hired her.

She had left the job a year and a half ago.

She cited "personal reasons," but apparently her relationship with Sagara had become public knowledge.

She moved into her current apartment.

There was no way that her savings or pension could cover the price of that place.

She must have been bought off.

The two had completely severed ties. At least that's how it looked from the outside.

Now, however, the two of them were clearly doing something together.

This time it was a completely different sort of affair.

Money, that was the only possible motive.

Living high on her settlement money and pension, Miura Sachiko had known a period full of pleasures, even illicit ones. Before she realized it, there wasn't enough left for daily living expenses.

She was already afflicted. A normal job was impossible.

She had only two options for making money. She could sell her body, or she could share with others the very pleasures now eating away at her body.

As things stood, the advance of the symptoms had restored her to an attractive twentysomething, but these days, with teenagers a dime a dozen, even her bout of youthfulness wouldn't bring in enough cash. She was, in fact, a woman in her forties. No matter how hard she tried, it was bound to show.

That left her only the other option.

As the wiretap made clear, the exchange between ex-lovers wasn't a matter of love for sale.

Apparently, Sagara was also strapped for cash.

Paying off Miura Sachiko was the start of his money problems, and his debts had been snowballing ever since.

Their mutual desire for cash might well have made them all cozy and familiar again. This was largely guesswork on Sakamoto's part.

He couldn't be far off, though. And if he were, it didn't much matter. Just about any motive would do.

Last night—

Some of his men had pushed for raiding her apartment right away. Sakamoto had stopped them, however. Something bothered him about the way she'd said that everything was "right on track." A screwup would get them nowhere. They could lose their grip on what really mattered, the stuff.

For the same reason, they hadn't put anyone on Sagara.

Clearly, Sagara hadn't received anything yet. If something made him jumpy, and the transaction didn't happen, it would slip through their fingers.

They'd give him slack, and when it was time to rope him in, they'd rope him.

So far they'd read it dead-on.

Now here they were—Miura Sachiko and Sagara at the table.

3

"How's things?"

"Um . . ."

He could hear their words, faintly.

The conversation was utterly meaningless, though.

From behind his newspaper, he intently watched their hands.

But there was no sign of anything passing between them.

Anyhow—

Miura Sachiko carried only a small shoulder bag. There was no way she could bring many copies of the stuff in it.

That meant that something was going to happen.

Maybe she was planning on taking him to the hiding place. Or was it going to be a more elaborate operation?

The two had been very cautious, even on the phone. Both of them probably had their suspicions, but Miura Sachiko at least had clearly anticipated the possibility of police surveillance.

They couldn't afford to be careless.

They'd wait until the very last minute.

The two sat silently.

The coffee Sagara had ordered arrived.

Sagara made a show of taking a sip, grabbed the check, and stood up.

Miura Sachiko stood, too.

She cast a suspicious look at Sakamoto.

Sakamoto deliberately looked right back. He looked her over carefully, head to toe.

She turned away abruptly.

She went out of the shop right behind Sagara.

Sakamoto did his best to restrain himself; taking a deep breath, and then another, he stuck to his seat.

He then drained the rest of the coffee in one big swig, hopped out of the booth, and went to the register.

The waitress returned to the front with a sour look on her face.

Sakamoto pulled a few coins from his pocket and hustled out.

The Corolla stood right in front.

His partner flicked a finger to indicate their direction.

Apparently, they'd doubled back into one of the lanes to the left.

They were heading toward the love hotel area.

Sakamoto took off in pursuit.

Just when he thought he'd lost them, he spotted them ducking into a hotel.

Sakamoto paused.

He waited a full minute.

They didn't come out. They must have gotten a room.

He casually went over to the hotel.

He ducked under a mass of vines covering the entrance and went in.

A chime sounded.

A small window slid open to the left of the entrance.

"Just one person today?" The voice from behind the low-set window was that of an older woman.

"Can ya get me a woman?" he asked roughly.

All the while, out of the corner of his eye, he watched the numbers on the elevator just inside.

Number three stayed lit.

"May I ask who sent you here?"

The woman's voice had a hard edge.

"Nobody, it's just, you see . . ."

"May I see some kind of identification?"

Sakamoto selected a business card from among the many fake ones he kept with him, just in case, and slid it inside the window.

A call to the number on the card would connect to an operator at headquarters. The operator would make up something to go along with the number.

"May I see another?"

She was a shrewd one.

There were those who would use someone else's business card as a front.

Sakamoto acted a bit angry and tossed a handful of the same cards inside the window.

"You want to see my ID, too?"

"That's all right. It's just that we don't do that kind of thing here. Not our business . . ."

"Sure, but you can work something out, can't you?"

If this didn't work, he was going to have to reveal himself.

The problem was, he wanted to keep it all as quiet as possible.

Otherwise, everything would come out in the open.

"Well, sir, you're welcome to get a room for yourself. That's no problem."

"And?"

"Get yourself a room, then try a call to this place."

With the key that she pushed through the window was a flashy card.

Below "Massage—Real Live Girls!" was a phone number in large print.

"Sure, I get you."

Sakamoto swept up the key and the card.

The key was for a fourth floor room.

"You see, we aren't that kind of place. We don't want that kind of reputation, not around here."

Suddenly, she sounded all business.

"I get you. You mind if I stay overnight? I want to take a little nap before I call."

"Please take your time. There are videos available with the room, too."

She grinned at him obscenely.

Sakamoto headed for the elevator.

The elevator came down from the third, and he went up to the fourth.

He then hustled down the stairs to the third.

To his relief, the hall stood empty.

It was early on a weekday, so business was slow.

Still, as he picked his way quietly down the hall, cries of passion sounded from a couple of rooms.

If an employee noticed him, he could simply say he'd gotten the wrong floor. If they took him for a voyeur, that was all right, too.

There were six rooms to a floor.

Three of the six were occupied.

An ear to the door gave a pretty good idea of what was going on in there.

In two of the rooms they were clearly doing it.

One room was oddly quiet. Number 302.

The sound of the television indicated that someone was in there.

(Here goes nothing!)

The room key gave him a good sense of the hotel system.

The doors had cheap automatic locks.

Steeling his nerves, Sakamoto slid an appropriate master key into the lock.

A couple of twists and the lock popped open.

He bolted in.

In a single motion, as he pulled the gun from his jacket, he shut the door behind him.

A middle-aged man sat on the bed watching TV, necktie loosened, suit coat thrown aside.

It was Sagara.

Caught unawares, he sat there bewildered, mouth open.

As soon as he saw what was in Sakamoto's hand, he threw back his head.

"Sachi!"

A shrill cry escaped his mouth.

"Don't move!"

Sakamoto strode over to the bed.

He took him by the collar and pinned him to the bed.

"We know everything. Better cooperate!"

"Who are you? What the hell is this?!"

Sakamoto replied with the back of his hand, knocking Sagara flat.

Sagara screamed and rolled around on the double bed. Blood gushed from his split lip.

Sakamoto quickly switched the gun to his left hand and with his right pulled out his pale-green badge.

He stuck it in Sagara's face.

Sagara groaned. Then he bared his teeth, yellowed with tobacco. He wasn't giving up. He started shouting back.

"What the hell?! What the hell do you think you're doing?! I haven't done anything. I'm just here with a woman . . ."

Sakamoto slapped him hard across the other cheek. Sagara went on rolling around on the bed.

"I asked you to cooperate. When I want you to talk, I'll ask. Get it?"

"Hey, this isn't funny. I got my—"

Sakamoto gave him another punch as soon as he spoke. With a yelp, Sagara fell back on the bed, face in his hands. He kept his mouth shut, though.

"Good. That's better. Now, don't move."

Sakamoto slowly transferred the gun to his right hand.

He had a compact automatic, a Browning .380. The short muzzle was threaded to mount a silencer.

Its simple mechanism meant there was no risk of jamming, even with the silencer.

The gun was not actually loaded. It worked to make people think twice, though.

Because of its design, you couldn't tell by looking at it if it was loaded or not.

Most Japanese didn't know anything about guns, anyway. The sight of one was enough to stop them dead in their tracks.

So you didn't even have to use it. Just wearing one had quite an effect. Every cop was now packing something. And they could use it however they wanted.

"Where's the woman?" Sakamoto asked, looking around the room.

"What woman?"

Sagara bobbed his head stupidly.

Sakamoto asked again, "Where is Miura Sachiko?"

Sakamoto knew without asking that there was only one place she could be. He'd already noticed Sagara's eyes darting anxiously toward the bathroom.

"Miura? I don't know! Never heard the name. This is some woman I just picked up. I didn't ask her name. She's some whore. What do I care who she is?"

Lies poured out of him.

Sakamoto said, "That's a shitty way to talk about someone you've paid good money to keep quiet."

Surprise showed on Sagara's face.

"Wait! Just wait!"

Ignoring him, Sakamoto grasped the handle of the bathroom door.

He twisted the knob and kicked open the door.

There she was, Miura Sachiko.

She had probably just gotten out of the shower.

She'd pulled on some clothes without drying.

The thin blouse clung to her breasts, showing her nipples.

She stood there shivering, clutching her bag.

"Out there."

Sakamoto gestured with his gun.

Miura Sachiko started cursing at him.

"Who the hell are you?! I warn you, I'll really scream."

The corner of Sakamoto's mouth twisted slightly, but he spoke calmly.

"Go on, scream all you want. But it'll be the end for both of you."

"What does that mean? You plan to kill us?"

Sakamoto shook his head.

"Our policemen have the place surrounded. If they hear something, they'll come running. If that happens, I'm not going to be able to hold them back. You get my meaning?"

Sagara opened his mouth to speak.

But Miura Sachiko cut him off with a shrill voice.

"How would we know? We're not doing anything, so cut the crap!"

The television, still on, emitted a series of ecstatic moans.

Porn videos were running on the hotel cable channel.

"Listen here."

Sakamoto lowered his voice.

"We're after the stuff, not you. Cooperate with us, and I'll do everything I can to get you off. Think about it! This is it! My job is to get the stuff. Anyone buying or selling it, we take them to the station. But I don't need any scores. Get my drift? Now, if the whole squad finds you here, nothing much I can do. Some of the boys are pretty tough. Some of the young ones are just itching to take over for me. I just want you to know that there's not much hope for you if they come up here."

"That's crap!"

She railed back.

"You're full of crap. I know your game. But it won't work with me. Stuff? Give me a break. And just where is it? Huh? I'd like to see it."

(Damn!)

Sakamoto clucked his tongue.

Maybe he had rushed it. Maybe they weren't ready yet for the transaction.

And yet, if that were the case, why all the secrecy, why go to such lengths?

Could this really just be about sex?

The afflicted tended to lose all sex drive, though. It was unlikely that Miura Sachiko was after that.

So this had to be about something else.

"Out there!"

Sakamoto gestured again with his gun.

Miura Sachiko complied, but very reluctantly.

She went into the bedroom clutching her bag.

Her panties and stockings lay on the bathroom floor where she'd dropped them. She hadn't had time to put them back on.

Sakamoto tried to figure things out.

What had she been doing in the bathroom?

Was she freshening up for a romp in bed? Maybe she just felt like a bath?

He leaned over to examine the panties and stockings. Nothing unusual. He just got a good whiff of her.

She hadn't dropped anything else.

Chewing his lower lip, Sakamoto entered the bedroom.

4

Miura Sachiko's coat hung from a hook.

He rifled through the pockets. He turned up a handkerchief.

"Hand it over."

Sakamoto wrenched the purse from her hands. She made no effort to resist.

He opened the bag and dumped the contents on the floor.

Not a peep out of her.

Most of the stuff was cosmetics. There was a wallet and a passport. She must have just gotten the passport, not a mark in it. He found the wallet stuffed with bills. All of them were big bills, fifties and hundreds.

No doubt about it. She was planning to fly the coop. But he

hadn't found what he was looking for. Only one key in her key holder, probably for her apartment.

Sakamoto tossed the bag aside.

Miura Sachiko sneered at him.

She looked certain of herself. This didn't sit well with him.

Sakamoto issued a command.

"You, Sagara. Off with the clothes. Shoes, too. Toss me the jacket."

Sagara cast a couple of glances at the woman, as if uncertain. She didn't bat an eye.

Sagara handed the jacket over with a sigh. He started pulling off his pants.

A plane ticket turned up in the pocket of his jacket. Singapore Airways bound for Hong Kong. Departure, tomorrow. Passenger's name, Miura Sachiko.

"I take it this was part of your deal."

With these words, Sakamoto ripped the ticket in half. Then he tore it to shreds.

That got a rise out of her.

She screamed at him.

"What the hell, you creep! You don't get it, do you? Whatever you're looking for, we don't have it. Leave us the hell out of it!"

She suddenly started ripping off her skirt and blouse.

"Here you go! Do what you want! Why don't you rip up these, too? You're really getting off on having us naked, aren't you? Pervert! Think I'm hiding something?"

She wasn't wearing a thing underneath. Her body was still wet. The thick tuft of pubic hair looked at odds with her youthful body. That was the only sign of her age.

She hurled the bundle of clothes at Sakamoto.

It suddenly occurred to him that she was trying to draw attention away from Sagara.

Sagara still wore a shirt, underwear, and socks.

Maybe Sagara was hiding something, and she'd stripped, thinking her body would distract Sakamoto.

Even so, that would only buy her a couple of minutes.

In any case, Sakamoto was planning on stripping Sagara and checking inside his anus. Good place to stuff—

(That wasn't it!)

Sakamoto had a burst of inspiration.

She had something else in mind. She was trying to draw attention away from herself.

Stripping naked was intended to make him think she wasn't hiding anything—

Tramping over her clothes, Sakamoto went right over to Sagara.

He jammed the gun in his pocket, stripped a belt out of one of the hotel bathrobes, and tied up Sagara with it.

Caught by surprise, Sagara didn't protest. He let himself be tied up and thrown onto the bed.

Miura Sachiko screamed instead.

"You creep! You're some kind of pervert!"

Sakamoto went for her now.

He wrenched an arm behind her back.

She doubled over in pain and fell to the floor.

"Cut it out! You're breaking it! My arm—"

She spread her legs as she struggled.

Sakamoto stuck his other hand between her legs.

He probed with his fingers.

"Stop it! No! You pervert!"

He probed deeper.

Pinning her down, he wriggled his fingers deeper.

Finally, he felt something.

(What the . . . ?!)

Something soft and squishy.

Grunting like an animal, Sakamoto managed to pinch it between two fingers.

He tugged.

It slipped right out. It was a condom, slick and shiny. The end was tied off.

Something was in it.

Sakamoto leapt to his feet and tore open the condom.

A key fell to the floor with a clink.

There was a round tag on it, with 326 engraved on it.

Without warning—

Miura Sachiko grabbed him and started wailing.

"Give it back, please, please!"

Sakamoto knocked her to the bed with his shoulder. She fell on top of Sagara.

He held up the key and spoke evenly.

"So it's in a coin locker. Not a bad place to hide it."

Sachiko burst into tears. Probably just an act.

"So where is it?" he asked. "Where's the locker?"

"I'd never tell you!"

"Have it your way. We'll find it easy enough."

She looked up at him.

"Okay, then, what the hell. The locker is in the underground at Shinjuku station, by the west exit."

She glared defiantly at him, and her laugher rang with confidence.

"You see, it doesn't matter how hard you try to track down every copy. We'll just go on making them. It's all up here now."

With these words, she pointed at her head.

She threw back her head defiantly and burst into laughter.

Sakamoto nodded.

"We know that. Yeah, we know all about that. That's why we eradicate it at the source."

Sakamoto calmly pulled the Browning out of his pocket. He extracted a silencer from the other and began screwing it onto the muzzle.

At first Miura Sachiko watched with disbelief, and then her eyes went wide.

". . . shit, you're full of . . ."

"No shit," he said, shaking his head. He loaded the slugs. "This is the real thing."

He raised the Browning, aimed square at her forehead, and squeezed the trigger.

With a sound no louder than a cough, the 9 mm ball blasted from the gun.

Eyes wide open, Miura Sachiko slumped to the floor, dead in a second.

Sagara started to protest in a tremulous voice.

"Wait. Hold on just a second. I don't know anything. You see? I just needed cash. I never read it. Never! I didn't read any of it. It's got nothing to do with me. I don't know a thing. I didn't even look at it! You got to believe me. It's the truth."

Hands tied behind him, he fell off the bed trying to wriggle away.

He kept whining.

"See? You got to help me! It's got nothing to do with me, I swear. I'm begging you. She tricked me into this. She wanted money from me. You got to understand. I beg you—"

The Browning coughed again.

Red blood trickled from the small hole in his temple.

Sakamoto untied the belt around his wrists. He removed the silencer and slipped it back into his pocket. He placed the gun in Sagara's hand.

That's how it had to be.

There was no other way to prevent the destruction of the world.

Sakamoto stood over the two, looked down, and joined his hands in prayer for a moment.

He'd made it look like a lovers' suicide.

The police would take care of the rest.

He took the elevator to the first floor.

Looking flustered, a woman called to Sakamoto from the window.

"Leaving so soon? Is there something wrong?"

"No, no, nothing wrong. People on the third floor were making so much noise that it sort of turned me off."

"I'm really sorry. Please accept my apologies. The third floor? I'll make it half price for you."

Sakamoto paid and left the hotel.

The Corolla was waiting for him around the corner.

The passenger door opened, and Sakamoto climbed in.

"Shinjuku station, west exit."

The Corolla moved out.

"How'd it go?"

"I took care of them all right. Now for the stuff."

With rush hour traffic, the Corolla took thirty minutes to reach Shinjuku station.

"Wait here. I'll get it."

Sakamoto set out alone in search of the locker.

He found it near the underground entrance to a department store.

326—

He inserted the key. It wouldn't turn.

It must be out of money.

He plunked in some coins, and it opened.

Inside was a paper bag.

He pulled it out and looked inside.

A dozen odd pamphlets, thin, with yellow covers.

On the covers, about the size of a postcard, nothing was written.

Sakamoto drew a deep breath.

Then—fearfully, he took one.

(What is this thing, anyway?)

He felt angry all of a sudden.

(What on earth was all of this about?)

Why did so many people have to die, just because of some weird thing written by an insane Frenchman forty years ago?—

It made no sense to him at all.

He couldn't help thinking that it was some kind of lie, it had to be a trick, or maybe the whole thing was a sort of conspiracy.

(It's . . . it's just . . .)

Without thinking, Sakamoto opened it.

The first line, in rather large letters, read "The Gold of Time." It looked like a title.

There followed a dense series of very small, rounded, hand-written letters, which had been transferred with mimeograph paper.

He read a few lines without thinking and, then, flustered, tore his eyes from the page. He was angry with himself for feeling so flustered.

(It's just a . . .)

He clucked his tongue softly.

(Anyone who goes crazy over this stuff must have been damned crazy all along.)

No sooner had he thought this than he began to feel dizzy. It was probably just a wave of fatigue.

Looking at the stuff was strictly forbidden, even for cops, no, especially for cops.

Still, in the course of an investigation, some fragment of it might catch your eye.

To Sakamoto it looked like nothing but incomprehensible babble.

It didn't make any sense.

He felt sure of himself. There was no way a guy like him would lose his mind over this.

And so . . . his mind raced.

And so, just one copy . . . just this once. Before he realized it, he'd stuffed one of the copies in his pocket.

No one saw him. There was no one paying any attention to him.

A faint smile flitted across his lips.

He headed back to the car with the bag in hand.

For some reason . . . he felt good.

A sensation like being tipsy ran through him.

(The Gold of Time—what nonsense!)

1

ANOTHER WORLD

1

It was a raw cold afternoon.

Glowering clouds had darkened the skies for three days already.

Paris, April 2, 1948. In a timeworn café in Montmartre, André Breton was waiting for a certain young man.

He continued to wait.

But the man hadn't shown.

Instead, the café door was swinging open to the occasional gust of wind that would sweep in laden with dust. It swirled at Breton's feet.

Breton's left leg began to throb with an almost imperceptible yet persistent and wearisome pain.

The pain quickened his irritation. In about two weeks Breton would be greeting his fifty-second birthday. Greeting it was inevitable.

The young man wasn't showing.

The café window provided a view of the square.

Breton's eyes again started to wander slowly, right to left, left to right. But there was no sign of any one hurrying toward him.

He wouldn't be casually strolling. With a brusque gesture Breton pushed back his left sleeve. Three forty-five—

He was already forty-five minutes late. He should be running full out. Crossing the square, making a beeline for the café. Breton unconsciously rubbed at the seat of his pants where the velvet had worn smooth. As if the person he was waiting for might be conjured forth from the ragged patch.

(Why . . . ?)

As he asked himself the question, he became aware of its two meanings.

A sense of paradox overtook him. How unbearable to wait. But then how reassuring it was to go on waiting.

Breton remained caught between the two possibilities, unable to move.

Why was the young man not showing?

And why did he actually dread his appearance, even as he awaited him?

Why did he go on sitting here, then?

Each and every second brought fresh pain to Breton.

This was the worst. This weather pattern said it all. On a day like today he should never have left home. Today was not "the day."

There were only a few people in the square.

Not sign of someone running toward him.

Another five minutes had passed.

(Ten minutes more) Breton told himself. (That's all.)

Breton didn't know which route the young man would take.

But he doubted that he would be at a loss to find this place.

In any case, if he made it to the square, there'd be no way to mistake the café.

After all, the café—Café Blanche—took its name from the park.

"Sure I know the place. Place Blanche, right?" the young man had replied on the phone.

Breton didn't know if he had understood them to be meeting at the square or the café. But it didn't matter either way.

Breton had repeatedly given him both names. And they had agreed on three o'clock.

Breton's eyes flitted across the square yet again.

Directly across the square was the Cyrano.

It was a thoroughly ordinary café just like this one.

Naturally, Breton would recall its name. Even today the name Cyrano had lost nothing of its brilliance and luster in the memories of so many surrealists. But only in their memories . . .

Before they had "discovered" the Cyrano, it had been the Celta next to the Opera House. During the enlargement of the Boulevard Haussmann, the Celta had been torn down, and Breton and company had moved to the Cyrano. For the surrealists that café had been a public place for agitation. Headquarters. Church. Altar. Playground.

The Cyrano era had lasted till the start of World War II. In the Cyrano, dreams had unfolded, spirits had clashed, and poems had met, and amid the wild clamor, directives to overthrow the powers that be had been issued.

That is what the Cyrano had been at one time. None of them would forget it. In the present, however, the Cyrano had completely lost its power of attraction.

The War, the Occupation, and then "liberation" had wiped it all away. Stripped of its magic, the Cyrano had turned back into a mere pumpkin.

You could still see the Cyrano from here.

Breton slowly and calmly exhaled, as if reluctant to give up the breath he had unconsciously been holding.

Invisible forces still emanated from Place Blanche. You could feel it. Or at least many people still believed it to be so.

Breton felt it, too, without a doubt. But there was something very weak about it. Something was missing.

Was it an effect of the fever? Was it an effect of the humidity issuing from the mouths of people breathing?

Or maybe the fever had already spread to the point where even the ambient temperature had reached saturation?

If so . . .

Breton pushed back his sleeve with a panicked gesture to check his watch.

Five minutes had passed. But the young man hadn't shown. He hadn't come.

(Five minutes more.)

In five minutes it would be four o'clock. In another hour or so, the group would gather as usual. That was their routine. Even ruined by the war, the surrealists kept this routine.

But today he found the thought of meeting with them strangely disagreeable.

(Why?)

Best to leave, Breton advised himself. Five minutes more, and then he had best go.

On the imitation mahogany table a glass filled with red fluid had been casually yet deliberately placed in the manner of a still life.

That's—(Ah!)—Place Blanche.

Breton had not even once raised the glass to his lips.

He felt afraid to reach for it. But he was not at all loath to destroy the harmonious composition on the table. On the contrary.

He would like to knock over the glass, to dash its contents across the table. Locked in battle against this impulse, he could not lift a finger.

He was struggling.

(Why?!)

Why must he endure so much?

Why wasn't he coming?—

He . . . (Hu Mei . . . Who May . . .)

That is the young man's name.

That was the name he had used with Breton. Breton didn't know if it was his real name.

In conjunction with the name, Breton recalled two eyes, too large for the beautiful face.

(Who May.)

It rang with mystery.

(Who . . . ?)

Involuntarily he had asked the question back.

With a faint curl of the lips, the young man had thereupon traced his name in the air with dark delicate fingers, in three letters: *W-H-O*.

That he remembered distinctly.

The young man had been merely nineteen at the time.

The response had left Breton baffled.

February 1943. During his exile in New York. That had been their first encounter.

2

July 1940—the fall of Paris, and with the unconditional surrender to the German army and the establishment of the Vichy regime of the État Français, Breton and the others fled to Marseilles.

It was in the following year that, after meeting Lévi-Strauss on the island of Martinique, Breton sailed for America. He arrived in New York in August, at the height of summer. Breton was not the only exile. Due to the crackdown on artists, a number of other surrealists came to New York, such as Duchamp, Tanguy, Ernst, Masson, and Matta. Their presence made it possible to hold the first International Exhibition of Surrealism in the United States.

"I was there a short while, and yet . . ." In an interview with André Parinaud broadcast on Radio France, Breton would reminisce: "I knew true happiness in New York. For instance, the joy of occasional lunches in the company of my friend, the truly admirable Marcel Duchamp, far from the cares of the world. . . . And then I met with unexpected happiness, which took me totally by surprise but, well, I probably shouldn't speak too loudly of it in this context. . . . I simply wanted to say that . . ."

Surely this "unexpected happiness" was a reference to his meeting Elisa, who would become his second wife. Or so it is believed.

Yet in New York, Breton made another unforgettable encounter, which would bring him both great joy and extreme duress.

It was Who May whom he met.

February 1943.

Breton had a cocktail in hand at the time.

It was a small party in Manhattan, with about forty in attendance, at an apartment facing Sixth Avenue.

More than half of them were artists in exile like Breton.

They had already drunk all the champagne.

A new cocktail, "invented" on the spot, then made the rounds.

Liquid of an extraordinary color was poured into the glass in Breton's hand. An American art student, an aspiring sculptor, dubbed the drink V V V, or Triple V. *VVV* was the name of a journal of surrealism that Breton, Duchamp, Ernst, and others had launched the previous year in New York with David Hare as editor-in-chief.

The three *V*s or triple *V* were a declaration: "*V* as a vow to return to a habitable and thinkable world, Victory over the forces of regression and death currently unleashed on the earth, but again *V* beyond the first Victory . . . . Victory over all that tends to perpetuate the enslavement of man by man, and beyond that double *V,* that double Victory, *V* again over all that is opposed to the emancipation of the mind."

Clearly, however, in the instance of the art student naming the drink, *V* was not for victory but for vodka.

Breton swallowed the dreadful drink in a single gulp, and before he was aware of it, he found himself muttering curses, directed at Americans in general.

That was the moment.

The door to the apartment opened.

It was some late arrivals, Patrick Waldberg accompanied by a young man.

Waldberg looked around the room and then strode over to Breton.

"He begged me to introduce him to you."

Throwing his arm around the young man's shoulders affectionately, Waldberg thrust the young man at Breton.

"A poet. Unknown. Which makes him a prince among young poets. Don't you agree, Monsieur Breton?"

Waldberg's tone was somehow defiant.

Yet he himself was probably just this side of thirty.

Breton frowned inwardly.

Waldberg had been born in California. As a boy, he had moved to Paris, whence his command of French. He had formed close ties with a number of poets, painters, and other artists. He had a talent for "close ties"—indeed.

He had also been among those who had fled the war and come to New York. Breton had met him two years previously. He had approved of his commitment to surrealism. Waldberg was full of talent.

That was something even Breton had to admit. Yet, for the moment, that was as much as he would admit.

Waldberg would make a fine critic at least. Or so Breton thought. He might only amount to a fine critic.

"Youth in itself implies poetic genius. By its very nature. Surely everyone is a poet, and there's absolutely no reason for anyone to hesitate to call himself one."

Breton was fully aware that his response might sound sarcastic.

But he did not, in fact, have any doubts that youth bore genius.

Two months previously Breton had traveled to Yale University to deliver a lecture titled "The Condition of Surrealism between the Wars."

In that talk he had loudly proclaimed—

"Surrealism was born of an unlimited belief in the genius of youth."

Nevertheless—

From the time he had arrived in New York, he had had his fill of "works" sent to him or sprung on him by self-professed poets and artists. Almost all of them were without any merit, immature, inferior, self-indulgent, nothing more than products of disorderly minds.

And so Breton found it difficult to respond civilly to the young man whom Waldberg had presented to him as a "poet."

Still, there was something about the young man that sparked curiosity.

Maybe it was because he was so clearly not of European descent. And above all it was his eyes.

A pair of dark eyes, seemingly large enough to absorb the world itself, cut Breton to the quick. Breton could not restrain the racing of his heart.

There was no resisting the force of inspiration in that gaze.

"Indeed—"

Waldberg merely nodded toward Breton, oblivious to his response.

"Indeed, there is an aura of genius about this young man, Monsieur Breton."

With a supercilious smile, Waldberg excused himself and walked off to get a drink.

Breton found himself alone with the young man, face to face.

"So, your poems, are they in French?"

Breton asked, rather perfunctorily.

The young man's eyes appeared even rounder and larger.

"They are. I was born in France, you see."

He replied in perfectly fluent French.

"Ah . . . so you're not American?"

The young man shook his head. He stared intently back at Breton, the vague trace of a smile flitting across a face that could truly be called beautiful.

Breton involuntarily shrank before that face.

He didn't know why. A strange emotion moved him.

Breton sipped his Triple V cocktail in an effort to conceal his emotion, however, and continued with questions.

"Your, um, name, then, is?"

"My name is Hu Mei."

"Who . . . ?"

Then it happened. The young man traced the letters *W-H-O* in the air. Breton gulped down his Triple V. He immediately regretted it. But it was too late. The ball of alcohol burned through his nose and throat.

Drawing a deep breath of air, Breton asked in a ragged tone.

"Who? You mean, you want me to guess who you are?"

It seemed to him a childish word game all too common among youths and poets. Or so he thought at first. This one was after all very young. Despite initial impressions, he might prove a disappointment.

Smile unwavering, the young man tilted his head.

"That is the name, my name."

Once again the young man drew some sort of figure in the air with a finger.

"That's how you write it in Chinese characters." He traced the same character in the air. "It is an ideogram. But I don't know what it means."

"Are you Chinese, then?"

Breton posed the question, feeling that the young man was being rather evasive.

"My mother came from Indochina."

The young man continued in impeccable French.

"My father was French. I was born in Paris. That's all I know. I never knew my father, and my mother died before I was old enough to remember her well."

At a loss for a suitable response, Breton raised the glass to his lips. This time, however, he fortunately remembered what was in the glass and lowered it hastily.

Who May had been raised in the Chaillot area. He hadn't lacked for money. His mother had made a good living. But she had died of an illness before he reached the age of twelve. Who May had then been adopted by a man named Jean-Pierre Carron who worked in the import-export business.

Carron was French with some Vietnamese blood.

It wasn't entirely clear why Carron ended up raising Who May. At least no one had ever explained it to Who May.

Carron had no family. That was one explanation. But it hardly amounted to a full explanation.

In any event—such was the story that Breton heard from Who May.

Breton, however, didn't take it all that seriously. But then there was no particular reason to doubt it, either.

Presently, as the threat of Nazi invasion mounted, Jean-Pierre Carron had immediately recognized the danger and sailed for the free land of America, taking Who May with him.

And then war broke out—

Unable to return to their former country, they had no choice but to settle in New York.

"So, how about a drink?"

Waldberg had returned, bearing a peculiar-looking cocktail in each hand.

"Incidentally, how is it that you two became acquainted?"

Taking advantage of the diversion, Breton asked Waldberg while he was handing one of the glasses to the young man.

"He," Waldberg replied, beaming, "was my student."

"Your student, was he?"

"Yes, at an English school for foreigners. In a class designed primarily for native speakers of French, for a short while I offered an extracurricular course. A course on poetry—"

Waldberg placed special emphasis on the word *poetry.*

"At the end of the course, I gave the students an assignment—for everyone to write a poem in English. And then I had each of them read their poem aloud and offered comments. It was really quite fun."

(It must have been) thought Breton. And he nodded his head.

Waldberg was the perfect person for it. He would adeptly play the role of instructor and make the course "fun."

"That was the first time I heard Who May's work. The English was quite accurate, yet it had a strange sort of rhythm that stuck in your head. So I spoke to him after class about it."

Who May had then confided in Waldberg about his ambition to become a poet.

"I read a number of his efforts. They were really quite good. I would quite like to have you read one of them, Monsieur Breton. There is no doubt that he is a poet. He has the soul of a poet."

"I see . . ." Breton adopted an ambiguous expression, assessing Waldberg and Who May.

"As soon as I can make time . . ."

But Breton had no intention of making time.

He did not believe what Waldberg had said about the young man harboring the "soul of a poet."

Nevertheless—

Four months later, it turned out that Breton would learn the truth.

The young man was indeed a poet. At least he had a formidable skill with words. Whether he had the soul of a poet or not, he had within him all the requisite technique and ability to become a poet. And not just that, but something beyond that—

On that first day, however, Breton had not detected it. There had been no time to detect it.

Once Waldberg had introduced him to Who May, Breton found an opportunity to excuse himself in order to speak with Fernand Léger.

By the time he thought about them again, there was no trace of Waldberg and the young man.

A peculiar feeling washed over him, as he keenly recalled the slanderous remarks constantly launched against the surrealists to the effect that they were just a "band of homosexuals."

3

That day—

New York was once again aglow in July sunshine.

It was the kind of day when everything appears born anew.

Drawn out by the lively weather, Breton strolled north along Fifth Avenue.

A pleasant breeze spun through his hair like a fine comb.

And in the distance the Empire State Building showed sharply against the sky, alive with light, towering over the city.

It had just turned noon.

Crowds of men and women streamed from the buildings to enjoy their lunchtime.

It was a peaceful scene.

The abundant good cheer that filled the city held Breton.

Before such a scene Breton's thoughts took an unexpected turn.

The turn grew into a fissure, and a profound abyss opened wide before his eyes.

(I am . . . where?)

At this very moment the entire world was choking on the stink of blood and explosives.

The newspapers and radios madly clamored every hour of every day about the situation.

And yet, for Breton strolling up Fifth Avenue, the spate of news reports, whether gallant or painful, was absolutely without reality.

(Where . . . is here?)

Breton continued walking.

He pondered. And thought.

His thoughts turn to France, trampled and stained.

There the mind was subject to defilement, and being stifled to death. And if you tried to resist, you had to be prepared for annihilation, not just of the mind but also of the body itself.

That was precisely why—they had fled. Holding on to what they had to preserve, they had come here.

But what an abyss, what a profound gap! His eyes went dark. Fear overtook him.

The reality in which he should actually be living was so distant. Too distant.

Breton walked.

Quickening his step, he weaved his way through the crowds on Fifth Avenue. In New York Breton had taken on a position as radio announcer for the Voice of America broadcast directed to Europe. Because of this job, he followed regular hours, leaving for the radio station at the same time every day.

The job entailed far more constraints and obligations than Breton had ever imagined.

Despite that, he had assumed the position voluntarily. And he took the job seriously and worked zealously. There was a reason for this.

In the first place, there was no other way for Breton to prolong surrealist activities than by securing this site of expression, the medium of radio. In any event he was aware that such gains were possible in this situation. He therefore went to great lengths to be scrupulous in all matters.

There was another reason.

To the resistance fighters in distant Europe he wished to express as much solidarity as possible, sending a message in his own voice, on the radio waves of Voice of America.

His thoughts inevitably ran deeper.

Was seeking asylum abroad permissible as an attempt to find refuge, or was it simply desertion?

Under the burden of such painful doubts, Breton spoke into the mike. He cried out.

Be that as it may, it was really himself that he was trying to persuade.

His efforts, however, were by no means successful.

Breton walked.

The lunch hour had arrived, but he had no appetite.

He wanted merely to continue on and on like this, walking.

He was free today until two. He had to be at the radio station again at two.

The green of Central Park came into view ahead.

He crossed Fifty-Ninth Street.

Yet—

The temperature continued to rise and rise. Sweat beaded his brow.

He wanted to take off his jacket somewhere.

With that in mind, seeking a bench in the shade of the trees, he started down one of the smaller paths in the park.

Just then he heard a voice behind him. Someone was calling his name. It was a rather high-pitched voice. He didn't recognize it.

With a sense of coming to himself, he turned around.

A slight young man came bounding into the park, fairly bouncing toward him.

(*W-H-O . . .*)

The three letters popped into his head.

There was no mistaking it. It was he.

Who May. Actually, he didn't know if that was his real name.

In any event he had succeeded in inscribing his existence into Breton's memories with three letters of the alphabet written with a finger in the air.

"—Monsieur, Breton."

He struggled to catch his breath.

Looking admiringly up at Breton, opening his large eyes even wider, he continued to speak.

"My apologies—you don't remember me—but I . . ."

"I remember you quite well."

Breton gave him a broad smile.

"Are you not the Mr. Who whom Waldberg introduced to me?"

The young man's eyes became rounder still.

"You do me an honor."

The young man bobbed his head awkwardly up and down like a wooden doll.

And then, after opening and closing his mouth a few times as if to draw a deep breath, he abruptly stopped.

"I have favor to ask of you!"

His tone of voice was desperate.

"Please, there is something that I must ask of you—Mr. Breton! I need your help!"

Breton raised an eyebrow involuntarily.

(My help?)

He could not repress a certain hardening of his heart.

This was because he had recently heard a number of similar pleas.

The group of refugees had been living here for more than three years already. In the course of three years all of them had faced one sort of problem or another. Quite a few of them had been plagued with financial difficulties in particular.

Many of them came thronging to Breton due to his "fame." It happened almost every day.

Consequently, he had, quite frankly, grown tired of such entreaties.

There was nothing he could do.

It was of course annoying, but even more than that, Breton simply didn't have the means to offer assistance to others.

They did not understand this, however.

These philistines fervently believed that there was a sort of one-to-one correspondence between fame and money. However he put it, his words fell on deaf ears.

On the contrary, in response, he became an object of resentment and hatred.

As a consequence, faced with this young man, Breton's first impulse was to shrug his shoulders brusquely.

"I am sorry, but you—"

Breton spoke very clearly to him, choosing his words carefully.

"You seem to have chosen the wrong person. Is that clear? At present I can probably do nothing more than disappoint your expectations. I hope you understand, but this can only be exceedingly uncomfortable for both of us."

Breton saw Who May's face flush with bewilderment.

Clearly, Breton's rather oblique refusal had not gotten through to him.

Who May's response took him by surprise.

"Fine! It makes no difference to me, really."

"It makes no difference?"

"Exactly! Whatever comments you give me, I will not feel that you have disappointed me. Truthfully! Mr. Breton, I know that there is no one else but you. Will you . . . ? I beg of you!"

(Comments . . . ?) Breton realized his mistake. (So that's what it was.)

Waldberg had, with certainty, called him a poet. But as yet "unknown"—Breton then spied a bundle of paper, probably a manuscript, sticking out from the cloth bag slung across Who May's shoulder.

"I see."

Breton muttered at him with a sigh. He had been mistaken, but if that was his favor sticking out of the bag, it was even more depressing.

But Who May bore a look of desperation.

"Mr. Breton! Please help me. You are the only one who can help me. At least I know of no one but you. I beg you. I absolutely must have your diagnosis."

"Diagnosis?"

Breton knitted his brows.

He could not determine whether the young man had used the term *diagnosis* simply to affect a grand turn of phrase, or whether he meant to refer to Breton's training as a psychiatrist.

"You mean to say . . ." Breton asked him with great deliberation. "You are ill?"

Who May's enormous eyes rolled in a fit of terror, enlarging as if to encompass the universe itself.

"Perhaps . . . I don't really know, but . . ."

The words cut short in his mouth.

He clenched the cloth bag slung over his shoulder in both hands.

"If you truly are ill, that's beyond my abilities."

Breton continued to test him.

"I was never a good doctor. I never healed a single patient."

"That's fine, I don't expect you to cure me. I want a diagnosis. From you, Monsieur Breton! I can't think of anyone but you. There is no one else! I absolutely must have your diagnosis. You're right! I am, there's no doubt, I am ill!"

Indeed—the young man looked ill.

Yet it was likely that he evoked his illness to prove his good health.

"It is impossible in the world today to find anyone who is young and not ill. Youth itself is a kind of illness, if you ask me."

Breton forced himself to smile for the young man.

Of course, if he truly were an invalid, there was no point in banging on about it. It might even be dangerous. Such thoughts also crossed his mind.

(In any event) Breton glanced at his watch. He was free for another hour. (I suppose I have no choice . . .)

"All right, then, let me take a look."

Breton pointed at the bag clutched in Who May's hands.

"Are those your medical charts?"

Who May started to blush.

In a moment deep crimson suffused his entire face.

"Come with me," Breton said to him. "Let's find a bench."

They walked awhile and finally found a place to sit.

With trembling hands, Who May took the cloth bag from his shoulder. And then, impatiently, he pulled out a bundle of about ten pages or so.

"How old are you?"

Breton asked him as he took the pages.

"Nineteen. But I will be twenty in February. Ah . . ."

Perhaps from excitement, his voice rose sharply.

"Mr. Breton, I implore you. I . . . I just found it. It was by chance. I made a discovery. It came to me in a flash. Something, someone . . . ah! It began to whisper to me, yet not to me . . ."

Irritated with Who May's incoherent babbling, Breton raised a hand to interrupt him.

"What exactly did you discover?"

Who May's eyes fell on the bundle of papers now in Breton's hands.

"A way to use words or, rather, a way to make them—of course!"

"Make them! You're saying you make words!"

"Sometimes—yes, but I don't know. I myself cannot judge. How best to make use of this discovery . . . I haven't a clue. Words are not something one can make all alone. That much I know. And yet . . . and yet! I can make them! It's true! That's why I need your diagnosis!"

Who May chattered on without stopping, like one possessed. Then he suddenly fell silent.

Breton shook his head slightly as if coming to himself.

His eyes fell on the manuscript.

It was fine typing paper. Yet the lines of words were written by hand in dark blue ink.

The first lines were written in a very methodical, almost fussy hand, but gradually the letters became disordered as if leaping across the page.

At the top of the first page in slightly larger letters was written "Another World." That apparently was the title.

Below was a signature—

Who May

It was evidently a poem in prose.

And yet—even so—

From the very instant he laid hands on the manuscript, rather to his surprise, Breton became aware of something somewhere stirring his emotions.

He had yet to read a single line. Nevertheless, he had a sense of premonition. It was a premonition that might be described as unusual and ominous. It ran like a chill up his spine.

(Ridiculous.)

He had exactly the same feeling as when he had laid hands on a new work by Benjamin Péret. Or like that when he had first cut open the pages of a collection of Rimbaud's poetry.

In any case—Breton shook his head hard from side to side. It was surely an effect of the afternoon heat.

The first stanza was as follows.

4

A fish. Dobaded. Its eyeball sliced down the middle. Sections quivering. Images reflected on the split lens are stained with blood. Dobaded. The city of people mirrored there is dyed madder red. Reversal of pressure, dobaded, and there you go! It's taking you there. . . .

(Dobaded?)

Breton kept on reading, although his thoughts were still ensnared by the unfamiliar word.

(Why?)

(Dobaded.)

The word was repeated again and again, now as a noun, now as a verb or adjective.

(Dobaded.)

The discovery that Who May had spoken of, his "making words"—was this it?

(If so, it showed no interest in others . . .)

(Dobaded.)

(It is still there . . . yet . . .)

(No, wait!)

(Dobaded.)

(This may be some sort of spell . . .)

(But . . . no, this is absurd . . .)

(Dobaded.)

(Wait! What was that—?)

(Dobaded! It's a bit—no, it is absurd!)

(Dobaded.)

(Dobaded!)

(. . . this, dobaded! What on earth . . . this, this thing!)

(Dobaded.)

(Dobaded.)

(Dobaded . . . dobaded . . . dobaded . . .)

(. . .)

(Dobaded!)

About an hour later Breton returned.

From another world . . . not of this earth, but of this universe, yet an entirely different world. He had come back here, to New York, Manhattan, a bench in Central Park. Dobaded.

(. . . dobaded.)

There was no room for doubt.

Breton had experienced it. At the command of these verses, he had been transported to the world that Who May had named "Another World" and then had returned.

Dobaded.

All of a sudden anger irrupted in him.

He didn't know why. And because he didn't know, he became angrier still.

Nevertheless—

Dobaded—

(Shit!)

There was no doubt that the young man named Who May had discovered something, or at least something related to the usage of words.

Dobaded . . . (Shit!) . . . in any event there had never been any sign of someone else who had thought to use words as he did.

(Of course not!)

His anger mounted still.

(Nonetheless, dobaded—what was this thing?! What could one call it . . . ?)

Breton held his eyes shut tight.

(Is this thing poetry?! Dobaded! No, it isn't like poetry. It is a spell! It is a sort of . . . hypnotism! It is like the use of words in hypnotism.)

Breton still could not open his eyes.

(In any case . . . surely, dobaded . . . shit . . .)

In any case, no matter how he struggled, there was no way for him, dobaded, to erase from his thoughts the lines that he had just read.

Whether it was a poem or not, there was no use denying the very obvious fact that Who May's discovery had imparted this experience to Breton.

The fact of it overwhelmed Breton.

(This thing . . .)

Overcome with frustration Breton cursed inwardly.

(He must have made a deal. That's how it was decided. At midnight he had carved summoning spells on the floor and summoned the devil. And in exchange for the secret of words, he sold his soul to the devil.)

As such thoughts crossed his mind, Breton grew angrier still, at his own foolishness.

(. . . in any case, dobaded . . . shit!)

Breton forced both eyes open wide.

In a rage he folded the bundle of papers still in his hands squarely in half.

Who May was there.

He stared at Breton with the same enormous eyes. A look of concern, clearly not feigned, colored his features.

Breton cast a glance at his watch. To his relief, it was about time for him to report to work.

Yet, dobaded . . . (Shit!) . . . his nerves were so thoroughly rattled that he had lost the will to make any decision.

Breton cast a glance at the papers that he had just folded in two.

In a rather weak voice he asked, "Was it really you who wrote . . . this?"

"I think it was me."

He answered in a roundabout way. And then he added: "I know it was I who held the pen. But . . . oh, please understand me . . . I have the impression that at the time I was doing no more than taking down notes. Which is to say . . . I don't really remember. It is so peculiar. I must be sick."

Breton snorted. That was the only response that came to him. But then words escaped from his lips, laden with overtones of contempt.

"If you think that you can impress me with your talent by deliberately adopting such a self-servingly poetic stance—"

Drawing a deep breath, Breton resumed, as if determined to spill his bile.

"Rest assured that it doesn't work with me. On the contrary, such posturing can only diminish your talent. That's really all I wish to say to you."

Who May remained immobile, as if paralyzed with fear.

He opened his mouth to speak but then dropped his head, blushing.

His appearance troubled Breton's feelings.

Clucking his tongue slightly, he withdrew a ballpoint pen from the pocket of his coat.

He held out the pen and the manuscript to Who May.

"Could you write your address or contact information somewhere in the margins? Or maybe a phone number?"

Who May nodded.

"You can reach me through the landlord of my apartment."

"Fine. If you could give me the room number, too."

In the same meticulous writing as in the first part of the manuscript, Who May wrote down the numbers.

Once done, he turned his eyes to Breton, looking at him expectantly.

"I would like to hold on to this manuscript, if you don't mind." Breton said to him. "I would like to read through it more carefully."

"Of course. I would like that. But . . ."

"But what?"

"It's just . . . that, well, what exactly are these words that I have written?"

"Is this something to ask me?"

"Oh . . . I don't know. I don't really even know exactly who I am. I am ill. That must be it. Please tell me! What in the world should I do?"

This time Breton really went into a rage.

"How on earth would I know?!"

Breton nearly screamed in response.

"Why is it so important to you, why? Of all things, this has nothing to do with me. It doesn't really matter to me who you are or whether you've fallen ill."

"Please forgive me, it's just, I . . ."

"Enough! Not another word! I've had enough. This is it for me!"

Breton snatched the bundle of papers from Who May's hands, waving it in the air as if to hurtle it to the ground.

"This is already far too much. So I will tell you, if you really want me to. This thing, this work, is completely outrageous, nothing but exasperating. Until now no one has seen fit for words to be used in such a fashion. That's right, no one. What is this "dobaded, dobaded" shit? Huh? Where did you pick it up? This, this sort of . . ."

Choking on his own anger, Breton glared at Who May.

"Oh . . . I don't really know. I just happened on it. It's a sort of way of doing things. I just tried making poems in this way. And then it all became clear to me. That other world, precisely as written here, suddenly became clear to me, and I understood. But, but . . . for me, it isn't yet . . ."

Shaking his head violently, Breton stopped Who May from continuing his account.

"So you don't even understand yourself? So you can't even evaluate your own work? Well, it makes no difference to me. Do whatever the hell you please. Dobaded, humph!"

Breton realized that he was becoming hysterical. He desperately tried to calm himself, but without success.

He couldn't keep himself from taking out his frustration on Who May.

"How can you, who writes this sort of thing, adopt such a superior tone? How?! It's unbelievable. A genius? Humph! Sure, there are lots of people who might hail you as a genius. But not me, not yet anyway. I still have to think it over. That much should be clear to you."

Breton took another glance at his watch.

He would certainly be late. Even though that no longer mattered to him, he didn't want to spend another second here. That had become a necessity.

Breton quickly fished a piece of paper from his pocket and wrote his address on it. He pushed it into Who May's hand.

"This is where you'll find me. Feel free to stop by anytime. If you don't feel like it, I won't insist on it, but—I would like you to promise me something. I would like you to show me, as soon as possible, anything else you've done—poems, prose, drawings, even books of trivial popular songs. Anything, no matter how trifling, don't hesitate to send it to me. Then I can think things over. Who you are . . . what you are doing . . . I need time to think through these matters. Okay? It will take a while. I will speak with you again after a while. Is that okay?"

As Breton made sure Who May understood him, Who May nodded, wearing an expression that could only be taken as aversion for Breton.

"I promise. But . . ."

Ignoring him, Breton got up from the bench.

Turning on his heels, he walked as fast as he could toward the park exit.

5

That evening Breton read "Another World" again twice.

Unable to contain himself, he reached for the telephone.

He wanted to speak to someone. If he could have pulled it off, he would have gone out and grabbed some unknown passerby. That was exactly what he wanted to do.

Instead, he chose David Hare.

Hare, a sculptor, lived in Roxbury, Connecticut. He had made a name for himself as the editor of *VVV*, the journal publishing the work of surrealist artists like Breton exiled in New York.

He was one who shared their vision.

He was busy at work.

Yet, sensing the gravity of Breton's situation, he leapt into his car and drove directly to New York in the middle of night.

Breton greeted him with eyes glazed over like those of a feverish invalid.

Hare arrived with a bottle of expensive red wine in hand.

Breton ushered him into the living room, bearing a corkscrew and two glasses. Sitting across from one another at the table, the two raised their glasses. Breton had yet to utter a word about the matter.

After refilling their glasses, Breton slid Who May's thirteen pages of densely written manuscript toward Hare.

"I would like you to read this first. I would like you to tell me frankly what you think of it."

" 'Another World' . . . is it?"

Smiling as he spoke the title, he began to look over the words.

Breton silently watched as his eyes moved rhythmically back and forth across the page. As soon as Hare reached the end of the page, he turned to the next. And then to the next. And the next.

Breton began to feel some qualms.

Hare continued to read. His pace remained smooth and even.

Within ten minutes Hare had reached the last page:

> . . . the moon dream becomes blurred. The earth turns red.
> Hurry! Dobaded. Before the wings of departure are submerged.

The lines ran out. Hare raised his head. The traces of confusion that flitted across his face did not escape Breton's notice.

"Indeed," Hare said curtly. "Fascinating. The style is fresh. Yes . . . not a bad attempt at all, I think."

(Attempt?)

Breton let out an involuntary groan.

To cover his slip, he took a gulp of wine.

Hare too reached for his glass. He took a mouthful, and then another.

"I sense genuine talent. There's no mistaking it. So? Do you intend to publish this work in our magazine?"

(Of course not!) (Why?!)

Breton was seething with anger.

How could Hare remain so calm—?

"I don't know . . ." Breton muttered in a deep voice. He then turned the question back at Hare. "What would you do?"

But Hare's opinion was already clear to him.

Hare was cool and collected despite everything. Or he appeared to be. In any event, his behavior was not of someone who had been profoundly moved.

The fact that he said "*our* magazine" betrayed his doubts about the work, mildly but clearly.

In other words, the implication was that insofar as he was but one of the participants in *VVV* he would certainly respect Breton's opinion, but he personally would not cast his vote that way.

That much was clear.

Anyhow—(Why?)

Why hadn't Who May's spell been transmitted to him? (Dobaded!) Was it because French was not his native language? Still, he would not have any trouble understanding it. The work that he had done with artists in exile like Breton provided ample proof. Perhaps there were completely different grounds for experiencing its value, in different dimensions?

"Let me just say . . . for me . . ."

Hare took another sip of wine, and gazing out into space, he proceeded slowly.

"I would wait another fifteen years and bring it out in a science fiction magazine."

"What! Fifteen years?"

To his dismay, Breton hadn't the slightest idea what Hare was trying to say.

"Science fiction?"

"Today, it isn't feasible. Readers haven't matured enough yet. There are some, but this is too avant-garde. This fantasy world called 'another world' is quite attractive. It is truly beautiful. It is full of an otherworldly sense of wonder. Unfortunately, however, it doesn't have a principal hero or heroine. Moreover, the vocabulary is too specialized. The absence of a hero is a fatal flaw in this genre. At least the editors who currently work in this genre in America think so . . . but in another fifteen years or so . . ."

"You are . . ." Breton replied, struggling to control himself. "You're dodging the question."

"Dodging? Not at all!"

Hare shrugged his shoulders as if surprised.

"I was doing my best to tell you honestly my impressions."

Breton groaned.

This time he made no attempt to hide it.

He had had some heated arguments with Hare in the past. He wasn't one to pick a fight with at this point. If he said he had spoken "honestly," then those were indeed his impressions.

Still, there was something that Breton didn't understand.

When it came to science fiction, the only works that came to mind were those of the Jules Verne variety. And he was fairly certain that American science fiction was considered vulgar and lowbrow. In fact, he himself couldn't think of even a single title.

"Science fiction . . . well, you're right, you could look at it that way. But—"

Backing up a step, Breton repeated his question.

"I would really like to hear your opinion as a surrealist. What do you think?"

Hare tilted his head slightly. "I see. But . . ." He looked rather at a loss.

Still, he looked directly at Breton and, as if coming to a conclusion, spoke again.

"As I understand it, I don't see any connection between this 'Another World' and surrealism."

"Why is that?"

Breton posed the question with unintentional sharpness.

"You yourself once pointed out, did you not, that 'the imagination aims to become reality'?"

"Indeed—I did."

The phrase had appeared in something Breton had written some ten years earlier.

Hare proceeded from there.

"In this 'Another World,' however, there is absolutely no sense of striving for 'reality.' It is escape. I have only the impression of a concerted effort to leave reality behind, or to obliterate it completely. Doesn't this run counter to the role that the power of the imagination is supposed to play in surrealism?"

Breton's silence prompted Hare to continue.

"His unique manner of expression certainly has its appeal. I even feel a certain sense of violence in the evocative power of his images. No one could deny his . . . Who May's . . . talent. But nevertheless—"

Hare nodded his head softly. It looked to Breton as if he was trying to convince himself.

"In particular, in 'Another World,' with his evocative use of images, rather than troubling or destroying our everyday perception of things, he seems primarily intent on their power to stupefy and immobilize. What do you think about this?"

" . . . "

Breton drained another glass.

"The vision of 'Another World' is truly overflowing with, well, strange and wondrous beauty. That much I admit. Above all, it dazzles. It verges on a sense of *vertigo*. But I can't help thinking that this vertigo is a sort of gimmick."

With a sigh, Hare neatly put the thirteen pages of manuscript on the table, casually placing them somewhat closer to Breton.

Then all at once he began again.

"These pages undoubtedly succeed in portraying a world entirely unknown to us. But, quite frankly, I am not convinced that it is all that worthwhile an accomplishment. I mean, I just don't have the impression that the vision presented here is particularly well grounded as a whole in psychic imagery or in the activity of the unconscious. So—what is this 'Another World'? I felt it to be nothing more than a fake, a sham, through and through. It is a world produced by relying merely on a sense of language or, if you will, on the magic of words. Or, to put it another way, how can a world produced with fake words amount to anything but a fake world? And if that is the case—"

Hare shook his head from side to side, slowly but with an aura of resolution.

"While this 'Another World' may work as science fiction or as fantasy, it is far from the spirit of surrealism. I don't see how we can look at it otherwise. This is my opinion, as a surrealist."

Hare had said his peace.

Empty glass still in hand, Breton was at a loss to reply.

An uncomfortable silence fell over the room.

(Dogma!) Breton cursed him inwardly.

Feeling himself in the grip of Hare's dogmatic pronouncements twisted something deep within Breton.

Dogma has the power to foreclose discussion and dissent. And the dogma brandished by Hare was that drafted by none other than the high authority, André Breton himself.

It was truly a farce. Breton frowned.

But now he was more astonished than angry.

Hare was calm. He had analyzed the work in all tranquility, offering his critique.

But then he had been speaking with André Breton.

Once again Breton felt the need to assure himself that he was in fact André Breton.

His astonishment then became greater still.

Hare had ended up lecturing André Breton himself about the nature of surrealism.

What could be more astonishing than that?

Breton finally came up with his own conclusions. There weren't many people who would go to such lengths to argue against Breton that a certain work ran counter to the spirit of surrealism. If they were intent on breaking with him, that was another matter. But what kind of person would argue down Breton without any such thing in mind? Hare didn't seem to be that sort of person.

Nevertheless, Hare had tossed precisely that kind of speech at Breton, quite coolly.

(Coolly . . .)

But had he really been so cool? Or had it been an act?

Had he been seized by some deep-down sense of anxiety or instinctive terror that had spurred him to such desperate denial? Was that why he could not help but cling to dogma?

(That's it.)

At last Breton found a reply.

He preferred to think that the deep red flush on his face was due to too much wine.

"Your analysis was on the mark. Probably . . . it's true . . . I agree with your very telling remarks about this work, that it is a fake world constructed with fake words. From the surrealist point of view, we should be exceedingly cautious in our evaluation of it. Thank you. Your comments were very informative."

The two stood up at the same time.

They then shook hands.

At that moment Breton noticed an expression of profound relief appear on Hare's face.

What had Hare gone to such great lengths to deny? Perhaps he had keener insight into the genuine character of "Another World"? What in fact was "Another World"?

After Hare had left, Breton picked up the manuscript pages, taking care not to look at the letters so finely written on them. He returned to his study and tucked it away in a desk drawer.

6

It was two days later that Marcel Duchamp arrived.

Breton had invited him to lunch.

That was merely an excuse.

Breton had once provided the following assessment of Duchamp, nine years his elder, in the catalog for a surrealist exhibition: "Our friend Marcel Duchamp is undoubtedly the greatest artist of the early twentieth century, which makes him a complete pain in the ass for many of us."

His feelings of friendship and appreciation had remained unchanged over the years.

Marcel Duchamp unexpectedly withdrew from the world of

art in 1923, leaving his opus *Large Glass* unfinished, and thereafter he became deeply absorbed in chess, and when asked about his work, as if to vanish in a puff of smoke, he would reply, "I am a breathing machine," yet he continued to garner attention and acclaim among surrealists for various experiments with images and word games.

Among those in New York, Duchamp was one of the few intellectuals for whom Breton felt boundless respect, and at the same time he still found him to be a pain in the ass.

In 1939, he published an anthology of his word experiments under the title *Rrose Sélavy.*

Surely, he wouldn't be overwhelmed.

It was hard to imagine anyone better than Duchamp for figuring out who Who May was, and what the world he had made ultimately was.

Without a word, Breton handed him the manuscript of "Another World."

As soon he began to read, Duchamp opened his eyes wide and let forth a shout.

"Genius!"

He read on.

Gradually, however, his look changed to one of disapproval.

Nonetheless, he continued reading until the end.

Setting the manuscript on the table, he shrugged his shoulders slightly.

"André, it's nothing to worry about," Duchamp said. "This is a sort of, well, psychic ability. But you need not worry."

"Psychic ability?"

Breton asked in surprise.

"What does that mean?"

"You must have heard of it. For instance, there are people who can move a box of matches on the table without touching it, or read what's written on a card facing down—"

Duchamp grinned broadly.

"—it's that sort of thing."

Breton looked at Duchamp. With a soft sigh, he shook his head from side to side.

"You mean to say that this 'Another World' is a kind of magic act like moving things with the mind or fortune-telling?"

"Not at all," Duchamp flatly disagreed. "It's not an act. It is real. There is no doubt that it is a genuine psychic ability."

"But . . ."

"There truly exist people who possess psychic abilities such as psychokinesis and clairvoyance. I am convinced of it. In fact, I have met with one such person. With her eyes closed, without moving a finger, with only the power of mental concentration, she proved able to lift my fountain pen about five centimeters above the desk. It was quite an amazing sight! And there was no possibility of a trick. I am certain of it. There really are people with psychic abilities in this world—"

"But if that's true . . ."

"Wait a minute."

Duchamp said, raising his right index finger and waving it from side to side.

"Such an ability is truly astonishing. It is a genuinely extraordinary ability that ordinary people could not hope to imitate. That is why those who see it are inevitably awestruck. And yet—that's all there is to it."

"That's all?"

"Precisely." Duchamp nodded gravely. "Are you still with me? What is the use of having such psychic abilities? Think about it. It is far easier to move a pen or a matchbox with the hands. As for cards, one need only flip them over to read them. Of course, it would seem useful for gamblers, but even then there are people who are skilled with dice and cards without any recourse to psychic abilities. In any event, it wouldn't be of much use in playing chess."

Rolling his eyes impishly, Duchamp went on.

"Such psychic abilities are really only 'different' for those like us. It is an 'extra' ability only in that it is beyond what people need. Consequently, even though it is amazing, no one out there actually takes it seriously."

Breton caught his breath.

He finally grasped the significance of what Duchamp was saying.

(That's it . . . indeed . . .)

Indeed, he had the feeling that the tangle of problems was partly unraveling.

And yet—

"But in any case he—"

Still uncertain what he wished to say, Breton began speaking.

"In any case, can't we say that he really did 'discover' a new way of using words?"

"Exactly!" Duchamp replied. "But he didn't make particularly good use of it. It may also be that there is nothing useful to be derived from it for us ordinary people."

Duchamp picked at the corner of the manuscript on the table with a fingernail.

"This man . . . Who May . . . isn't he Chinese? No matter, but what exactly did he think he was writing? Poetry? Well, this is nothing like poetry. It may be written with words, but this is painting. And, one might say, quite garish at that. Its fantasy is visually too primitive. Don't you think? That paranoid Catalonian would be delighted to crank out this sort of thing in reams."

That was a bit of sarcasm directed toward Salvador Dalí.

Dalí at that time was completely cut off from the surrealist group, and Breton had dubbed him Avida Dollars, an anagram of Salvador Dalí, meaning "greedy for money."

"That's what . . ."

Deep in thought, Breton muttered in reply.

". . . what he himself was saying . . . he didn't know what he should do with his 'discovery' of a new way of using or making words—"

Then he added, "He said he was 'ill' . . . and he gave me the manuscript because he wanted my diagnosis . . ."

"That makes sense—"

Duchamp nodded as if he understood the entire matter.

"This is true, he is indeed ill. Without a doubt. Incidentally, how old is he?"

"He said nineteen."

"Nineteen! Well, in that case, we've nothing to worry about!" Duchamp's voice rang cheerfully.

"He'll recover. His recovery is a sure thing!"

"Recovery?"

"Exactly! It's only natural. It is a sure thing!– After all, it is an illness. I wonder where he happened upon this spell, um, 'dobaded.'"

Apparently, Duchamp thought of it as a spell, too.

In fact, there didn't seem to be any other way of referring to it.

"In any event–" Duchamp drew a deep breath before continuing. "He will write something else–why don't we wait until then, André. We may be surprised; maybe this falling under a curse was a one-time thing. He may fully recover. That's what I tend to think. That's what will happen. Because he is simply ill–"

Duchamp shrugged his shoulders only slightly this time.

"Regardless, if he does send you a second work, let me know immediately. I'll hurry over. What a thrill it will be if we have another startling encounter with the unknown, and should the work disappoint us, in that case we will be happy for him, Who May. Don't you think?"

He then went on to add, "Well, then, what shall we do with this manuscript? I am not against including it in the pages of *VVV*. But there will be trouble . . . for sure. In any event, we need to keep a typed copy of it. I'd like to expose someone else to this menace."

With these words, Duchamp placed two hands on the table and thrust him himself up.

"All right!" He announced loudly as if putting it all behind them. "Let's go to dinner!"

At that time–

Duchamp probably did not actually believe that a second work would appear. And even if it did, he surely thought it would be a mistake to have high expectations of it. Both of Duchamp's predictions, however, would prove utterly wrong.

At the same time he would have to learn the hard way that another startling encounter with the unknown would not necessarily give them cause for joy.

And it was barely one week later—

2

THE GOLD OF TIME

1

. . . the second hand kept turning. It eventually met the long hand at the fifty-nine-minute mark. They overlapped, and then, with flawless precision, the second hand continued on, marking the passage of a new second.

The short hand was now nearly approaching the four-hour mark.

Bells chimed from across Parc Blanche.

Breton did not look up.

The movement of the watch hands held his attention completely.

(Only another minute.)

He did not want to change his mind again. He had no intention of changing his mind.

With the passing of each second Breton had made the same pledge.

He would wait until exactly four o'clock as marked on his watch. He would wait until then.

That means that when the second hand passed the long hand again, it would all be over.

That was the limit.

Only four seconds left.

He would then drink the last of the bottle of red wine on the table. He would stand, would leave the café—and he would forget.

Less than three seconds.

A gentle sigh escaped his clenched lips.

It had been a painful hour.

It was the first time that he had felt so much pain waiting for someone.

The pain of it came from his misgivings.

Even while he was awaiting someone, and very anxiously, at the same time he felt terribly afraid that the person would actually show.

Although he wanted very badly to see what he, Who May, would bring with him, he also rather hoped to avoid it.

And both feelings were equally genuine.

That's what made it so painful.

Although fairly torn in two, Breton nonetheless had endured a full hour.

But there was a limit.

Two seconds more.

Breton did not lift his head.

There was no sign of the café door opening.

He wasn't coming. He certainly wasn't about to arrive now.

The certainty of it soothed the ache in his heart.

Nevertheless—

Why hadn't Who May come?

Why hadn't he kept his meeting with Breton?

After all, it had been at his request—the meeting. It had been Who May who expressed the desire to meet with Breton.

It had been last night.

It was just past eight.

The telephone rang.

"Is this Mr. Breton? Mr. André Breton?"

He sounded at wit's end.

"I have to make a request of you! No matter what, I—of you—I—I'm sorry! Oh . . . you've probably forgotten me, but

I have met with you before. With you—yes, well, no matter what, I—"

Breton hadn't forgotten. As soon as he heard his voice, Breton remembered.

At the sound of "I have to make a request," it all came back to Breton vividly.

"Monsieur Who, please calm down."

Breton answered rather harshly.

Once Who May had stopped gabbling so frenetically, Breton went on.

"Of course, I remember you, Who May. How could I forget? I even recall quite well the time that you ran up to me at the entrance of Central Park, to express your concerns, and with rather the same words, 'Please I have a request!' So don't worry about it. First, take a deep breath, and then please tell me exactly where you are, and how I can contact you by phone. But take it slowly, okay?"

He heard Who May exhaling loudly at the other end of the phone.

And while still exhaling, he began chattering.

"Oh, Mr. Breton! You really do remember me, don't you? Really you do!"

"Really I do. So—"

Breton prompted him.

"Yes! Yes, Mr. Breton. I have returned, to Paris, that is. About three months ago. I am currently living in the Chaillot area. I have rented an old apartment. I obtained your address from Mr. Arshile Gorky. That's right. Mr. Gorky wanted very much to see you. He asked me to tell you about this in the letter that he wrote. I don't know if you have heard, but last year his studio caught fire, and most of his works were destroyed in the fire. What's more, he had to have an operation for cancer. Things are really terrible for him. Oh my . . . and all this even though he is such a fine artist . . . really I just . . ."

"Hang on a minute."

Breton asked in surprise: "Did you say Arshile Gorky? Are you acquainted with him?"

It came as quite a surprise.

Breton knew Gorky quite well. In fact, he had known him quite a long time.

What surprised him was the combination of Gorky and Who May.

Gorky, a painter, had been living in America.

Breton first met Gorky in 1944 when he sought refuge in New York. The sculptor Isamu Noguchi had introduced him to Breton.

Born in Armenia, Gorky had immigrated to America at the age of sixteen. He stood out from the crowd, sporting a luxuriant moustache that lent him a decidedly foreign air.

His name had originally been Vostanik Adoyan, but apparently he had taken the name Arshile in honor of an Armenian nobleman who had done a great deal to preserve Armenian literature, and Gorky, which meant "heartless" in Russian, was also the name of his favorite writer. Or so someone had told Breton.

In any event—

When someone showed him a collection of Gorky's sketches, at a glance Breton recognized in them the rare quality of genius. They had truly inspired in him wonder and admiration.

Breton promptly decided to include Gorky at the forefront of surrealism, and the following year, 1945, the catalog for the first solo exhibition of Gorky's work held at Julien Levy's gallery included a short essay titled "The Eye-Spring: Arshile Gorky."

Characterizing Gorky's works as "heterogeneous forms in which human emotions are directly deposited," Breton lavished praise on him, writing, "of all the surrealist artists, Gorky is the only one who maintains direct contact with nature—sits down to paint before her to reveal the very rhythm of life."

And yet, for all that, there seemed to be something about Gorky himself as an individual that did not really agree with surrealism as a movement.

Gorky's spirit was, for lack of a better term, *wild*.

It combined the tenderness and ferocity of the wild.

As such, it appeared at once risky and overly sentimental for the surrealist movement, which was based on a certain intellectuality.

Breton nonetheless went to great lengths to bring him into surrealism.

And as Gorky began to frequent Breton's circle, surrealism had an actual impact on him.

Even after he returned to France in 1946, Breton continued to worry about him.

Accounts of the fire and Gorky's operation for cancer had already reached his ears.

Still, he never imagined that he would hear the name Arshile Gorky from Who May.

There were reasons for this—

By the time Breton met Gorky in 1944, Who May had already vanished without a trace from Breton's circle of friends.

And one week after that day in June 1943 when Breton had made Marcel Duchamp read Who May's "Another World"—

Breton found a large envelope stuffed in his apartment mailbox. It had not been delivered by post.

There were no stamps or postmark on the envelope.

It was addressed, however, to Breton, and instead of a return address there was only Who May's name, and nothing else.

Probably he had dropped off the envelope himself.

In any event—

As soon as he spied Who May's name, he immediately telephoned Marcel Duchamp as promised.

And Duchamp, as promised, hurried right over.

He was in very good humor.

He took the envelope from Breton with an extravagant gesture, exhaling sharply in anticipation.

"So this is it!"

He tore open the envelope.

A manuscript appeared, handwritten in fine letters on typing paper, just like "Another World."

There was a title on the first line.

It was titled "Mirror."

Duchamp read the first page and then passed it to Breton. His heart pounded in his chest. His feelings were mixed.

> Look!
> Your eye, your eyes, both your pupils,
> Staring at your eye, your eyes, both your pupils.
> Look!
> They are staring. Your eye, your eyes, both your pupils. . . .

It—

It had begun with a phrase that repeated endlessly like a Möbius strip.

And then without warning . . .

". . . foolishness."

Duchamp mumbled impatiently about halfway through reading it.

Hearing his voice, Breton raised his head. Their eyes met. And then they simultaneously looked away. They continued reading in silence.

In the midst of reading Breton became aware that the numbering of the pages did not follow the usual order. The first page was 1. The subsequent pages ran in the usual sequence of 2, 3, 4, and so on till 10, but the next page was 9, and after that, 8.

As Duchamp passed him the pages, the numbers continued to decrease, and the last page was 2.

In other words—this meant or, rather, indicated that from the last page you were to return again to the first page, 1.

1 . . . 2 . . . 3 . . . 4 . . . 5 . . . 6 . . . 7 . . . 8 . . . 9 . . . 10 . . . 9 . . . 8 . . . 7 . . . 6 . . . 5 . . . 4 . . . 3 . . . 2 . . .

Eighteen pages in all, and without end—

In keeping with this schema, Duchamp, reaching the last page marked 2, once again picked up the first page that he had already passed to Breton and began to read again.

Breton followed him.

It was entirely natural to do so. It was a structure that made it possible to continue reading endlessly.

The manuscript went back and forth between Duchamp and Breton time and again. Time and again . . .

All of a sudden—

Duchamp slapped the table hard with one hand.

At the sound, Breton returned to himself, pulling his eyes away from the lines of words.

Duchamp was glaring at the ceiling, a page of the manuscript still gripped in his fist.

"I remember reading something a lot like this."

Duchamp fairly spat out the words.

"In some passages said to be decoded from Mayan pictograms, there were repetitive incantations much like these. Indeed . . . truly like . . ."

". . . incantations."

Breton murmured in reply. Once again—spells.

Surrealism is not unaware of the value of spells. In fact, the concepts of wizardry, black arts, and arcane teachings are a profound source of energy for surrealism.

Indeed, Breton had once declared, "In the depths of surrealism I seek the truth within arcane teachings."

But—nevertheless, nevertheless—

"Is his name really Who May? The name sounds Chinese or Mongolian, or something like that. If so, it may be that he attained some knowledge of the ancient arcane teachings of the Orient and is putting it to use in these passages."

Duchamp asked.

"He . . . Who May is in fact of Oriental descent. But his father is French, and he said that he was born in Paris."

Breton shook his head.

"He's definitely French. It's clear from his grasp of French usage."

Duchamp chuckled slightly.

"Certainly, he knows how to use French. That much is evident. But—there is no one else who uses French as he does. I doubt there is anyone else like him."

Sharply, as if angry, Duchamp raised his voice.

"What do you think, André? What on earth do you think it is, this—this *thing* written in French?"

2

Such a question left Breton at a loss.

It was easy to answer, and yet not so easy.

The answer was already written on the first page of the manuscript, as a title. "Mirror"—that was the answer.

"What do you think this *thing* is, André?"

Thus pressed, Breton reluctantly muttered, "Mirror, isn't it? It . . . it's a mirror. That's how it seems to me."

Duchamp burst out laughing. It was uneasy laughter.

His usually handsome features appeared distorted with laughter, somehow demonic.

"Mirror! Mirror! Mirror! But why? How can you make a mirror with words?"

Duchamp yelled.

"This thing is indeed a mirror. I saw myself reflected in it. Was it the same for you, André? Did you too see yourself reflected in it?!"

Breton clammed up. And he lowered his eyes.

"Why is it? How is it? How can a mirror be made using the French language? I cannot even make a guess. Yet it is nonetheless possible. And the proof lies right here before us. It would seem that, with words, with the French language, something that reflects light was somehow possible. But! But still—"

Duchamp could not find the words to continue.

His laugher gradually took on a chirping sound, like a bird.

Breton wanted to say something. He wanted to reply. But there was nothing he could say.

Reading the text was nothing other than reading oneself—that was all one could say.

No one can truly read the author's text. People always read the words, the text, as a reflection of themselves.

For example, one might consider the term *woman*. The

"woman" thus portrayed is nothing but "woman" for the individual reader, inseparable from each reader's life experiences and mind-set.

In this respect, all words are like mirrors. Words present an image of the reader. Words can only present an image of the reader.

He wished to approach Duchamp at such a conceptual level of theory.

Words are mirrors—

And that's why . . . that's why . . . But, no, this was different.

(This *thing* was different!)

Breton's cheeks trembled slightly.

This—what now stood before his eyes—was not a product of such a conceptualization.

No—I'm not really sure—it may be—an incantation, or it may be similar to hypnotism . . . an optical illusion generated by the skillful use of words—but, in any case . . . in either case . . .

Just as Duchamp had said, it is undoubtedly some *thing,* made of lines of words that could transform the French language into something that reflected light, into a veritable mirror. It is not a concept. Words . . . are sending back a reflection, connecting the "image" of the reader himself to that site where the magical moment of stringing words together conjures forth a boundary.

In any event—it was a "work" that possessed definite qualities.

For a long time the silence deepened between the two men.

Neither one of them was about to look at the manuscript still lying on the table.

Both sat there, gazing off into space.

Duchamp was clearly in a bad mood. He had been laughing, but as soon as he stopped a deep crease appeared between his eyebrows.

He seemed to be deep in thought. Or maybe he was trying not to think. It was surely one or the other.

"Well, that's that."

Duchamp finally parted his lips. He spoke as if to himself.

"Let's meet with Who May. And we'll ask him. We'll get the answer from him. We'll just have to have him tell us . . . why he wanted to write something like this . . . why he thought something like this could be written."

"That's fine by me."

Feeling like he'd been saved, Breton stood up.

He went to his study, to get the manuscript of "Another World."

Who May's contact information was written on it. He found the manuscript.

Breton picked up the phone on his desk.

Duchamp came into the room after him.

Breton put his ear to the receiver. He gave the number to the operator.

The connection went through. The phone began to ring.

After seven or eight rings, someone picked up the phone at the other end.

Who May had said that it was his landlord's number.

Breton gave his name and asked the landlord if he could call Who May.

"Who May? Is that someone's name?"

The landlord didn't know Who May.

Come to think of it, Who May was supposed to be living with his stepfather.

"Could you wait one minute?"

Searching his memories, Breton just managed to remember the stepfather's name.

"Carron, that's it, I'd like to speak to Mr. Carron's son."

"Carron, I know. You mean the guy with the Oriental son?"

"That's right."

"They're not here anymore."

"Not there? Have they moved?"

"Probably. It was last night. They packed up and cleared out of here late at night."

"Where to?"

"I don't know anything about that. They said something about going out west but . . . they didn't tell me where."

Breton bit his lip.

In that case, Who May had come by to drop off the manuscript the night before he left.

"Did they leave anything, a message of any kind?"

"Well, they seemed in quite a hurry. I don't think that they had the time to leave messages."

It sounded like he was covering up something.

He gave the impression that some sort of serious trouble had suddenly fallen on the father and son.

"Is that right . . . ?"

Breton's voice dropped off.

He asked the landlord please to contact him if he heard where they'd gone, and hung up the phone.

He looked at Duchamp again.

"Not there, is he?"

Duchamp, who had been listening to the exchange, raised an eyebrow.

"That's right." Breton nodded. "He's vanished. Gone somewhere—"

Duchamp shrugged his shoulders.

"It's a shame. A bloody shame. I really wanted to see him—"

Still, even as he spoke, an expression of relief flitted across his face, as if he'd been relieved of some burden.

"By the way," he added. "I think we talked about it before, but what do you intend to do with it? Are you thinking of putting this—'Mirror'—into print?"

Breton gazed at Duchamp.

Then he slowly shook his head side to side.

"There's no way. I know that. At least it is not a task for a surrealist to publish this. Or, even if it were, not now . . . not yet . . ."

"You think that it's too soon, don't you?"

"It may be too soon, or it may be its day will never come. In any event, I think it's clear that 'now' is not the time. If something like this fell into the hands of the American military, Who May would surely be carted off to some secret base for the fabrication of new weapons. Don't you think?"

"It's possible."

Duchamp grimaced.

"If they made use of his ability, they could make propaganda more effective than bombs. First, they would have to give him instruction in Japanese and German. But they'd do it. The Americans do that sort of thing."

"But—"

Pointing at the manuscript of "Another World" on the desk, Breton continued.

"I don't intend to change my position about this. Maybe another work—if we could meet with him again and see what he comes up with next, maybe. But until then, I'd like to keep all of this under wraps. I still can't figure out what this is."

Duchamp cast another glance at "Another World" on the desk.

"Another work, you say. To be honest, 'Another World' and 'Mirror' are enough for me. More than enough. It's already plenty. My impression hasn't changed either. I'm still wondering what in the world it means to make a mirror out of words."

A timid smile flitted across Duchamp's face, as if he were embarrassed by what he said.

And that was all.

That was all—for they had no more news of Who May after that.

Not a word from him, or even rumors of him, reached Breton.

The following year, in 1944, the final edition of the surrealist journal *VVV* was published in New York. There was a reason for this being the last one. Above all, Breton and Duchamp feared that if they continued to publish this journal, they'd eventually succumb to the temptation to publish Who May's work.

In the summer and fall, Breton traveled to Canada with Elisa, the woman of his dreams whom he had met in New York.

It was the happiest time of his life. He soon heard of the liberation of Paris. And in high spirits, he began writing *Arcane 17*.

The Great War dragged on. Yet it seemed that the world had suddenly turned toward the future and become brighter.

In 1945, Breton put his energies into traveling widely. He traveled throughout the American Southwest, to Nevada, Arizona, and New Mexico, and wrote "Ode to Charles Fourier" during these travels.

That was also the year in which he officially divorced Jacqueline Lamba and made Elisa his new wife.

The day when he could return to France was approaching.

Late that year and early into the next, Breton traveled to Haiti and Martinique where he became a keen observer of voodoo rituals. Learning that these magical practices were adaptations of hypnotic techniques brought over from Europe, he felt as if a huge burden had been lifted off his chest.

For he had not forgotten. Both "Another World" and "Mirror" were tucked away in the bottom of his trunk.

Yet he had not once reread them. Maybe it was because he didn't have the time for it. Or maybe it was because he hadn't bothered to make time for it.

Either way, he could not possibly forget.

His deep attraction to magical practices in Central America was due to Who May's influence. The psychic wound that Who May had inflicted on Breton had, oddly enough, pushed him deeper into the world of malignant spells and incantations.

Yet through them, Breton learned to his surprise that these puzzling magical practices were very much rooted in the body. And this knowledge provided some measure of solace.

(. . . maybe) he would think. Maybe within the verbal operations of Who May's work, which appeared so magical, there lay hidden a very trivial trick to be exposed. (That's it . . . surely.)

If you took the time to calm yourself and looked closely at it, you would certainly see right through it without any difficulty.

However—there was no time for that, not yet. He didn't have that kind of time.

In Haiti, Breton's speech served as the trigger for the outbreak of a large-scale general strike.

In Paris, the publication of Benjamin Péret's "Le Déshonneur des poètes" was met by great indignation on the part of the Resistance fighters who had continued to fight during the Occupation of France.

March 1946—

Breton returned to Paris.

The terrible reality of the postwar world immediately fell on him, swallowing him up.

The birth of the atomic bomb cast a cloud over humanity, darkening the end of the Great War.

His former comrades had split into various factions, some hostile and some friendly. Thus began the days that severely taxed Breton—battling for an applied surrealism while fighting against social realism, and then critically confronting a situation in which the return to power of those authorities who had collaborated with the Vichy government was simply ignored.

That year passed in the blink of an eye.

He had actually begun to forget.

Until last night, at eight . . . when he had heard that voice on the phone—

3

It was unbelievable all the same.

How was it that Who May, who had completely vanished from sight, had had an opportunity to meet Arshile Gorky?

Even more important, why had Who May simply dropped out of Breton's sight?

And why did he now want again to meet with Breton in Paris?

"I met Mr. Gorky in Connecticut. David Hare let me stay with him, and that was when he introduced me to Gorky."

"Hare?"

"Yes, I came back on my own. To New York . . . but there was no one there. This was after you had returned to Paris. I did get your message, though. You said to contact David Hare—and so I decided to give him a call. He was very kind. He talked to me a lot once he had read my works. He gave me some sound advice as well. I stayed in his house in Connecticut some two weeks, and then I got on a ship bound for France."

Breton had left the message when leaving New York. At the time, beyond returning to Paris, he had no idea how or where he would find a place to live.

He trusted Hare, however. And so he gave him Who May's name.

Breton himself had long forgotten about the message. But it had all worked out after all.

Breton now understood.

He knew that David Hare had been quite close to Arshile Gorky.

The year after the Bretons had met Gorky, Hare offered him a room in his home, and during his stay there Gorky completed his *Plough and the Song* series.

Hare was truly generous about such things.

Breton was surprised that Who May had received Gorky's address, but if Hare had been involved, it wasn't unthinkable.

"—that's all very well." Breton asked: "But why did you disappear without telling us? 'Mirror' did reach me. Marcel Duchamp and I were both quite taken by surprise with it. We really wanted to ask you some questions about it. So we called the apartment number you had given me, but you and your father had already cleared out of there."

"I must apologize, Monsieur Breton. Jean-Pierre Carron, my father, ran into trouble in his business dealings with an Italian gentleman—and we had to leave New York. And so we fled all the way to California."

"Fled?"

"We were in fear of our lives. My father was penniless at the time. We couldn't tell anyone where we were living. I have to apologize . . ."

"I see."

"I parted with my father in San Francisco. He told me that if we stayed together, I could be implicated in his troubles—so I returned alone to New York."

(His father?)

Breton tried to imagine the stepfather whom he had never seen.

A man whose business with an Italian man in America involved the sort of troubles that put a price on his head, so it seemed.

"That much I understand, but—"

Glancing up at the clock, Breton continued.

"You said that you're in the Chaillot area, right? So no time like the present. Come to my house. You're more than welcome here. I would like to hear more about this 'request' of yours. And there are many other things I would like to talk about."

"That's not possible. I can't go anywhere right now."

"Why is that?"

"Right now, Monsieur Breton—right now I am writing. I can write. I have found a completely new key. It's such a—oh, how I can write with it!"

"A key?"

"Monsieur Breton—oh, please listen to me. I am fearful. Truly fearful. If I do write it, what will happen to me . . . I really don't know. It scares me. I am terrified."

"What are you afraid of?" Breton replied somewhat exasperated. "What key have you found? What are you trying to write—this time?"

"Time. I can write time. I have found the way to do it, the words for it."

"Time!? But that's . . . no, wait."

Breton cleared his throat to suppress the impulse to yell at him.

"Time is, after all, a fairly common topic, isn't it? You're surely aware of all the poetry and prose about time. And then—there's film, too. The art of film is, by its nature, an art of time. Putting that into words, for instance—"

Breton was doing his best to rebut him.

If one considered Who May's first work in the same manner, it was a "picture." Regardless of whether it was a simple picture or not, it was unmistakably a "scene" written with words.

If, when Who May said he was "writing time," he meant transforming cinema into words—then he could use the same arguments that he had used with Hare and Duchamp.

Immediately, however, from the other end of the line came a firm rejection.

"That's not it at all! Mr. Breton, that's not what it is!"

"It's not?"

"What I am trying to write is not an illusion of time. It is time itself. I can put into words time itself, duplicating the time that binds this world. I can produce another time with words. I have discovered the key for it!"

". . ."

Feeling overawed, Breton was at a loss for words.

"Monsieur Breton, you have to believe me! It's the truth! I truly can write it."

"I understand," Breton replied in a strangled tone. "So, that's what you're now trying to write?"

"That's right, Mr. Breton!" Who May replied excitedly. "I have already written down the title. And then, well, I became afraid . . . I didn't know what to do. I felt that I had to call you—"

"And what exactly is the title?"

"I called it 'The Gold of Time.' That's right. There is an amazing resemblance between the qualities of gold and of time. I have come to understand why alchemists were so taken with gold. They didn't want gold. They were trying to control time, life itself!"

"What do you intend to do? That is—from here on . . ."

"Yes. Listening to you, I have reached a decision. I will write it this very night. I will try writing it. I already know how. It is already finished in my head. I only have to write it."

"Tonight, you say? So you will have it finished by to-morrow?"

"That's right. I will write it! And I would like you to look at it first! Tomorrow! Please!"

"All right. That's what we'll do."

Breton thought a bit and made a suggestion.

"Tomorrow at three—you know Place Blanche in Montmartre. A café of the same name has opened there. I'll wait for you there. How's that?"

Who May repeated the place and time and promised to be there.

"I will definitely be there. Without fail—oh, Mr. Breton, truly . . . I will! Time! I will create time with words! It's unbelievable, I never would have thought it possible, until today. But I can do it. I can! It can be written . . ."

If Who May said he could do it, he could—a chill ran through Breton as he thought about it.

After all, he was the one who had created a "mirror" with words.

He had hung up the phone but couldn't remember when.

He became aware that he was staring into space, slumped deep into the chair in his study.

A chill ran down his spine.

He hurried off to the bedroom where Elisa awaited him.

All night long—he tossed and turned with nightmares, awakening at dawn drenched in sweat. He couldn't remember ever feeling so wretched.

And so he had made his way to Place Blanche.

He sat down at this table at exactly three o'clock.

An hour—

(Who May, your time's up.)

Breton raised his head.

He reached for his glass and drank down the wine in a gulp. It was utterly flavorless to him.

Yet the glass of wine washed something away. He felt his spirits lifting.

(So that's it. The matter's settled.)

He pondered.

(He wasn't going to show. Such a thing . . . even for Who May . . . is just not possible. It was all illusion and delusion on his part.)

A trace of a smile appeared on Breton's lips.

He stood up.

Oddly, he no longer felt the cold.

(Who May.)

Breton summoned him in his mind.

(You truly produced something astonishing. But that was the end of it. Duchamp was right after all. You made a "mirror" of words, but what then? That was as far as it went. That's as far as your "special abilities" could go—)

Breton left the café.

He crossed Place Blanche and headed home.

(Indeed, there was no reason to be afraid . . . writing time? . . . "Gold of Time"? . . . But you couldn't deliver after all, Who May. It's all over. Or maybe I should use your turn of phrase and say, You're cured.)

Duchamp's conclusions came to mind.

The demon possessing him must have fled. No doubt of it. Making "time" with words proved too large a delusion for even a demon to bear.

The cold wind continued to blow relentlessly.

Yet Breton's cheeks felt pleasantly warm. And the icy chill in his heart seemed to melt away.

(Indeed, now is not the time to fight each other over illusions. Today we have to face up to reality—the reality of the postwar world—)

Breton held his head high in the cold wind.

(Yes, indeed!)

At that time—

Breton had no way of knowing.

But he was mistaken.

Who May had already written "Gold of Time."

But there was good reason why he could not deliver it to Breton. He was already dead by then.

Well, it is not exactly true that he died.

His heart was still beating. But he had lost consciousness and all physical responses.

He was but a lump of flesh, faintly breathing, his head resting on the manuscript that he had just finished, his large eyes open wide.

Late that night, his roommate, an Italian art student, returned drunk to the apartment and found him in that condition. He called the police.

Who May was taken at once to the hospital.

Judging from his condition, the doctors suspected that he had been taking some sort of drug.

The police searched Who May's room. But nothing turned up.

Although they thoroughly interrogated the art student who had found him, he knew absolutely nothing.

The student had known Who May fairly well. He had heard that Who May's father was in America. He knew of no other relatives except the father.

Ultimately, the responsibility for Who May fell to him.

His name was Enrico Caldocchi. He had only recently come to France. He had gained fairly good conversational skills but almost no reading skills.

He initially thought that the document that Who May had left was a will.

The policeman took a look, shrugged his shoulders, and rejected the idea.

"It's a poem of some kind. It makes no sense to me."

Three days later—

Who May's heart stopped without his ever regaining consciousness.

Even though he'd been told it was just a poem, Caldocchi still thought that there had to be some sort of will or testament in it.

Caldocchi thus went through the letters addressed to Who May, thinking to send the poem to someone who had been close to him.

He knew that the father was in America.

So he first looked for letters from America. There were three of them.

Caldocchi then wrote out a number of copies of the poem left by Who May. He couldn't read French, but it was easy enough for him to write the words. The handwriting was very neat and easy to read.

He also made a number of copies for other people who seemed to have been friends with Who May.

He then put them in envelopes and addressed them.

After mailing them, Caldocchi decided that his responsibility ended there.

He called a secondhand store to get rid of Who May's personal belongings.

With the few francs he received, he went out into Montmartre and drank a toast to his departed friend.

4

March 3, 1948—

Philippe Sadeico received an envelope.

The sender's name was Enrico Caldocchi. The name wasn't familiar. Thinking that it could be from one of his customers, he opened it.

Sadeico owned a small restaurant on the Boulevard de Magenta. It was nothing fancy but had a reputation for good food. A lot of the young people in theater came there, and every night at closing time the place was still jumping.

He often received letters from customers, either appreciative or apologetic.

Sadeico had no interest in theater or the arts. But he was fond of these young people, and they were fond of him in return.

But that was not the kind of letter he pulled from the envelope.

At the top of the page was written "The Gold of Time." And then Who May.

(Who May . . . that's right!)

Sadeico remembered.

The youth, the stepson of that businessman, Jean-Pierre Carron. The memory gave Sadeico a jolt.

With a furtive glance at the bedroom where his wife slept, he stuffed the letter in his pocket.

Who May's mother was a highly sought-after prostitute. An Oriental woman. Both Carron and Sadeico had been customers of hers.

But she was dead now.

Carron was a bachelor. He'd been quite the playboy at the time.

He had adopted her son.

It was obvious what he had in mind. Who May was as beautiful as his mother. He had a lovely physique. Carron had a reputation for swinging both ways.

Sadeico felt no aversion to beautiful boys either.

He had invited Carron and his son to his restaurant many times.

He hadn't been able to get between them.

Carron and Who May seemed to get along very well together.

Sadeico was persistent, nonetheless, and wrote a number of letters to Who May.

When the Nazis invaded, however, father and son fled for America. He hadn't heard from them since.

What on earth could Who May want of him now? What's more, the letter had been sent to him by someone else. Caldocchi . . . clearly an Italian name.

(Surely . . . he can't intend to blackmail me, to expose me for some wrong.)

Sadeico became uneasy.

"Hey, I am going out for a while!"

Calling to his wife, he hurried out.

It was less than a three-minute walk to the restaurant.

The boy on janitorial duty had already begun cleaning up the restaurant.

Sadeico sat at one of the tables and pulled the letter out of his pocket with trepidation.

"The Gold of Time"—

He had no idea what that meant.

He began reading nonetheless.

"The shade of the shadow of light. The depths of the depth of light. Equinoctial tipping of light. Around behind light, at the time it arrives here. Time is gold. Gold itself has the same aspect as time. . . ."

Before he had read half of the first page, his head began to throb in pain.

(What is he getting at?)

He felt angry.

A code? Or some sort of poem?

(Come on!)

Nobody was about to get Sadeico to read a poem. Let alone something incomprehensible like this that didn't even seem like a proper poem.

Maybe Who May had lost his mind?

Probably one of his friends sent it to him to let him know.

(Whatever it is . . . ugh!)

Sadeico put the letter back in his pocket.

(I don't get it. Nothing to do with me.)

The mother probably had some sort of illness. She passed it along to the son, and now it's finally starting to show.

Sadeico felt a chill run down his spine.

(It's not funny. In that case, I too . . .)

He suddenly wanted to take a leak. He stood up and went to the back of the restaurant.

While he pissed, he looked at his thing and shivered again.

He felt thoroughly depressed.

When he went back into the restaurant, a customer was coming in.

It was Jacques Lesage. He was a member of an avant-garde theater group. He often showed up at Sadeico's place. Today he was too early. Nothing was ready yet.

"Sorry, Jacques. At this hour, we're not cooking. Only cold plates," Sadeico said.

"That's fine with me. Whatever you can give me. I haven't eaten all day."

"Too much to drink again?"

Laughing, Sadeico went into the kitchen.

Fresh bread had just arrived.

He put some cheese and sausage on a plate with it and carried that and a glass of wine to Lesage's table.

"Thanks."

He immediately started to dig in.

"By the way, Jacques." He suddenly had an idea and took the letter from his pocket. "What do you think of this?"

". . . ?"

"Just give it a read for me. I can't make heads or tails of it. I can only assume that he's crazy."

Lesage took the letter.

Chewing all the while, he started to peruse it.

At that moment, his young assistant called Sadeico from the kitchen.

Sadeico left the table and went inside.

The cleanup was finished. Sadeico gave the boy his pay for the day and came back into the table area.

Lesage was still reading the letter. Even though he'd come in with an empty stomach, he had forgotten all about the food in front of him. He wore a blank expression on his face.

Sadeico began to feel uneasy again.

"What do you think? What's it about?"

In response, Lesage shook his head from side to side a couple of times. Then finally he looked up.

"Who is this . . . Who May?"

"Just a name. The son of a friend."

"This son . . . is he a poet?"

"A poet? So you think this is a poem after all?" Sadeico asked, feeling somewhat relieved.

"A poem . . . it is . . . certainly . . . but then I am not sure . . ."

"That's only natural. He's crazy, I'm sure of it."

Lesage just shook his head.

"Where is he living now?"

"I really don't know. I only know that he fled to America with his father before the Nazis came. But I don't know if he's come back, or if he's still there. This letter arrived out of the blue, this morning, addressed to me."

Lesage went on shaking his head. Then he spoke.

"This . . . letter, or . . . whatever, do you mind if I keep it?"

Sadeico frowned.

"I don't mind. But . . . well . . . is there anything, anything written there that might be compromising for me?"

"Anything about you? No, nothing at all. It's hard to describe . . . but no, in any case . . . there's someone I'd like to show this to."

"It's okay, then," Sadeico nodded. "Just take it, fine by me."

Lesage jumped to his feet.

Without a word, he ran out.

The bread and cheese were still on the table, half eaten.

"What the hell!?"

Sadeico cursed.

"They're all crazy!"

By the end of the day, however, Sadeico had forgotten all about it. It had been an unusually busy day.

The same day, March 3, in the afternoon—

A young man came to visit Antonin Artaud at the psychiatric clinic at Ivry-sur-Seine.

A member of an avant-garde theater group, he had appeared in some of Artaud's plays staged by his group. It wasn't the first time that he had paid Artaud a visit.

After his attack in Dublin in 1937, Artaud spent most of the next ten years locked away in asylums, but two years previously, through the efforts of friends, among them Breton, he had been released from medical incarceration.

He had been transferred from the psychiatric hospital in Rodez to this clinic.

Even while in the clinic, Artaud remained exceedingly active. The previous year he had published "Van Gogh, le suicidé de la société," which was awarded the Prix Sainte-Beuve.

His condition had stabilized, and it appeared that it would continue to improve.

On that day, the weather was fine, and Artaud greeted his visitor in high spirits.

The young man stayed with Artaud for about an hour and then returned home.

The next day—

Artaud was found dead, sitting in his chair in his room at the clinic.

Actually, when the nurse found him, he was still breathing. Staring at the ceiling, he was actually still breathing. His heart was still beating.

But he had lost consciousness. All trace of consciousness had completely left him.

In his fist, Artaud was gripping a letter of about ten pages, filled with writing in a fine hand.

5

The fate that befell Arshile Gorky was too cruel to describe as bad luck.

After losing well over thirty works to a fire in his studio in January 1946, Gorky was informed the following month that he had colon cancer and underwent an operation.

Fortunately, the operation was successful, but thereafter he had to live with all manner of special equipment for cleaning and relieving himself, such as an artificial bladder tied to his side that continually emitted gurgling sounds.

But Gorky rose to the situation.

Upon his release from the hospital, he immediately picked

up his paintbrushes, and in the late summer and early fall, on a farm in Hamilton, Virginia, he made sketches for more than three hundred works. To continue his work, he returned to Sherman, Connecticut, and rented a barn not far from the studio that had burned down.

Yet he continued to be deviled by misfortune.

Some two years after his operation, on June 26, 1948, he was involved in a car accident when gallery owner Julien Levy and his wife were driving him home from New York. He suffered a fractured back and neck, which rendered him impotent and made it impossible for him to use his right arm and thus to paint.

Gorky fell into a profound spiritual depression as a consequence.

Having already reached the limits of her tolerance, his wife finally left him. She felt that it would be better for their two daughters to avoid being swept up by Gorky's misfortunes any further.

Alone, broken physically, shattered emotionally, he dragged himself back to the converted barn in Sherman that was his studio.

During his absence, dust had covered everything in the room.

When Gorky finally managed to get himself into a chair, he noticed an envelope covered with fine dust on the desk.

The address was written in exceedingly clumsy letters.

The sender's name meant absolutely nothing to him.

Due to the paralysis of his arm, Gorky used his teeth to tear open the envelope.

A sheaf of papers was enclosed.

As Gorky smoothed out the folds of the pages on the desk, tears came to his eyes.

(Who May . . .)

It was a name dear to him.

Two years previously, the young man had given solace and encouragement to Gorky in his time of great loss.

It was the surrealist David Hare who had introduced him

to Gorky. The young man had shown a more profound understanding of Gorky's art than even Hare had.

The young man stayed at Hare's house for some time. During his stay, he frequently came to keep Gorky company in his studio.

The young man was writing poetry.

He had shown one of his poems to Hare. It was written in French. But Gorky nonetheless understood something of it. Or, rather, for Gorky it was less a matter of understanding it than one of feeling that the strange words were speaking to him from the beyond.

(Dobaded.)

He remembered it still. Along with the strange words, he recalled Who May's beautiful countenance with those oversized eyes.

He had later returned home to France.

Gorky had received one letter from him, which had included a request for the address of André Breton.

André Breton—!

The prince of surrealism. Gorky had had enough of surrealists. He couldn't help thinking that his association with them had brought tragedy upon him.

He had once explained it to a fellow artist, Saul Schary: "It was a great mistake to associate with the surrealist crowd. They're a terrible lot. They're the sort who think nothing of sleeping with each other's wives. It was a horrible mistake to let my wife associate with that crowd."

Of course, Breton had praised his work. Yet that hadn't been for Gorky's sake.

Breton had merely used Gorky for the sake of surrealism, that is, for the sake of Breton himself.

At the time Gorky hadn't seen it, though.

He had been blinded by flattery.

(André Breton . . .)

He could easily imagine how advantageous Who May might prove as an offering on the altar of surrealism.

He considered warning Who May.

But then he reconsidered.

Who May's life was his own. He should be the one to determine how to live it.

Gorky telephoned David Hare, requested Breton's address, and sent it to Who May. In the letter, he also asked him to tell Breton to come visit again.

Gorky wished by all means to show Breton the artificial bladder hanging at his side.

How would Breton react to that? Would he make a show of sadness? Or would he just laugh? Or maybe he would come up with some pithy remark such as "your very existence is now surrealism"?

As he had expected, however, Breton never contacted him.

He had had no news from Who May in quite a while either.

Gorky had begun to forget him. There had been other things on his mind.

(Who May . . .)

Gorky slowly perused the densely written letter, word by word. The writing was not Who May's.

Had Who May had someone write for him?

But—why?

Could it be that Who May had suffered a similar fate to Gorky? Gorky mused.

(If that's the case, surrealism must be to blame.)

As he pondered, Gorky continued to read.

He understood. It was clear to him.

It was probably not Who May who had written out the words. But there was no doubt that the words on the page had been written by Who May.

And then—it was nightfall.

Before he knew it, the morning sun was streaming into the barn.

Just before dawn in mid-July—

The ring of the doorbell awoke Isamu Noguchi at home in bed on MacDougal Alley, Greenwich Village.

Rubbing his eyes, he went through the garden to the front door, and there stood Arshile Gorky.

He had clasped in his arms, as if dear to him, a dirty old rag doll and an equally soiled and shabby envelope.

The tears that suddenly began to stream from his eyes took Noguchi by surprise, and he brought him directly into the house.

But Gorky refused and raised his voice as if agitated.

"This is all there is. This is all that is left to me in the world! All there is!—"

Once Gorky had calmed down, he asked Noguchi to take him back to the converted barn in Sherman, Connecticut.

Noguchi called Wilfredo Lam and put Gorky in the car. On the way, he stopped with him at a psychiatric clinic, and after Gorky underwent electroshock therapy, Noguchi drove him home.

Gorky held on tightly to the doll and envelope the entire time.

Some days later, on July 20—

Gorky's oldest friend, the artist Saul Schary, decided one night after dinner to call on him to see how he was doing.

Schary later gave the following description of Gorky at that time: "He was extremely agitated. His eyes . . . were deep in color but glazed over as if flashing with light, and his face was splotched with red and white patches. He was very irritable, as if something was hounding him."

Gorky chatted with Schary for a couple of hours that night.

Schary finally excused himself late at night, but, exhausted from the hours of talking, he forgot his glasses at Gorky's house.

In the next morning, Schary rang Gorky to ask if he could come and collect his glasses.

"Of course. Come over immediately."

So Schary set off.

Gorky was as irritable as the night before. Yet at the same time he looked rather happy.

Gorky retrieved Schary's glasses, and as he handed them to him, he spoke resolutely.

"Schary, my life is over. I'm not going to live anymore. There's no need to."

Startled, Schary tried going inside to cheer him up. But Gorky cut him short.

"Schary, would you mind leaving now? There's something I have to do alone. Just once more, that . . ."

With these words, Gorky led Schary to the door. He walked out to the car with him. He then took Schary's hand and said with great affection, "Good-bye, Schary."

Schary felt obliged to drive off.

Gorky's condition continued to bother him nonetheless.

So he stopped off at Peter Blume's house on his way home.

Blume, who had just gotten out of bed, was shaving.

Schary told Blume about how Gorky had seemed to him.

"It's possible that he means to kill himself."

The word spread quickly among the other artists in the Sherman area.

Upon hearing this news from the Blumes, Yves Tanguy's wife, Kay, became worried and called Malcolm Cowley. Cowley rushed over to the Blumes' house.

Finally, after a brief discussion, they all decided to go check on Gorky.

They all went in Cowley's car.

They arrived at Gorky's place close to noon.

But the place was silent. No one was there.

In the barn, they found a rope hanging from the rafters. But that was all. There was no sign of Gorky.

They split up and broadened their search.

Nearby were the remains of a site that had been prospected for uranium. They walked the temporary roads that had been carved out.

As they were passing by one of sheds where there was a stone crusher for uranium ore, a small dog dashed out barking.

It was one of the two dogs that Gorky kept.

Attracted by the barking, they hurried into the shed beside the stone crusher. They peered inside.

Gorky was hanging there by the neck, dead.

One of the group who found him, Malcolm Cowley, later said that he looked like a wax doll.

At Gorky's feet, a crate lay overturned, which he had stood on to hang himself. There was a stack of similar crates nearby, and on one of them he had written, "Good-bye my loves."

Someone telephoned for the state troopers.

Someone else went into his studio to see if he had left anything behind before deciding to kill himself.

There was a painting that looked pretty much complete. At the corner of the canvas, he had written the title "Last Painting," but with a knife he had slashed the surface of the painting this way and that.

On his desk, a shabby doll and an envelope had been neatly placed.

Kay Tanguy reached for the envelope. She thought it might be a will.

Her husband Yves stopped her.

"Better to not touch anything until the police arrive."

6

The day of the funeral—

Arshile Gorky's sister Vartoosh had flown in from Chicago with her husband, Moorad Mooradian.

But among those who attended the funeral there was not a single face familiar to her.

Due to Breton's endorsement, the surrealists had flocked around Gorky.

They had largely driven away his old friends and acquaintances.

This was still a source of unhappiness for Vartoosh.

She finally spotted Saul Schary in the crowd.

Schary was one of the few friends who had remained close to him to the end. Naturally, Vartoosh had also known him a long time.

Vartoosh approached Schary, crying. She hugged him and

then asked, "Where have all of his friends gone, Saul? You're the only one here that I know."

Schary placed a hand on her shoulder and told her in great detail everything that he knew about Gorky's last few days.

"On the desk was a tattered doll and an envelope containing some sort of poem. Beyond that, we didn't find anything resembling a will or testament."

"A poem, you say?"

Her voice became slightly shrill.

"Is it something written by one of those surrealists?"

Saul Schary shook his head.

"I'm not sure. It's in French. I can't read a word of it. Apparently, however, your brother read it repeatedly just before he died. The pages and the envelope were quite worn and dirty. I wonder what it's about."

"French? That definitely sounds like the surrealist crowd. Probably one of these surrealists wrote it. I'll bet that they were writing something nasty about my brother."

"I don't think so. I don't think it's like that at all."

Aware of the surrealists around them, Schary lowered his voice.

"I think it's some kind of literary work. In English, the title would be something like 'Gold of Time.' If you'd like to read it, I'll get it to you. Yves Tanguy has it right now."

But Vartoosh vehemently refused the offer.

"I have no desire to read it, none at all. Please pass it along to the surrealists."

Schary followed Vartoosh's advice.

After the funeral, Schary called on Yves Tanguy and told him that Gorky's family wished to have the poem sent to the surrealists in Europe.

Tanguy took Schary's request to heart.

His understanding was that Gorky's family wished to share with his surrealist "companions" a work that Gorky had enjoyed reading till the day he died. So Tanguy set to work.

Tanguy typed up a number of copies of the poem and sent them to all the surrealists he knew.

In late 1948, Sylvia Carney, a female surrealist who had met Tanguy during his exile in America, was found dead in her bathtub.

The police made inquiries to determine whether it was suicide, murder, or death by natural causes, but ultimately the cause of death remained uncertain.

The following year the poet René Malle hung himself.

In 1952, Pierre Mabille, a doctor who joined surrealism in the field of art criticism and devoted himself to anthologizing obscure "arcane" works, died in Paris.

In the same year, Roger Vitrac, a poet and playwright who introduced surrealist humor into the world of theater, also died in Paris.

Also in the same year—

A leader of the surrealist movement, hailed as one of its great poets, Paul Éluard, died in Paris.

In 1953—

The Czech poet Jindrich Heisler, acclaimed for his delicacy with words and images, also died in Paris.

In the same year, poet and painter Francis Picabia, who had been at the forefront of Dada and surrealism, died in Paris.

In 1955—

The well-known surrealist artist Yves Tanguy, born in Paris but naturalized in America after taking refuge there during the war, died in Woodbury, Connecticut. Paper was found rolled into his typewriter, apparently to type poetry.

In 1957—

Oscar Domínguez, best known for his "decalomania" and his period of "cosmic objects," committed suicide in Paris.

In 1959—

The greatest of the surrealist poets, on whom Breton had lavished his praise, Benjamin Péret, died in Paris.

Another poet whose talents had won Breton's admiration, Jean-Pierre Duprey, killed himself in Paris in the same year. One day he began suddenly saying that his other self had appeared. He was soon put in a mental hospital. After his release, he completed a manuscript titled "La Fin et la manière," which he asked his wife to send to Breton, and then hung himself. "La Fin et la manière" was published six years after his death.

Also in that year—

The surrealist critic, theorist, and artist born in Vienna, Wolfgang Paalen shot himself in the head one stormy night in Mexico City.

A keen reader of contemporary physics, he insisted that it was necessary to explore both the arts and sciences to unlock the secrets of the universe.

It was said that not long before his suicide he told his friends that he hadn't known that the secret of time had been resolved, but now that he knew he could no longer remain in this space-time.

In 1962—

The Swiss-born surrealist painter Kurt Seligmann died of a self-inflicted gun wound. Seligmann, already known for his Ultra-Furniture, had assisted Breton and the other refugee surrealists during the war. After his Ultra-Furniture project, he immersed himself in the study of the occult, and in the months before his death he had laid the groundwork for spiritual techniques of harnessing space-time energies. But before he could bring his experiment to fruition, he passed away.

And then in 1966, André Breton died.

The epitaph on his tomb reads—André Breton 1896–1966 "I seek the gold of time."

1970—

As if following Breton, Marcel Duchamp died in Neuilly-sur-Seine on the outskirts of Paris.

In the year after Breton's death, it was said that Duchamp continually repeated the words of Breton's epitaph, "I seek the gold of time."

In 1970, Georges Malkine, an artist known for his deep involvement with surrealism from its beginnings, died. He had all but abandoned painting, but then in 1949, while in America, he found inspiration and revived his career as an artist, continuing to paint until 1966, not long before his death.

And then in 1982—

The American science fiction writer Philip K. Dick, whose otherworldly descriptions were exceedingly close to surrealism, died of a heart attack of unknown origin.

Before his death he had become obsessed with the idea of harnessing the dreadful potentiality latent in the time-travel paradox by means of alchemical transformation and apparently revealed that he finally got his hands on suitable material to do so.

But he died before he could actually begin such work.

3

UNDISCOVERED CENTURY

1

It was Friday afternoon.

With a red pen, Mishima Keiko was editing the proofs of a column to be carried in a women's magazine. At a workstation along the wall, another temp, a designer, was working on the layout for a special insert called "A Complete Guide to Orgasm" for the same magazine.

Everyone else had cleared out.

All was quiet.

From the headphones strapped over the designer's ears, a faint drumming could be heard.

It must be incredibly loud for him.

With that sort of work, you'd need something to numb your mind.

Sakakibara Kōji slugged down the last of his cold instant coffee, snapped shut the book he'd been reading, and stood up.

Mishima Keiko briefly glanced his way and then returned to making red lines.

The fact was—they had time on their hands.

Five people worked in the office, including Sakakibara, the

president and chief editor. They took on a temp or two when necessary.

That's all there was to Kirin Publishers.

They had only one regular publication, the *Kirin Quarterly Magazine of Poetry and Art*. They also published some paperbacks, mostly editions of poetry and criticism in translation.

A major newspaper had once introduced them with the headline "The conscience of the publishing world."

They truly took pride in their work. They put their heart into every volume they handled.

But you can't live on the dictates of conscience alone.

And so they took on side jobs. They did some editorial work for other presses. They did setting for printing.

Their card read, "Planning, editing, publishing, finish work." In other words, they'd do anything.

Their ambitions lay entirely in publishing.

In reality, however, they depended on side jobs for 70 percent of their income.

Six years earlier, Sakakibara had worked in the editorial division of a major publishing house on literary magazines.

He held a degree in French literature.

He had written on Valéry for his undergraduate thesis and on Mallarmé for his graduate thesis.

Naturally, his interests lay primarily in that area.

Within the editorial division, he focused his efforts on foreign works. In each issue, he introduced literature from another part of the world. He was one of the first to draw attention to Latin American literature.

His efforts had had a definite impact.

But Japanese writers began to complain.

They pointed out that writers received very little for contributing to literary magazines, and so if foreigners took any part of that small share, there would not be enough for Japanese writers.

And so, one day—the senior editor informed him that they were cutting his section.

He argued against this move. At the top of his lungs.

Eventually, the editor-in-chief himself entered the fray.

"One of our distinguished contributors has expressed his concerns over the direction that we have taken with this magazine. And he'll encourage others to withdraw their contributions."

The distinguished contributor had considerable clout in the literary world.

He could indeed put the squeeze on them.

All the more outraged, Sakakibara took on the editor-in-chief. The editor-in-chief simply replied, "I understand. I will take your opinion into consideration."

One week later—

Sakakibara received notice of his transfer. His new section was producing an entertainment magazine for teenagers.

The idea was for him to pour his rebellious energy into something more challenging, a magazine with circulation figures twenty times greater than prior magazines.

Sakakibara made a bold decision.

With friends from college, he started his own company, Kirin Publishers.

Six years had passed.

His partner, Kasadera, who started the company with him, was making the rounds of publishers.

Until last month they had had regular work for a weekly magazine, but that had been cut off in the name of updating the look of the magazine, and so he was looking for some work to replace it.

Kojima was out picking up manuscripts. Miyagami had finished his proofreading and was on vacation.

The desks for the five employees formed a cluster in the center of the office.

Against one wall were two workstations for part-time designers. Bookcases lined the other walls. The lower shelves of the bookcases were reserved for cartons full of returned books. The piles of cartons that had accumulated over the years had gradually spilled onto the floor, like a glacier eroding everything in its advance.

Sakakibara stood at the window looking down on Waseda Avenue.

The office was on the third floor of a building near Takadano-baba station.

He watched the endless streams of students flowing into the university below.

(But with so many students out there . . .) He thought gloomily. (Still no reason to get our hopes up.)

In any event—even if the numbers were small, they had regular readers. What really mattered in life was to hold to your goals regardless of what others thought.

Even if it meant something as worthless as a "complete illustrated guide to orgasm."

Just then—

The phone rang.

Mishima Keiko picked up.

"Hello, this is Kirin Publishers."

She had wandered into their office four years ago.

She had still been a student at the time. She was a devoted reader of *Kirin Quarterly*.

Her visits had become more and more frequent.

Sweet and lovable, she soon became a favorite of the editors. Gradually, she began to help with various tasks. She was a college senior. Upon consultation with Kasadera, he made her an offer to work with them. She accepted with enthusiasm.

Despite the low pay, she gave it her all.

(Sometime . . .)

Sakakibara thinks a lot about it.

(Sometime . . . before Kasadera beats me to the draw . . .)

"Boss."

She called for Sakakibara.

"It's a Mr. Tomari from Hakuden Agency—"

"Hakuden Agency?"

Naturally, he knew the name.

It was one of the largest agencies in the advertising industry. Kirin had had no dealings with them.

It couldn't be a request to publish an ad.

If so, they had made a mistake. Kirin never advertised on that scale.

Kirin placed advertisements in newspapers and small magazines targeted for book lovers. Most of these were exchange ads. In exchange for carrying their ad, Kirin gave them similar advertising space.

That largely sufficed.

Even if Kirin placed advertisements in a large national newspaper such as the *Asahi*, it wouldn't help them move books at all.

It might seem a shame, but things actually worked better that way, because the group of readers who bought their publications was exceedingly limited. They had little to do with the so-called general public.

And so they had no reason to do business with the likes of Hakuden.

Sakakibara took the call nonetheless.

"Hello, this is Sakakibara."

"Hello! My name is Tomari. I work for the Hakuden Agency companies."

"Yes?" He sounded short of breath. But he went on in a somewhat nasal tone. "What can I do for you?"

"Okay! My apologies for calling you out of the blue. You are Mr. Sakakibara, aren't you?"

"This is he."

"Well then, great! We are working on behalf of the Seito distribution group, and right now we're developing plans for an academic business campaign for next year, and—"

The Seito distribution group, that meant the Seito department store chain.

No doubt about it, it was a huge corporation.

They owned a chain of supermarkets and rental units and had recently expanded into the leisure and recreation business.

Business with them seemed even more unlikely.

"Well now—" The agency's representative chattered on

energetically, as if eager to make his point. "In the context of this project, we would really like to have your company help us out, and that's why I am calling you today—"

It was not what he had expected.

"By help out, you mean, you want us to work with you?"

"Do you think that would be possible?"

It was quite a combination, Hakuden Agency and Seito. And to be asked was astonishing.

But . . . still . . . Sakakibara thought there had to be some kind of mistake.

"Well . . . you see, we do finish work related to print runs, and that's only for publishers, and so we've not much experience with advertising . . ."

Sakakibara spoke frankly.

"Print runs?"

The Hakuden agent gave a short laugh.

"You must be joking. That's not what we're looking for. On this project, we're hoping for your full participation—"

"About this project . . ."

"If at all possible, I'd like to meet with you tomorrow to discuss the details—"

"Sure, that would be fine with me."

Come what may, he had nothing to lose by hearing him out. Still . . . it didn't entirely make sense to him, and Sakakibara wished to make things perfectly clear.

"Well, we're in the business of publishing, and consequently, we only deal with the material end of things. And so, even after talking with you, I am not entirely sure that we can do anything for you—"

"That's not at all true. As a matter of fact, the request for Kirin to join the project came directly from the head of Seito. If you'll excuse my saying so, we hadn't ever heard of your company before then."

"It came from Seito?"

"Yes, from the advertising division. They heard that the name of your company, Kirin, came from a painting by

Salvador Dalí. It's all beyond us, quite frankly. We were actually hoping for some guidance from you in these matters."

(I see . . .) Sakakibara nodded inwardly.

At least they know something about Kirin Publishers.

And, judging from the initial conversation, the work had something to do with cultural production.

In which case the request wasn't entirely off the mark.

And even if it was somewhat off the mark, under the current circumstances Kirin Publishers couldn't afford not to take on anything that came their way.

"Sounds good to me," Sakakibara replied. "As for tomorrow, is there any particular place you'd like to meet?"

"That's great news! So, well, it would be great if you could come directly to the Seito department store. . . . And I'd like to meet early, if that's okay by you. I could wait for you at the entrance to the advertising section on the third floor of the Ikebukuro store, just before ten."

"Ten o'clock, on the third floor of the Ikebukuro store?"

"Perfect, I'll see you then."

He hung up.

"Has some new work come our way, boss? Is it really with Hakuden?"

Mishima Keiko had brought him a fresh cup of instant coffee.

"Yeah . . . apparently a request from Seito department store."

"What! What would they want with us? They don't want to buy us out, do they?"

Sakakibara sipped his coffee.

"Keiko, could I ask you to come with me tomorrow?"

"Tomorrow? But it's a Saturday."

"And at ten in the morning."

Keiko made a face.

"I'd really like you to come. And it's a store we're going to. After the meeting, we can hang out shopping."

"But if we're just going to hang out—"

"It depends on how the meeting goes. If . . . if, for instance, they agree to pay us more than five hundred thousand yen, I think maybe there'll be shopping."

"Five hundred thousand? Well, it's pretty much impossible then."

Keiko stuck out her tongue at him.

"But I get it. I'll go with you. And I'll take a day of vacation next week instead."

As it turned out, Sakakibara ended up buying Keiko an Italian handbag the next day. And they had dinner together.

This was because they offered Sakakibara far more than he had expected. Yet, as a consequence, Keiko missed out on taking a day off the next week. There wouldn't be any more days off for her.

2

He had arranged to meet Mishima Keiko at the entrance to Seito department store.

It was Saturday, the 15th of December.

People thronged in front of the store even though it hadn't yet opened. It was the peak of the holiday gift season.

Sakakibara felt rather down about it.

Kirin Publishers would give out year-end bonuses next week. There would be something for everyone but not enough for anyone to feel in the mood for holiday shopping.

In fact, they were thinking about throwing an office party rather than giving bonuses.

It took him awhile to spot Mishima Keiko.

It wasn't because of the crowds.

He wasn't accustomed to seeing her in a dark blue business suit and a beige overcoat.

He'd only seen her in casual clothes. Her appearance took him by surprise. But it was a welcome surprise.

"I hardly recognized you."

Sakakibara's tone conveyed how impressed he was.

"Weren't you the one who told me to wear something proper?"

Keiko laughed, looking him over head to toe, in turn. She nodded in approval.

"You're looking pretty sharp yourself."

Sakakibara stood stiffly in his finest suit.

Unaccustomed to wearing a tie, he felt it choking him.

"As for this—"

Keiko said, opening her coat to show him her outfit.

"It's something that my mother bought for me before graduation, for job interviews. But I've never had an opportunity to wear it—"

Sakakibara had recruited her for Kirin Publishers before she'd had any chance to interview for other jobs.

Sakakibara made a wry smile.

That's surely why he felt so responsible for her.

A responsibility that he intended to live up to in other ways, too—

"Let's go."

It was ten to ten, time for their meeting. Sakakibara steered her toward the entrance.

The main entrance was still locked.

He found a security guard who let them use the employee's entrance.

The area inside the employee's entrance was crawling with clerks getting ready to open.

They finally made their way into the store and took the elevator to the third floor.

Clerks were rushing to and fro there as well.

Department stores may look pleasant and placid to the shopper, but behind the scenes a war rages.

They wandered a while before finding signs for the advertising division, and as they approached, a man dressed sharply in a three-piece suit hurried over to them.

"Mr. Sakakibara?"

"Yes."

"Ah, glad you could make it. The meeting has just begun. I am Tomari, the one who spoke to you on the phone yesterday—"

"Sorry if we kept you waiting."

They hurriedly exchanged business cards.

"And this is . . . ?"

Tomari turned to Keiko, looking her over with obvious interest.

Keiko gave him a slight bow and introduced herself.

"My name is Mishima, Mishima Keiko, executive secretary to Mr. Sakakibara. I hope you don't mind if I also attend the meeting today?"

(Executive secretary!?)

That threw Sakakibara in a spin. She was putting on quite a show.

He was painfully aware of her intentions. She was doing her best to bolster Sakakibara, who seemed somewhat overwhelmed by the whole situation.

"Yes, of course. He's lucky to have such a lovely secretary. I'm quite envious. Please, do come in."

The two of them followed Tomari to the meeting room.

Every head turned their way when Tomari opened the door.

It was an expansive room. About twenty men were seated around a large table.

As you'd expect of ad men, they were impeccably dressed and looked sharp as tacks.

In other words, they weren't the sort of guys that you'd expect to see in Sakakibara's circles. And as far as Sakakibara was concerned, they weren't the sort of guys he wanted much contact with.

But it was too late to back out now.

And in any event—he'd promised to hear them out.

Two seats had been left open for them.

"This is Mr. Sakakibara, president of Kirin Publishers, and his executive secretary, Ms. Mishima."

Tomari introduced them.

Some of the men nodded.

Some of them stared openly at Keiko.

Copies of the project dossier were handed to Sakakibara and Keiko.

On the cover, stamped as confidential, was written "Seito Marketing Group Autumn Cultural Venture Plans: The Twentieth-Century Avant-Garde Art Exposition."

Leafing through the pages, he found the section devoted to Kirin Publishers:

"Kirin Publishers: stock value: ¥100,000; number of employees: five with the president; address: Takada-no-baba, Shinjuku; . . . primary mission is the publication of translations to introduce contemporary foreign art, especially poetry and criticism, with emphasis on France. Responsible for *Kirin Quarterly*. Special issues include *Deformations of Art: Contemporary Surrealism, The Alchemist's Beard: A Tribute to Dalí,* and *Finger Winter* (poems). On Tsujimi's recommendation, their staff is ideally suited to this campaign. To be negotiated."

Sweat began to bead on Sakakibara's forehead.

They knew all there was to know about Kirin Publishers. They knew everything and were still interested in negotiating with him.

Nonetheless . . . the part about "on Tsujimi's recommendation" concerned him. Tsujimi was Tsujimi Yūjirō, general owner of the Seito Group. He was reputed to be an art connoisseur. Apparently, he had focused his interests on literature, too.

"Well, then, I would like first to thank you for taking the time to attend this meeting, our second, concerning the Autumn Cultural Venture. Now . . ."

The meeting began with this introduction by the director of the Eighteenth Division who was serving as project leader on the Hakuden Agency side, and then Seito Advertising presented the agenda for the day.

It was only later that Sakakibara learned who was who. At the time he had absolutely no idea who was the client and who was the agent.

They simply launched into the meeting without any such introductions.

In other words—even though they had been invited, there seemed no reason for them to be there.

With the exception of an occasional glance at Keiko from one of the young men, no one seemed particularly interested in their being there.

The next item on the agenda was the budget report.

There was a seemingly endless list of figures related to media, for television and newspaper coverage.

Sakakibara gradually became irritated.

And anger followed.

It just wasn't right to call them out on a Saturday morning without a word of explanation and leave them sitting around.

He was tempted to walk out.

Had he been alone, he probably would have. He didn't really care what they thought of him. Besides, the job had come out of nowhere. Since he hadn't been counting on it anyway, why put up with this?

In any case, he didn't like their way of going about it.

What sort of negotiation could there be, if it just amounted to tracking down some company and writing it into their plan?

It seemed clear that they thought "negotiation" meant they'd call and he'd come running, and that's what really pissed him off.

But Keiko was there.

If he acted like a child, she'd be embarrassed, too. And so he managed to behave himself.

Still, she must be feeling pretty annoyed, too.

Sakakibara bit his lip.

He focused the presentation on the writing board, staring at the rows of astronomically high figures.

Then it happened.

The door to the meeting room swung open.

He heard a voice.

"The president has arrived."

Silence fell over the room.

A moment later, with the grating of chair legs, everyone stood up.

Sakakibara instinctively followed suit and stood up. Keiko got up, too, smoothing the wrinkles from her skirt.

There—

The one they called "president" flew into the room as if on wings.

It was Tsujimi Yūjirō.

Sakakibara recognized him from his media appearances.

He looked younger and somewhat smaller than on TV. But he was even more energetic in person.

"Please, everyone, take your seats—"

His voice was strong and clear.

As he spoke, Tsujimi advanced to the front of the room and turned to face them.

"Thanks for coming. We're onto the fall plans?"

"Exactly! Mr. President, we'd like to thank you at this time for considering Hakuden Agency—"

With a wave of his hand, Tsujimi cut short the stiff salutations by the head of the agency and looked over the room.

"By the way, is the head of Kirin Publishers, Mr. Sakakibara, here?"

"Um, yes."

It was Tomari's turn to jump to his feet.

"He's right here, sir."

Sakakibara stood and bowed for good measure.

"I'm Sakakibara."

He introduced himself bluntly.

Tsujimi broke into a big smile in response.

"Hello! What a pleasure. I am Tsujimi. Good to meet you. I am a great fan of your business. I've had the pleasure of reading every work you've published. You do truly fine work. But—how are sales? Sorry, I hope you'll forgive my bluntness. It doesn't matter, does it? If great books were sold in great volume, that would be the end of it. It wouldn't be a great book anymore. That's the standard. We do business with the masses, so we know something about it. Of course, bad products won't sell. That's clear enough. That's the standard. Every generation has its standards. If you go below it or above it, you won't sell. That's why we're putting so much effort into cultural ventures. If you're just selling, it's no good. You have to return to basics. You make money with the standard and invest on top of it. If you don't, the standard itself will drop. And that's not good for business. You have to aim a little higher, you need to set trends. Distribution alone is no good. You'll be beaten by specialty stores. And so we have to take initiative to protect high-quality goods that don't turn an immediate profit. This is our position. And that's the way I think we have to look at the market today—"

Everyone listened attentively to his "views."

Some of them were bobbing their heads earnestly.

(What the hell!)

Sakakibara wearily lowered his head.

(The masses? Standards? Back to basics!?)

He looked over at Keiko whose hands were trembling on her knees. She was trying to repress a fit of laughter. Even more than the president's speech itself, it was watching Sakakibara's reaction to it that struck her as funny.

Seeing this took a load off his mind.

It was foolish to get angry over it.

He no longer cared how it turned out.

They have their business, and we have ours, regardless of how much we sell.

He felt much calmer.

Sakakibara raised his head.

"By the way—"

Tsujimi was speaking to a well-built man next to him who looked like an executive.

"Have you worked out the budget for Kirin Publishers?"

"Yes, here are the figures we've come up with."

The man handed a slip of paper to Tsujimi and indicated the figure.

"I see . . . hmm . . ."

Tsujimi cocked his head. Then he spoke.

"That's fine. Okay, then, let's go with this. You have five

employees at Kirin, don't you, Mr. Sakakibara? Fifteen million yen for your services for one year, plus an additional twenty million yen for editorial and publishing fees. How does that sound? And if you're short on staff, Hakuden Agency can lend a hand—what do you think?"

"That's not a problem, of course! We'll supply any additional staff."

It was Tomari who had replied.

3

(Thirty-five million yen!?)

When he heard the amount, Sakakibara closed his eyes for a moment as a wave of dizziness washed over him.

(Did he really say thirty-five million yen!?)

In his wildest dreams he had never imagined that much.

For the first time in his life, to his shock, Sakakibara understood the expression "an embarrassment of riches."

But—still—when he said "the entire staff," "a yearly retainer fee," what did that mean exactly?

He suddenly felt the sting of the little gems that adorned Tsujimi's speech— "that's not how you sell" and "investment" and "back to basics"—which bothered him even more.

"Wait a minute, please!"

Without thinking, Sakakibara had raised his voice.

Even the smallest creature has its pride. And so far they had gotten by pretty well on their pride. If they sold that off, what would be left of them?

"Yes, what is it?"

Tsujimi looked up from the documents, and with a smile plastered on his face, looked squarely at Sakakibara.

His expression of supreme confidence rankled him.

"Without some discussion of the work to be done, it's a bit difficult to talk money. Don't you agree?"

Mishima Keiko jabbed a finger into his thigh. He felt it, of course, but it was too late for him to back down now.

"You mentioned retaining our services for a year, but our company has remained autonomous through various projects. For instance, even though it's small potatoes, we publish a quarterly magazine. We also put out books. It's not a matter of money. We're simply an editorial production company. We wish to pursue very specific work. Which means that we cannot accept certain constraints."

After this outburst, Sakakibara sat back down.

Silence filled the room.

The Hakuden Agency representative, Tomari, was staring at the ground, face beet red.

The head of the advertising division for Seito department store looked anxiously around the room: some men looked away, others looked uncomfortable. But there were some who stared coldly back at him, with expressions of contempt.

But—

Strangely enough, Tsujimi Yūjirō didn't look ruffled in the least.

The smile remained plastered on his face. He spoke up.

"Of course! You are absolutely right, Mr. Sakakibara! But we're not trying to buy your company. If you were merely a production company, we would never have made this request. We would like for your company to continue with its usual editorial activities. This is strictly 'another project.' We're asking you to devote your spare time to this project. We're interested in your participation in it. And what is more, we feel that this project entails materials that are ideally suited to your company's expertise. That is why we've come to you. That is what I meant by 'retainer fee.' I appreciate your position. I may have misspoken. The term *retainer fee* is somewhat misleading. How shall we rephrase it? Shall we call it something like an 'exclusive contract fee'?"

(Exclusive contract fee . . . ?)

It still doesn't make any sense.

What exactly was being exclusively contracted?

Nonetheless, feeling that his objections had been too neatly parried away, he found himself at a loss for words. Hunched over, Sakakibara glared rather sullenly at Tsujimi.

"Even more importantly . . . what sort of project are we talking about?"

As Tsujimi spoke, he looked around the room at the Hakuden and Seito executives.

"It would seem that matters have not yet been properly explained to Mr. Sakakibara—"

"No, sir, they haven't!"

The panicked response came from Tomari.

"But—we were just about to begin filling him in on the details! We started with the reports related to media—but that was surely a mistake. I hope you'll accept my apologies. But, we can, well, get started immediately—"

Tsujimi cut off Tomari with a wave of his hand.

"There was no need to have Mr. Sakakibara sit through your discussions of media arrangements. Now that that is understood, shall I explain things to Mr. Sakakibara myself? Surely, that would be the most expedient."

"Oh, no, sir, it isn't necessary for you—! But, well, then—!"

The division chair of Hakuden Agency leapt from his seat, flushing.

But Tsujimi ignored him and motioned to Sakakibara.

"Shall we go, then, Mr. Sakakibara? You're in for quite a surprise. I am very certain of that. Come on—"

Thus prompted, Sakakibara rose to his feet, still feeling uncertain.

Mishima Keiko also stood up.

Tsujimi had already turned his back to the room and was on his way out.

The tall man, the secretary who had shown them to the room, guided him.

"This way, please."

The advertising division and Hakuden Agency executives looked utterly confused as Sakakibara and Keiko left the conference room.

Tsujimi was already well ahead of them.

Store employees scattered before him and bowed deeply as he passed.

The secretary scurried ahead to press the up button of the employee elevator before Tsujimi.

The elevator arrived. The secretary cleared it of employees and ushered in Tsujimi, Sakakibara, and Keiko. The door closed.

The elevator reached the eighth floor without stopping.

The door slid open.

There—

The ambiance was entirely different from that of the third floor they'd just left.

For one thing, there was not a person in sight.

Deep shag carpeting covered the floors.

The gentle indirect lighting imparted a sense of softness and indistinctness.

"This floor is reserved for executives."

Tsujimi informed them impassively.

"Where shall we take them?"

The secretary whispered discreetly.

"We'll talk in my suite," Tsujimi said.

"As you wish."

He scurried ahead to the end of corridor where he opened double doors of heavy wood.

It was what one would expect of a presidential suite.

It was beautifully appointed. Not in the least flashy. The furniture was simple. But one could tell at a glance how expensive it was. The room had an aura of power and influence.

An imposing desk overwhelmed the left side of the room.

The right side was a reception area.

"Please, take a seat."

Tsujimi directed them toward the sofa.

Stacks of worn and battered wooden crates were piled in the reception area, conspicuous for their incongruity with the rest of the room.

The labels in French slapped on the sides suggested they had come from abroad.

In any case—

Sakakibara and Keiko sat down together on the sofa.

Tsujimi sat facing them.

"By the way, before we talk business, could you please introduce me to this young lady?"

Tsujimi smiled pleasantly at her as he made this request.

"Please excuse me. This is Ms. Mishima, a member of our editorial staff.

It was Sakakibara who rushed to introduce her this time.

It wouldn't do to present her as his "secretary." They knew everything about the company. He would only invite suspicion if he introduced her as his secretary.

"My name is Mishima Keiko. I am an editor at Kirin. Pleased to meet you."

Keiko introduced herself frankly this time.

"I see. I see. Well, I see that Kirin's good taste extends beyond its books. To its employees as well. Very lovely taste, indeed."

Tsujimi was brimming with good spirits.

"Well, now . . . let's get right to it—"

He then turned around and addressed the secretary. "Mr. Sano, could you please bring us something to drink?" And he turned toward them again.

"What I am asking of you in particular—you see, some people in our international art section uncovered something very interesting in Paris—"

Tsujimi's eyes opened wide in excitement.

"You see, Mr. Sakakibara, they found materials related to surrealism that have never before been discovered."

"Newly discovered materials?"

At the word *surrealism,* Sakakibara leaned forward.

"Exactly. And that's only part of it."

Pointing at the stacks of crates, Tsujimi began to explain.

"Our international art section had long been in contact

with a dealer in European antiquities, and about six months ago this elderly art dealer passed away—"

He spoke with an air of indifference.

"His son took over the business but rather foolishly started to talk about selling off the entire collection that his father had spent years putting together, in one big lot."

The buyer in the international art section had taken a look, and, eventually, he managed to buy up nearly everything in the store, just like that.

"As it turns out, the old man had been a patron of Dada and surrealist artists in his youth and developed a wide range of connections. A lot of interesting things turned up. For instance, we discovered a letter that Salvador Dalí wrote to André Breton in 1958."

"Really?!"

Sakakibara's eyes glittered with excitement.

Because Dalí had completely broken ties with the surrealist movement in 1939, if the letter was genuine, it would create a major sensation among scholars of Dalí and Breton, regardless of the actual contents.

"That's not all. There are diaries and letters, unpublished manuscripts, sketches, small oil paintings, objets d'art—a mixed bag of materials, by well-known and unknown artists. . . . We couldn't possibly sort it all out ourselves. In any event, there is certainly enough there to put together a large-scale show, which we propose to call *The Twentieth-Century Avant-Garde Art Exhibition*—well, that's what we have in mind. And this is why we have requested your assistance, Mr. Sakakibara."

The more he heard, the more it piqued his interest.

They hardly needed to beg him. Even without payment—not that that would be feasible—he would have snapped at the chance. Sakakibara found his eyes drawn to the stacks of wooden crates.

Then—

A cart of refreshments arrived.

There was an assortment of coffee, tea, soft drinks, and various alcoholic beverages.

"What may I serve you?"

The woman pushing the cart asked of Sakakibara.

But his mind lay elsewhere.

"Mr. Tsujimi, would you mind if I took a look?" Sakakibara asked without taking his eyes off the crates.

Tsujimi's face eased into a smile.

"Yes, of course—you might begin with the crate on the top right. There's an old leather trunk in it. Apparently, it belonged to André Breton—"

"Breton! Did it really?"

"If you decide to participate on this project, we'll have everything shipped to your offices. Or we can set aside a special room for you here. What do you think?"

Sakakibara drew a deep breath. And then he took another.

"Just let me know how to proceed. We're eager to offer whatever assistance we can."

4

Ultimately—the agreement with Tsujimi, president of Seito department stores, was worked out as follows.

First, Sakakibara and the staff at Kirin Publishers would be responsible for the conceptualization of the *Twentieth-Century Avant-Garde Art Exhibition,* which meant developing an overarching theme for the entire project.

To start this work, however, they would have to sort through and organize the piles of materials that the Seito international art section had shipped from Paris.

The real draw of the exposition would be paintings by bigname artists such as Dalí, De Chirico, Magritte, and Tanguy. But they were nothing new. There had already been two or three large public exhibits of their work in Japan.

People might be drawn to such exhibits, but the exhibits alone wouldn't be anything special.

The real significance of the exhibition lay entirely in the materials that had been recently discovered.

There was quite an assortment of materials. In addition to

such visual materials as paintings, designs, and objets d'art, there were numerous diaries, letters, and unpublished manuscripts. Well over half of them were by completely unknown artists.

They were going to have to organize and analyze them to determine their worth.

The Kirin offices were not large enough to undertake such work.

Fortunately, there were two unoccupied rooms on the fifth floor of the same building. Seito rented these for them. These provisionally became their new offices.

Once these were furnished with desks, chairs, file cabinets, and shelves, they finally set to work on the materials.

The international art section took charge of storing the artworks. But there still remained close to ten cartons of materials.

The bulk of these were written materials. About 70 percent of these were printed materials such as books and pamphlets. The remainder consisted largely of hand-written materials such as unpublished manuscripts, memos, and diaries. The great difficulty lay in making sense of them.

About eight months until the opening of the exhibit—

But they didn't have much time at all to put the materials in order, when one took into account the number of days necessary for preparations at the department store end of things.

On top of that—

They were putting off the work that Kirin was actually known for, editing and publishing.

As it turned out, Kirin Publishers had taken on everything from fliers to pamphlets.

And that wasn't all.

Tsujimi Yūjirō had thrown another challenge at Sakakibara.

"These materials, all of them, belong to you. You may do with them whatever you wish. Think of them as part of Kirin's assets. That is, at least until the campaign comes to a close next December."

"Until next December?"

"Until that time you may handle them as you would any-thing else. There's no need to worry about us. The only thing we ask is that you design the publication and put it into print. As long as you do a decent job of it, we'll be entirely satisfied. Personally, of course, I know that your company is capable of more than a decent job."

". . . which is to say?"

"Let me put it more concretely. Personally, I have very high aspirations. With these new materials, I think it's possible to write the history of the twentieth-century avant-garde from a thoroughly new perspective . . . and to produce a new series on surrealism, for instance."

"A new series on surrealism?"

"Don't you think such work would be truly worthwhile?"

"Basically, you're saying that it's okay for us to publish everything?"

"And if necessary, we can offer financial support. If you complete a volume or two in time for the grand opening, we can display them at the exhibition, and our distributors can help to set up special displays for bookstore sales. What do you think?"

Tsujimi did not fail to add that if Kirin Publishers was not able to show some success within the year, he would withdraw their publication rights and find some other publisher.

Sakakibara was eager to give it a go.

The response was a foregone conclusion. He promised that they'd give it their all.

It was too much work for five people, however.

Sakakibara hired a couple of graduate students from the French Department of his alma mater on a part-time basis. He met with the students and their supervisor to assure that they could take a one-year leave beginning in the spring.

Their task was to skim the materials, sort them by content, and provide brief summaries.

The new year was soon upon them.

Even throughout the holiday week, the lights remained on well after midnight in the third floor offices and the fifth floor workspaces. Everyone was absorbed in his or her various tasks.

The deadline for the submission of the initial plan was only two days away.

But it was almost complete.

Sakakibara shifted his focus to establishing the overall theme for the exhibition on surrealism and related materials.

And then it came to him—

"The Undiscovered Century."

And as a subtitle he opted for "An International Exhibition on the Age of Surrealism."

He had already sent the conceptual designs to Tsujimi.

That is—

In order to establish the twentieth century as the undiscovered century, they would present it as traversed by intellectual projects that remained "unfinished"—Marxism, Freudianism, and surrealism.

Sakakibara's idea was to stress their "unfinished" nature. And then he would show that the raison d'être of surrealism lay in its being a project awaiting completion.

He felt confident about this approach.

The piles of never-before-seen materials from Seito gave quite a boost to his confidence.

Now, in the third-floor offices, Mishima Keiko was producing a clean draft of the proposal. A clean draft no longer involved writing by hand or using a typewriter. She was busily typing on their newly acquired word processor.

Another person was working alongside them on the editorial floor, Miyagami. He was busy working on the ads for the spring issue of *Kirin Quarterly*. Prominently featured among the advertisements in the spring issue were announcements for the next issue, a special issue on surrealism, and for the publication of their eight-volume series of books on surrealism.

All of the other employees, including Sakakibara, were in the fifth-floor workrooms.

The two graduate student part-timers were organizing and

classifying materials to produce a detailed list and index for the surrealism exhibit catalog.

The other three, Sakakibara, Kasadera, and Kojima, were about to start in on the looming task, André Breton's trunk.

It was—

It was a large old-fashioned steamer trunk, the leather binding thoroughly worn and covered with scratches.

Beneath the stout straps on both sides, the initials "A. B." were embossed.

No one had touched this trunk until now.

As a consequence, expectations were running high, but at the same time, they all felt a sense of foreboding about it.

The trunk . . . without a doubt . . . its very existence was cloaked in an aura of fascination. The trunk itself seemed to be a sort of powerful object, ready to spring to life before their eyes.

That's why—

Sakakibara had suggested in the project proposal that they use this trunk as the symbol of the exhibit.

The trunk would appear, for instance, on exhibition brochures and posters, and as a logo on other visual materials. They were toying with the idea of placing the trunk right where visitors entered into the exhibition space, providing no other explanation but the words "Breton's trunk."

He was keen on pushing this scheme.

Breton's trunk was undoubtedly the perfect symbol for conveying the concept of the "undiscovered century."

In any event—

They were now going to raise the lid.

It felt like Pandora's box.

There probably wasn't all that much in the trunk, since one person could easily lift it.

Kasadera cut the cords binding it and carried it over to a large worktable in the middle of the room.

As it tilted, they could hear the contents sliding and knocking.

Sakakibara and Kojima gathered around the table.

Kasadera unclasped the thick leather straps.

The lock had broken and no longer held the lid. And so, as soon as he removed the straps, the lid opened halfway.

Sakakibara reached over and pulled the lid back until the trunk was fully open.

From within—

An unpleasant odor filled the room.

"All right, let's check every item, one by one. And Kojima, could you take care of writing it all down?"

Passing the notepad to Kojima, Sakakibara looked inside.

Letters and notes lay scattered, pages yellow and brittle. There was also a bundle of what looked like letters.

Alongside them lay a necktie, twisted and kinked.

As he sorted through things, he found a side pocket, and in it, an old wristwatch. The hands had stopped at eight sixteen.

At the bottom a picture postcard turned up, bearing a photo of the Empire State Building.

Sakakibara began with the bundle of letters.

There were a dozen or so of them. He noticed that the rubber band around them was new. Someone had bound them recently.

This meant that someone had looked through the contents before they had.

Come to think of it, it made sense. The buyer for the Seito international art section who acquired these materials must first have taken a look, and in Tokyo, the art staff and even Tsujimi Yūjirō had surely opened the trunk for a look.

It wasn't at all surprising that someone had put a rubber band around the letters, but Sakakibara couldn't help feeling disappointed nonetheless. It was the sort of disappointment an archaeologist might feel upon finding a Coke bottle inside an ancient tomb that he had just excavated.

Clucking his tongue slightly, Sakakibara removed the rubber band.

He passed half of the dozen odd letters to Kasadera.

Most of them seemed to be addressed to Breton. A number of them had been sent to a New York address.

Judging from the postcard of the Empire State Building that had turned up, it seemed likely that Breton had had the trunk with him during his sojourn in America.

Sakakibara set at once to looking through the letters, checking the names of all the senders, and reading them to Kojima to write down.

Among them was one envelope without any sender marked on it.

It was addressed to Breton's Paris address.

The postmark was so faint as to be almost illegible, but he could make out 1953 or 1958.

Sakakibara slid the letter out of the envelope. There was only a single sheet of paper. And the message written on it was exceedingly short. This was all there was to it: "'The Gold of Time' is in America. I know where it is. But I don't have any intention of getting it."

That was it.

The signature read Avida Dollars.

Avida Dollars—which meant greedy for money.

It came back to him. Breton and his group had coined this name for Salvador Dalí when he turned his back on surrealism and began to sell himself as "the wise Catalan prince of staggering genius." It was an intentionally malicious gesture on their part.

It was an anagram of Salvador Dalí.

In which case—

This was probably the letter from Dalí to Breton that Tsujimi Yūjirō had mentioned.

Sakakibara read the sentence over and over again.

Something else came to mind.

In 1966, the year in which André Breton had died—

A certain phrase had appeared as an epitaph for the famous writer: "I seek the gold of time."

5

"Hey, take a look at this."

Sakakibara handed the letter to Kasadera.

He told him about the connections that had come to mind.

Kasadera tilted his head to the side. He said, "Well, let's worry about that later. Let's stick to cataloging the contents of this trunk tonight."

". . . Yeah, okay."

Sakakibara reluctantly agreed.

But once the idea had flashed through his mind, it stuck with him, continually in the back of his mind. It was a knot that promised to untangle if he could just pull the right thread.

Only he had not yet grasped the right thread.

Sakakibara returned to his tasks, fighting back his impatience.

After they had gone through all the letters, setting aside those that they might make use of, they went on to the next task.

Next were the miscellaneous memos and notes.

The bulk of them were covered with diagrams and designs and rapidly written notations. They were very hard to read.

"There's no way. Let's leave these to the students."

Kasadera voiced his opinion.

Sakakibara also gave up on them.

They decided to have the graduate students decipher them and set them aside in a large briefcase marked for the students.

Next—

A hand-written manuscript emerged.

It wasn't Breton's handwriting, though. It was written with perfectly formed letters, bold yet neat.

It was signed Who May, which sounded like a joke.

They found another manuscript with the same signature.

Both of them seemed to be prose poems.

One bore the title "Another World," and the other "Mirror."

At the top corner of the manuscript "Another World" were

written an address and phone number. The address looked like New York.

Surely, it was something related to Breton's time of exile.

"What exactly is this?"

Kasadera read the manuscript two or three times, then frowned.

"Who May . . . is what it says. It must be someone's pen name?"

One of the graduate student part-timers working at another desk turned when he heard Kasadera's remark.

"Did you say Who May? There's something here by Who May as well."

"Is that so?"

The student stood, walked over to the sorting shelves along the wall, and pulled out an envelope from the piles of materials that had already been classified.

"Who May, as in 'and who may you be . . .'? It's right here."

On the envelope was written "Long poem, to Antonin Artaud, from Who May (1948?)."

"To Artaud, no less?"

Sakakibara's eyes opened wide.

"Yes. We found it among the items belonging to Antonin Artaud. But it's not the same handwriting. I thought that it may have been dictated, and so I included it with the Artaud items—Who May sounds like the sort of pen name that Artaud might have used, doesn't it?"

Put that way, it actually made sense.

Sakakibara took the envelope and pulled out the contents.

A sheaf of yellowed pages emerged. The other manuscripts were written in a fine hand. But this one looked different. The hand was obviously different from the two other manuscripts found in Breton's trunks. The writing was clearly legible but not as smooth. It looked like it had been written very slowly and deliberately.

In any event—

Sakakibara set the sheath of papers on the worktable.

Indeed, it had been signed with the name Who May.

"L'or du temps."

(L'or du temps . . . !)

Sakakibara groaned.

"L'or du temps" was "the gold of time."

The inexplicable letter that Avida Dollars, that is, Salvador Dalí, had sent to Breton had spoken of "the gold of time"—

And then, in his epitaph, Breton was said to be seeking the "gold of time"—

Now here was yet another "gold of time" but—in this instance, it was not some mysterious reference. Rather, even if they don't really understand it, it was a concrete title for an actual poem—which had appeared before their very eyes.

And so ultimately—

Did Dalí's "gold of time" and Breton's "gold of time" refer to the same thing?

And then did those two actually refer to the manuscript belonging to Antonin Artaud, titled "The Gold of Time"?

There was no way to know. Still, it was hard to believe that these were mere coincidences.

Who was this Who May, anyway?

Indeed, who may you be . . . ?

Was it one of those riddles that the surrealists were so fond of?

There was no way to be sure. There just wasn't enough information at hand.

Sakakibara lined up the three documents on the worktable, the two manuscripts from Breton's trunk and the manuscript found among Artaud's belongings.

Three references to "The Gold of Time"—

Three manuscripts by "Who May"—

Two sets of three that formed a single link.

"Do you think that Who May was Artaud's pen name, as he suggested?" Kasadera said.

"If that's the case, we have a way to explain the connection with Breton. What a discovery that would be!" The graduate student who had first discovered Who May said excitedly.

"In any case, we're definitely going to use these three. Well, it will depend on content, but we can probably use it as a central theme for one of the volumes on poetry in the book series. Needless to say, we can make a hell of a lot out of it if we find actual proof that this was by Artaud."

Kasadera gazed into space.

"I'll try to come up with something. I'll leave no stone unturned to trace connections to Artaud. If necessary, I can do a comparative analysis of word frequency or grammatical patterns."

The student was overflowing with enthusiasm.

It was possible that if they explained the situation, the university would allow them to use the computers for linguistic analysis.

If the results were good, they would have support for their speculations about this being a work by Artaud.

If that were indeed true—it would be a truly important discovery.

Sakakibara's heart was pounding.

But there was another pressing question.

Not only was there the question of who Who May was, but they also had to figure out the meaning behind "the gold of time."

Just then the door to the workspaces opened.

Mishima Keiko and Miyagami had come up.

Miyagami was carrying a large tray with both hands. He had brought cups of coffee for everyone.

"We're finished below. Here, for you."

Keiko returned the original copy of the proposal that she had entered on the word processor to Sakakibara.

"So, how are things moving along here? Is there anything that I can help with?"

"Let's see . . ."

Sakakibara looked at the clock.

It was already close to two in the morning.

"It's about time to call it a day. There's always tomorrow—"

As he looked around the room, Kasadera nodded with a look of exhaustion.

"Great, then, about these manuscripts—"

Sakakibara was comparing the three manuscripts laid out on the table while sipping his coffee, deep in thought.

Then he spoke.

"I'm going to take these home for the time being, to look them over. Could you make me a copy of them?"

"No problem, I'll do it right away."

Mishima Keiko reached across and took the manuscripts.

"Sorry, but, could you do one for me, too—" Kasadera called after her.

Kasadera had already translated six books from French. Of the Kirin staff his reading skills in French were by far the best.

Not counting the graduate students, and after Kasadera, Sakakibara and Keiko had the best French skills. Of the two, she had the best conversational skills.

Kojima and Miyagami had better abilities in English and Spanish than in French. Between the two of them, they covered both North American and Latin American literatures.

While Keiko made the copies, Sakakibara and the others began cleaning things up.

They first put Breton's trunk carefully back into its crate and stored it.

Sakakibara and Kasadera took care of putting all the original materials taken from the trunk into hard cases, labeling them, and filing them in the cabinets.

Mishima Keiko had completed the copies.

"I made one for myself, too," she said, handing a thick stack of papers bound with a clip to Sakakibara and Kasadera.

The original manuscripts, like the other materials, were stored in cases, which Kasadera put away in the cabinets.

The students finished filing things on the desk.

"All right, let's go."

"Good job, everyone."

"See you tomorrow."

It was late at night in January. It would be cold as hell outside.

Everyone pulled on a jacket or overcoat and filed out of the room.

Sakakibara wore a rugged leather bomber jacket. He grabbed his motorcycle helmet, shut off the lights, and followed the others out.

Sakakibara lived near Waseda station, only one stop away from Takada-no-baba on the Tōzai line. It was only about three kilometers from the office. It only took him about ten minutes when the subway was running. But if he missed the last train, it was a thirty-minute walk.

It was too close to justify taking a taxi. Hearing the destination, some drivers would refuse the fare.

It wasn't worth their while.

And so Sakakibara commuted on his motorcycle.

The bike was a Honda CBX 650 that he had bought second-hand. It had a large frame, American style.

Sakakibara had received his two-wheel license in high school before there were size limits. Nowadays, it was hard to get clearance to ride the big bikes, unless you had a lot of time on your hands or a real passion for it.

"So, boss, are you headed home?"

Kojima, who had been chatting with Miyagami and the students, saw the helmet and looked disappointed.

He turned to Kasadera and pretended to lift a glass to his lips, to convey "Join us for a drink?"

"No thanks, not me. I'm eager to get home to read this stuff."

He slapped the bag containing the manuscript copies and waved good-bye.

"Not me either. I'm too wiped out."

Mishima Keiko also passed on the invitation.

The elevator arrived.

The seven went down together.

"Take care, see you."

"See you."

Kojima, Miyagami, and the two students spotted a bar behind the station and ducked in to get out of the bitter wind.

It was an area frequented by students, and so there were a lot of places open, even at this hour.

The other three remained outside.

"Keiko?"

After seeing Kojima leave, Sakakibara decided to make his move.

"Do you need a ride tonight?"

She was renting an apartment in Kami-Ochiai.

Like Sakakibara, she lived only one stop away from Takada-no-baba on the Tōzai line, but in the opposite direction. Likewise, it was too far to walk and too close for a cab.

And so, after the last train, someone needed to see her home.

Usually, Sakakibara or Kojima would take care of seeing her home.

In the warm months, Sakakibara often drove her home on his motorcycle. Even though it was out of his way, it was a quick hop on the bike.

But it had been very cold lately.

Kasadera lived in Shibuya, and so it was not too much out of his way to stop at Keiko's home in Kami-Ochiai. Because he went home by taxi, Kasadera had pretty much taken over the task of escorting her home, to the point where he seemed to feel that it was his right to do so.

He had evidently intended to take her home tonight.

Not only will the ride be cold for Keiko, but also Sakakibara will have to go twice the distance. If he is going to offer to escort her home, he needs some sort of reason.

He has his reason—of course. He has a really good reason. But it's not one that he can speak about openly.

He has been returning home well after midnight lately, day after day.

Frankly, he had to work up the nerve to ask.

In fact, it was unusual. He was very aware of that. But even though he was aware of it—he couldn't stop himself asking.

He could blame it on the cold weather. It was too cold for him to ride alone.

That's also why he expected to be turned down, because it was too cold.

And yet—she accepted without any hesitation.

"Thanks. I appreciate it."

Kasadera, who was trying to hail a taxi, turned around and looked at them in surprise.

But he didn't say a word.

A taxi stopped. Kasadera waved good-bye and ducked into the taxi. The door shut behind him.

Kasadera wasn't driving, but his taxi sped off in the night, with an angry screeching of tires.

6

While the engine of the CBX 650 warmed up, Sakakibara went back to the third floor offices to get another helmet.

It was a red jet helmet. It was pretty much Keiko's helmet. He rarely gave a ride to anyone else.

It occurred to him that this was the first time this year that he had taken her.

Probably he had hurt Kasadera's feelings. But Sakakibara had been suffering in silence long enough.

He handed her the helmet and fastened her purse and his bag to the grab bar.

The rear seat was rather small, but since it was an American bike, there was no uncomfortable bump between the two seats.

He should have warmed the engine a bit longer, but it was already quite late.

In any case, it was throttling well, and so he cut the choke and eased the CBX 650 out of the parking space reserved for him alongside their building.

He threw a leg over the seat. Mishima Keiko slid onto the seat behind him at his signal and held on to him with both arms.

He put it in gear with his foot. It made a grinding sound. The intense cold had probably affected the lubrication of the clutch. Easing the throttle open, Sakakibara drove onto Waseda Street. He kept it in low gear awhile.

But as they passed the intersection in front of Takada-no-baba station, the engine started to race and roar.

A group of men wandering drunkenly into the street to flag a taxi leapt out of the road as they passed and yelled after them.

He put it in second. The bike gathered speed.

They quickly arrived at the light at Kotakibashi. He turned right and continued straight.

And then—

It caught his eye.

(Snow . . .)

From behind him came Keiko's voice at almost the same moment.

"It's snowing!"

Large flakes of snow, mingling with a fine drizzle, danced gracefully down from the jet-black skies, spinning brilliantly on the wind in the light of the streetlamps.

"It's snowing!"

It was an enchanting scene.

Sakakibara eased back on the throttle.

It wasn't because it was slippery.

Rather, he wanted to enjoy this marvelous moment as long as possible with Keiko beside him.

As they slowed, a taxi impatiently honked from behind. Sakakibara didn't speed up at all.

On the contrary, he slowed further, the snow rushing at them and swirling around the CBX like a river of stars.

Their destination was all too rapidly approaching.

Besides, he couldn't keep her out in this cold wind much longer.

The lights of her building appeared ahead.

Sakakibara put on the right blinker, turning the CBX into the apartment complex where Keiko lived.

Everything around them was silent.

Sakakibara stopped twenty meters short of her apartment and cut the engine. It would be tiresome if people in her building complained about the noise.

She got off the bike. She pulled off the helmet.

Sakakibara put down the kickstand and got off.

She didn't say a word.

Sakakibara unfastened the straps holding her purse.

Just when he handed it to her—

She threw herself into Sakakibara's arms.

She spoke.

". . . I'm cold."

Not sure what to do, Sakakibara wrapped his arms around her.

". . . tighter, hold me tighter . . ."

She spoke in a whisper.

". . . don't go . . . please . . ."

Sakakibara was at a loss.

He was uncertain about her intentions.

He spoke without thinking, stupidly.

"But why?"

He felt her trembling in his arms.

"You have to make me say it?" She scolded him.

The flakes of snow had grown larger.

They settled on her hair like crystals before melting away. Sakakibara gently brushed the lingering snowflakes from her hair.

". . . I'm cold."

She repeated.

". . ."

Sakakibara nodded without a word.

She slipped out of his arms, turned, and started to walk ahead.

He pulled off his helmet.

He hurriedly took his case from the rear seat, put it and the helmet under one arm, and grabbed the key and locked the handlebars with the other.

He followed her.

Catching up, he walked at her side.

He wondered if he should simply walk beside her or put an arm around her, but for some reason he felt too shy to do that.

It was a neat and trim building with relatively few apartments. He had heard that many women lived there. Maybe that was why the corridors and stairs were so clean.

It wasn't the first time that he had been invited to her room.

He had been offered tea or sake on other nights. But nothing had happened.

Sakakibara wasn't one to press his luck with women. He tended to worry more about hurting a woman than about losing out—which was a nice way of putting it, when in fact he was secretly afraid of being hurt himself.

At times Sakakibara became exceedingly angry with himself. But then that's how he was. He wasn't going to change.

That is why nothing had ever happened between them.

He probably looked like a guy afraid of women. Or maybe he just looked clueless. But it really wasn't either. It wasn't that he wanted to run away, and it wasn't that he didn't feel something for her . . . but . . . he couldn't help feeling like an utter coward when face to face with Mishima Keiko.

That's how strong his feelings for her were. He was terrified that she'd reject him. And so he went on day after day telling himself, "I'll do it today, I'll do it today."

Ultimately, however, before he could make up his mind, she'd lost patience and picked that day for him.

Her apartment was on the third floor. It was 304. He'd never forget it. The nameplate on the door read simply Mishima.

They took the stairs rather than the elevator.

Their shoes, wet from the sudden snowfall, left a dark damp print on each step. Each one dampened Sakakibara's sense of confidence.

He kept thinking about Kasadera's face as he waved goodbye to them before speeding off in the taxi.

They reached the third floor.

Mishima Keiko took the key from her bag and unlocked the door. She opened the door and silently gestured at him to enter.

He awoke once, near dawn because he heard Keiko murmuring.

"... I'm cold ..."

But she was just talking in her sleep.

Her body was still pressed warmly against his, her head resting on his chest.

Beneath the covers with her, drowsy with satisfaction, Sakakibara felt himself drifting back to sleep.

He awoke to dazzling sunshine.

The white lace curtains glittered with light.

The aroma of coffee reached him.

Then it all came back to him.

He threw back the covers to leap out of bed only to find he hadn't a stitch of clothing on.

He got out of bed anyway.

He spotted the clothes he had shed the night before, now folded neatly on the bed stand.

She had even left him a fresh pair of underwear and T-shirt.

He heard her voice.

"Sakakibara-san, are you awake?"

She spoke with same tone that she used with him at work.

"Uh, yeah ..."

Sakakibara answered, feeling somewhat hesitant.

"Come in here once you're dressed. I went out and bought underwear at the convenience store, I hope it fits."

"What time is it?" He asked her while getting dressed.

"It's past nine, about nine-forty. But more important, have you taken a look outside yet?"

"Outside ... ?"

"Yes, outside! You haven't seen it yet!"

Her voice rang with excitement.

And then she came flying into the bedroom.

"You haven't seen it yet? Come on, hurry up!"

She grabbed him by the belt he'd just put on and dragged him over to the window.

(. . . !)

Sakakibara's jaw dropped.

Snow hadn't entirely buried the neighborhood, but every rooftop was covered with a mantel of white that shone brilliantly in the light streaming down from a cloudless sky.

"Wow!"

An almost inarticulate noise escaped his lips.

It was truly miraculous.

It felt like some unknown power was celebrating their union.

Sakakibara gazed absently at the scene for some time.

Then he returned to himself, becoming aware of the weight of her hand on his shoulder.

He turned, but her eyes were cast down, no longer gazing up at him.

He was about to say something, but, as if anticipating his words, she turned from him and moved quickly toward the dining room.

"We should get moving. The train will be packed because of the snow—"

Her apartment was a typical two-room studio.

There was a bedroom and a dining room.

A cute little table with two chairs stood in the middle of the dining room.

The interior was simple. It said a great deal about her personality.

By the time he had washed up, breakfast had appeared on the table, coffee and toast, bacon and eggs, with a small salad on the side.

The announcer on the television droned on about how unusual snow was in the city.

Scarcely exchanging a word, they tucked into the food while watching television.

Ten past ten—

They left her apartment.

On the street nearby, Sakakibara's CBX was covered with snow.

It had begun to melt, but the streets were still too slippery for the bike. He had assumed as much and had left his helmet and grip in her room.

They walked side by side to the Ochiai metro station.

"Let's take different trains."

At her request, he took the first train to arrive. As expected, it was jam-packed.

He managed nonetheless to force his way into the crowded train and endured the ride to the next station.

The snow had pretty much melted away in the area around Takada-no-baba station.

With thoughts of Keiko, who would surely be arriving on the next train or the one after that, Sakakibara headed for the Kirin offices.

He first poked his head into the editorial offices on the third floor.

The door wasn't locked. But the lights were on.

When he opened the door wider, he spotted two men, half asleep, one on the floor, one on the sofa.

The one on the floor had a blanket pulled over his head, so Sakakibara couldn't tell who it was, but it was Kojima on the sofa.

When he noticed Sakakibara, Kojima's eyes opened wide.

"Ah, boss. And a good morning to you. You made a good choice returning right away last night. All that snow. We couldn't even get a cab."

He scratched his head, as if looking for an excuse.

"And Miyagami?"

"Ah, Miyagami and the other temp went upstairs to the workroom to sleep."

Well, that explained things. When he went up to the workroom to wake up Miyagami and the student, Mishima Keiko arrived.

They probably wouldn't get much work done that morning, not until those guys' hangovers wore off.

It was already one in the afternoon.

But . . . Kasadera hadn't come in yet.

The trains should be running on schedule by now.

(Strange—)

An unpleasant thought crossed Sakakibara's mind.

The expression on Kasadera's face as he climbed in the taxi last night remained clear in his mind.

Sakakibara reached for the phone. He dialed Kasadera's number.

It kept ringing . . . seven . . . eight . . . nine rings.

He lived in a small house left to him by his parents. He lived alone. Still, it was one floor, and so it shouldn't take him long to get to the phone, no matter where he was.

Maybe he had just left for the office.

Sakakibara hung up.

Sometime past two they finally got into the swing of things.

"I wonder what's happened to Kasadera?"

Keiko whispered to Sakakibara when she brought him some tea.

Three o'clock rolled around.

Sakakibara called Kasadera's home once again.

But there was still no answer.

Six o'clock went by.

Kojima and the others went out for dinner. Sakakibara sent Keiko with them and stayed by the phone.

Kasadera wasn't going to show.

Sakakibara ran out of cigarettes.

Thinking maybe there was a fresh pack in his bag, he un-zipped it.

The copies of the manuscripts were right on top where he'd thrown them last night.

He pulled them out and fished around until he found a pack of Mild Seven on the bottom.

He tapped one out and lit it.

Again he tried Kasadera's number. Still no one there.

He spread out the manuscript copies on the table.

But he was too tired to make out the words. He finally gave up and put them back in his bag.

The group returned from dinner.

That day—they ended up working well past two in the morning.

4

THE SHADE OF THE
SHADOW OF LIGHT

1

The day after the funeral, there came a call from Kasadera's mother.

If there was anything that Sakakibara wanted from among the books and papers that he had accumulated, she wanted him to take it.

She said she'd take the remaining books to a used book dealer.

Kasadera Tōru had been the youngest of three brothers.

His parents were currently living with the eldest son and his wife in Shizuoka. The middle son was in Nagoya.

Apparently, they had found a buyer for the house in Shibuya where he had been living alone.

"I see. I will come take a look," Sakakibara replied.

It was Friday.

The entire staff at Kirin looked worn out from helping at the funeral the previous day. And so anyone who hadn't an urgent task to complete had been given a respite from the Seito job.

But Sakakibara came in just after ten nonetheless.

He felt agitated at home alone.

Kasadera was dead. And there was no apparent cause.

It was Sakakibara who had found the body. Actually, Kasadera was still alive when he found him.

After two days without word from him, Sakakibara became worried and went to his house in Shibuya.

There was a light on in his house. But the front door was locked. He tried calling from a nearby public phone a few times and then tried shouting from outside. There was no response, though.

Newspapers and letters had piled up in his mailbox.

The lady next door came out.

She recognized Sakakibara. She said that she hadn't seen Kasadera coming or going the past couple of days.

The evening newspaper from the day before was in the mailbox. He had taken in the one from the night before.

That meant that he had returned home that night . . . that snowy night.

He used the neighbor's phone to call the police. They broke the lock on the back door and went in.

The house was warm. A strange odor laced the air.

The light was coming from a sitting room that he used as a study.

He was there.

A burner on the gas stove was on.

There was Kasadera, stretched out on his back sleeping, his legs under the kotatsu, a low table equipped with a heater.

The room reeked of alcohol.

They soon realized why.

On the kotatsu lay the pile of photocopies of the manuscript, a French-Japanese dictionary, and a pad of paper. Beside them was a bottle of whiskey and a glass.

It was all too obvious what he'd been doing.

That night he returned home well past two in the morning, and while having a nightcap, he'd started reading the manuscripts signed Who May.

The bottle of whiskey had been left uncapped. It was now empty. The glass was empty, too. Later they discovered that he hadn't drunk the whiskey. It had evaporated in the heat. That explained why the place reeked.

At first Sakakibara thought he had drunk too much and fallen asleep like that. But that wasn't it. Kasadera wasn't sleeping at all. He was lying there with both eyes wide open, staring into space.

His one hand was still clutching one of the three manuscript copies.

The policemen contacted the station immediately. A police car and an ambulance showed up in no time.

At that time he was definitely alive.

Although the heat from the gas stove and the kotatsu had thoroughly dehydrated him, he had a pulse and was breathing.

"He'll be okay. He'll get through this," pronounced the doctor in the emergency room.

His diagnosis was not entirely wrong. The treatment successfully pulled him through the worst of the crisis. At least this is what the doctor said. He was on the way to recovery physically.

But—he never regained consciousness. The doctor shook his head and started an urgent search for other causes. But before he could determine what was wrong, without any warning, his heart ceased beating.

It happened about ten days after they'd found him.

The police ordered an autopsy and began a rather half-hearted investigation into the cause of death, accident or suicide.

Sakakibara was called in for questioning.

If suicide . . . he could definitely imagine a motive. In any case, he could guess why he'd been drinking.

In a roundabout manner, Sakakibara mentioned it to the police. But they didn't take him seriously.

For one thing, he hadn't left any sort of note behind.

On the pad of paper on the kotatsu, he'd been making some notes in what appeared to be French and Japanese, but these were all related to the contents of the manuscript.

The police had already verified this.

He had written the title "Another World" in Japanese on one manuscript. On another manuscript he had jotted *kagami* to translate the title "Mirror."

It was obvious from the way he had scribbled these words that he had been very excited.

On the last manuscript he had translated the title "The Gold of Time" in Japanese. But he had not made any other notes on this one.

He had been holding the copy of "The Gold of Time." It was as if something had happened while he was reading it.

Apparently, the doctor did not think he had died from excessive drinking. The examination suggested that he'd probably only had about one glass of whiskey.

Besides, no matter how much he'd been drinking, drinking couldn't explain his condition.

The doctor tended to think that some sort of violent shock had left him physically and mentally incapacitated. But no one, including the doctor, could figure out what sort of violent shock could have put him in such an unusual condition.

In the end—both the causes and the effects remained unexplained, and the death was attributed to an "accident." Any lingering doubts about suicide vanished. The investigation came to an end, and the body was returned to his family.

Then yesterday the funeral ceremony had been at last held, after a delay of five days.

The call from Kasadera's mother had come at about eleven in the morning.

Sakakibara promised to come by sometime after one.

He had assumed that no one would come to work today, but Miyagami turned up.

He had received the cover illustration for *Kirin Quarterly* and decided to come in.

Now that he had the image, he had planned on doing the cover layout that afternoon.

Sakakibara asked him to go with him.

Sakakibara was familiar with Kasadera's collection of

books. There were some valuable volumes. It would be a waste to let them go.

Miyagami worried that he'd fall behind on his deadline, but the offer of a free lunch swayed him.

At twelve-thirty, after lunch and a cup of coffee, Miyagami went to pick up a small van from the rental car office on Waseda Avenue.

They filled the back with empty boxes and headed for Kasadera's house.

His elderly father and mother greeted them.

They guided them into Kasadera's study where only shelves of books remained.

The desk and chest and kotatsu had all been removed.

Sakakibara and Miyagami began silently to sort through the books.

They decided to take the draft of his translation of the manuscripts and his notes.

By just after four they had filled all the boxes. The books that they didn't want would go to a used bookstore.

The task left them feeling utterly depressed. He had founded Kirin Publishers along with Sakakibara. Kirin wouldn't have been possible without his efforts. Memories of those tough days came back. And then, on that last night . . . the expression on his face as he turned and looked at him . . .

Kasadera's mother brought them tea.

Sakakibara had intended to pay for the books, but she refused adamantly. "If I took your money, it would be as if you and Tōru had been complete strangers," she said.

"Tōru relied on you more than on his own brothers. And the fact that it was you who found him, it was as if he had called out to you."

She continued to speak fondly of him. Sakakibara let Miyagami carry the boxes so he could listen to her.

It took about an hour for the conversation to wind down.

"I hope you'll excuse our intruding on you today."

Sakakibara stood up.

"As soon as an opportunity arises, I would like to call on you again in Shizuoka."

The elderly woman bowed deeply in reply. The elderly father came out to see them to the entrance.

"You know . . ."

The woman whispered in Sakakibara's ear as he put his shoes on.

"You know . . . the young woman . . . the one who helped out with the reception the other day . . . named Mishima, Mishima Keiko?"

"Yes, that's her."

The old woman smiled slyly at him.

"She's quite pretty, isn't she?"

" . . ."

"Our Tōru seemed really taken with her . . ."

Sakakibara stiffened.

"We were just reading a bit of Tōru's diary, the two of us, you see. The young woman's name came up again and again. Isn't that right, dear?"

"That's enough, Tomiko."

Her husband stopped her from going any further.

"If the young woman heard this, wouldn't she feel terrible? Please excuse us. It's better to forget all about it."

Sakakibara bowed his head and slipped out the entrance.

Darkness had already fallen outside.

It was cold.

It felt cold enough to snow.

Sakakibara barely spoke a word during the trip back to the offices in Takada-no-baba.

He was dead tired.

As they carried the boxes from the van into the building, it actually began to snow.

He thought of Keiko. He thought of what the woman had said.

Miyagami spoke up.

"I'll return the van and walk home, but do you want me to

drive you home first? It'd be pretty dangerous on your bike with all this snow."

"That's okay, thanks anyway. I have a few things left to do."

"Okay, see you then."

Miyagami left.

Sakakibara sat with his elbows propped on the desk and stared into space for some time.

Then he picked up the phone.

Keiko picked up immediately.

"Hey, where have you been?"

Sakakibara explained what had happened.

"I see . . . is that what happened? . . ."

Keiko's voice trailed off. But, as if rallying her spirits, she invited him over.

"Why don't you come over now? Let's have something to eat together."

Ever since that day, he hadn't had much time to talk with her. Of course, it hadn't been just that.

But they were finally past that stage.

If he spent some time with her, if he spent some time alone with her, it would do a lot to lift his spirits.

He should do it.

"Should I bring something?"

"That would be great. Could you bring something to drink? I have some whiskey but no beer or wine—"

Whiskey really didn't appeal to him just then.

"Okay, then. I'll get something."

He hung up and looked around the silent empty office.

The boxes they'd carried in were stacked along the wall. He opened one.

Right on top in a bundle were the notes that Kasadera had been jotting down that day, the copies of "Another World" and "Mirror" that had been lying on the kotatsu, and the copy of "The Gold of Time" that he'd been holding when he died.

Sakakibara took the papers and slid them into a large envelope. He turned off the heat and lights and left.

He selected a bottle of white wine at a nearby store and then grabbed a bottle of red wine as well.

He was thinking that, if possible, he'd really like to get a bit drunk.

He hurried through the snow to the metro station.

2

The first bottle of wine was empty in no time.

But it hadn't taken the edge off his mind as he'd hoped.

Keiko's face was flushed red.

Sakakibara removed the cork from the second bottle.

As he stood to throw away the empty bottle, the envelope fell from his chair to the floor.

"Hey, what do you have in there?"

Keiko leaned over and picked it up for him.

"It's the copies you made . . . from before . . ."

Sakakibara opened the envelope to show her.

"It's Kasadera's copies. I guess he was going to translate them himself. These are his notes here."

". . ."

Keiko took the manuscript, nodding silently.

"I was going to read this over the weekend anyway—I really want to put it in the next volume. In remembrance of Kasadera . . ."

These past two weeks—

Every day had been a mess. He wasn't in the frame of mind to sort through the materials to catalog them.

But he had had plenty of time to think.

He had pretty much worked out in his head the structure for a book series based on the new materials.

The series would be called *Undiscovered Materials.*

The first volume, *Sources of Surrealism,* would provide a historical survey of surrealism from a new perspective.

The second volume, *Visions of Surrealism,* would include a range of visual materials from painting to cinema.

The third volume, *Forms of Surrealism,* would also deal with visual materials but with an emphasis on the plastic arts such as sculpture, objets d'art, and other objects.

The fourth volume, *Languages of Surrealism,* would contain word experiments, with an emphasis on poetry, but also including diaries and dream notebooks.

He had a number of possible titles for the subsequent volumes, such as "Oratories," "Realities," "Presents," and "Limits," in order to publish collections of treatises, letters and miscellaneous writings, and to present personal histories and biographies. His basic idea was to provide a definitive account of the development and contemporary legacy of surrealism, focusing on the vitality and limits of the undiscovered materials in order to pose new questions.

He wanted the fourth volume finished by the time of the Seito exhibition, if possible. At very least he wanted the first three volumes on display.

Subsequent volumes would be books for specialists. Actually, the fourth volume was also somewhat specialized, but the first three would surely attract the eye of the public due to the wealth of visual materials.

It was also part of Sakakibara's plan to use the revenues from the first three volumes to fund the later volumes.

Surely the completion of three, maybe four such volumes would fulfill his obligations to the head of Seito, Tsujimi.

He wanted to use Who May's writings in volume three or four, *Languages of Surrealism.*

Even if they couldn't actually verify that the texts were by Antonin Artaud, the materials were undeniably important, if only because they showed that these two masters of surrealism, Artaud and Breton, both had secretly possessed the same manuscripts. And then they also had in common the cryptic phrase "the gold of time."

In any case . . . the first thing would be to study the texts closely.

That much was clear, and they would have to determine if it could be rendered in Japanese.

With only a quick look at the texts, he had found all kinds

of odd word usage. While this contributed to its poetic value, it might make translation pretty much impossible.

Keiko got up to wash the wine glasses. Sakakibara then refilled their glasses with red wine.

The two of them again clinked their glasses in cheer.

"Keiko, have you read the Who May texts yet?" Sakakibara asked after draining his glass.

Keiko nodded slightly.

"I took a quick look at 'Un univers ténébreux,' the one that Kasadera translated as "Another World.""

"How was it?"

"Well, rather strange . . . it made a strange impression . . . how should I put it? It was like hearing a song from an unknown people dwelling in a mysterious land . . . and suddenly that land appeared before my very eyes."

"Really? It sounds great."

"But then . . . once I had read it . . . that was it. None of it left a lasting impression. I'm not sure, though. Maybe I was missing something . . . there were lots of odd words. For instance . . ."

Keiko pointed at the manuscript and said, "This . . . is read as *dobaded,* right? Where does that come from?"

Sakakibara shook his head.

"And?"

"At first I thought it was just a rhythmic word. But then, you see, it is used as a noun, as a verb, and even sometimes as an adjective."

". . . *dobaded,* huh?" Sakakibara pursed his lips. "I guess there's no way to translate it then?"

"Well, I don't think it's entirely impossible. If you come up with something good for *dobaded,* the phrases themselves seem fairly easy."

"What about the other works? Like 'Mirror' and 'The Gold of Time'—?"

"I haven't looked through them yet. There just hasn't been much of a chance."

She was right about that.

Sakakibara picked up the copy of "The Gold of Time" that Kasadera had been clutching right till the end.

"L'or du temps, huh . . . ?"

He read the title and skimmed over the first few lines, trying to translate them into Japanese.

"'In the shade of the shadow of light. In the depth of the depths of light. . . . Beyond, behind it. . . .' Well, even without a dictionary you can get a basic sense of it."

Gazing on the manuscript beside him, Keiko continued with the translation.

"'The darkness is out of reach. The light too eludes our grasp. . . .' Right?"

She looked into Sakakibara's eyes.

"Hey, what do you think? Shall we put our heads together on this?"

"Put our heads together?"

"Exactly."

With these words, Keiko disappeared into the bedroom. She soon reappeared with another copy of the manuscript.

"Okay, then."

Sakakibara nodded. He refilled the glasses, took a sip, and returned to the manuscript.

"This should be interesting. Let's give it a go. First, 'The Gold of Time . . . Who May' and then . . ."

"'In the shade of the shadow of light. In the depth of the depths of light.' And let's see . . . 'Equinox of light, on the other side. . . .'"

Translating line by line, the two of them made their way through "The Gold of Time."

Then—

Suddenly feeling as if the wine had hit him, Sakakibara raised his hands to cover his eyes.

"What happened? Are you all right?"

Keiko's voice sounded very far away.

". . . um, yes, I'm fine . . ."

He replied, or thought he had, but wasn't entirely sure.

In the darkness behind his eyelids something was spinning wildly.

He reached out to support himself on the table that was supposed to be right in front of him, but he couldn't feel a thing. Or, rather, he was surely touching it but could not feel it.

He brusquely opened his eyes.

Keiko's face was there. But it was all a blur.

Her mouth opened. Now her voice sounded exceedingly close.

"'In the shade of the shadow of light. In the depth of the depths of light. . . . Equinox of light. . . . Around to the other side of light, at the time you arrive here . . . time is gold . . . gold itself resembles time."

(. . . !)

The voice wasn't right. The voice—wasn't Keiko's!

Sakakibara opened his eyes wide. He couldn't tell if he had really opened them or not. But he kept trying and felt that he had.

The face before him wavered, back and forth, and then suddenly he saw it clearly.

(Kasadera—!)

He felt him. He had the distinct sensation that Kasadera was right in front of him—or something that looked like him was certainly there.

The face laughed.

It was joyous, heartfelt laughter. Or so it seemed.

(In the shade of the shadow of light. In the depth of the depths of light. . . . At the time you arrive here, time is gold, and the shadow of the shade . . . in the depth of depths. . . .)

The voice echoed through his mind.

Sakakibara then came to a realization. He gained some insight.

That voice . . . those words . . . each one contained the key to understanding the overall order. Each and every word . . . explains something about their order. That was the key to their endless combinations . . . and at the limit . . . therein is . . . a whole that is locked within that limit. . . .

In an instant—

Everything went black.

He shifted his body, but this time a distinct sense of his physical presence came over him.

He opened his eyes—

It felt strange. He had supposedly opened his eyes before. Yet they had opened again.

Something had been peeled away before his eyes.

Or that's how it felt to him.

A layer had been peeled away, and a new scene appeared.

Therein—

Was Keiko. Without a doubt, it was Keiko.

Kasadera had . . . vanished. Only a faint echo of his smile lingered. Exactly like the smile of the Cheshire Cat.

And yet . . . and yet . . .

Sakakibara looked at Keiko. He stared at her.

Her eyes were open as wide as possible.

Her face was pale. It was drained of blood.

"Kei . . . ko . . ."

He barely managed to speak.

But the expression on her face was stiff, so stiff that it looked about to crack.

Her eyes were focused intently on something, something behind Sakakibara. It was as if she were looking through him.

Sakakibara instinctively turned around.

Her gaze gave him the feeling of something behind him.

Is there something—there—!?

But he couldn't see anything.

There was nothing, no one, behind him.

His head was spinning, but now probably because of the alcohol. Sakakibara turned to face Keiko directly.

He placed both hands on her shoulders.

"Keiko!"

His shout verged on a scream.

Just then she blinked as if confused. Three times, four times, he shouted to her. Gradually, the focus of her eyes shifted to his face.

". . . !"

Her mouth opened wide in a silent scream.

She made an effort to push his hands from her shoulders.

Sakakibara held tightly to her.

"What happened!? Come on, it's okay!"

With these words, he tried to pull her into his arms.

". . . Ah, aah . . ."

Finally, she realized that it was Sakakibara. Now she threw herself into his arms.

They clung to one another, trembling in each other's arms. They were unable to move for quite a while.

"What happened—? What was it that happened!?" Sakaki-bara repeated somewhat deliriously.

"It's really you . . . suddenly . . . you were . . ."

As she began to speak, she was at once sobbing and speaking.

"Me—? What happened to me!?"

"You . . . you suddenly . . . changed . . . and you were no longer you . . . at least that's how it looked to me . . ."

"What did I look like!?"

". . ."

She didn't answer.

She breathed as if gasping for air.

He held her tighter and then found the courage to speak.

"Was it Kasadera—!?"

Keiko burst into tears as if unable to hold them back any longer. And he felt her entire body stiffen as if struck by lightning.

He must have guessed correctly.

That meant . . . it meant . . . that she too had seen his ghost.

"It's horrible . . . why? Don't say . . . don't tell me, you, too . . ."

"You should lie down in bed for a while—" He tried to get

her to her feet. "It must be the wine, the two of us just drank too much."

But Keiko shook her head violently in response.

"You saw it, didn't you? You saw it, too, didn't you!?"

"Try to keep calm, okay? Come on—"

"But you're right, you're absolutely right! It was Kasadera!"

"Stop!"

"He was smiling . . . he looked so happy . . . he was smiling at me . . . and behind him . . . I wonder where he was? The earth around him was a sort of red, reddish brown, all the way to the horizon . . . and the sky too looked reddish . . . the sun was very small but it was shining all the same . . . where was it?"

Earth . . . ? Sun . . . ?

That wasn't it at all! Sakakibara had seen something entirely different.

What Sakakibara had seen, or thought he had seen, was the ghost of Kasadera wearing a joyous expression, and nothing else.

"That's right . . . that place was definitely not our Earth . . . on the distant horizon was a range of mountains taller than any that I have ever seen . . . and Kasadera was flying in that direction . . . it's true! He really was floating in the sky!"

"Enough! I get it—"

". . . but . . . but . . . it wasn't only him . . . a great number of . . . a great number of others were with him . . . hovering . . . on air . . . in the sky. I couldn't see them but . . . I felt it . . . it wasn't just him . . . and I could almost see them . . . almost . . . almost . . . and when I could, then . . . ."

"Stop it now!"

Sakakibara pressed a hand to Keiko's mouth as she continued chattering as if in a feverish trance.

And then he helped her to her feet.

Were such things really possible—?

Sakakibara had never thought it necessary to deny the existence of ghosts because he had always considered the issue ridiculous and irrelevant.

He had always believed, and there had been no good reason to think otherwise, that ghosts and such existed only in the minds of those who saw them.

That was why, that was—(precisely!)—why Kasadera had appeared here and now before him.

That had to be it.

Kasadera who had waved good-night to Keiko and Sakakibara that night . . . the copy of the manuscript that he held in his hand . . . the notes that he had left behind . . . and then what Kasadera's mother had revealed of his feelings for Keiko . . . all these things, in combination with all the wine, had sparked a radiant illusion upon his retinas. There was no other explanation.

It was all due to his unnecessary feelings of guilt.

And Keiko too was surely prey to similar feelings of regret.

That's all there was to it.

We simply ignore it and move on. And that would be the end of it.

Holding Keiko, Sakakibara pushed open the bedroom door with a foot.

They fell into bed in each other's arms.

Keiko sighed deeply, her breath hot.

She wrapped her legs tightly around him.

They didn't even take the time to undress. Their hands were all over one another, arousing one another, and they rolled and grappled until they found themselves locked in an embrace that matched their bodies' passion.

It happened quickly.

In the heat of the moment they both reached climax quickly.

Still, they remained entwined. They could not move apart.

They feared the exposure that would come with separation. Someone was watching. Even though their minds told them it was impossible, they nonetheless burrowed deeper into each other's bodies, like small animals instinctively trying to hide themselves deep in their lairs.

Until the night began to give way to dawn light . . . they ravished each other, in flight from fear.

3

They married.

They held the wedding in mid-May, on the Saturday following Golden Week.

A small reception was held for their friends, acquaintances, and coworkers at Kirin Publishers.

The reception also celebrated the publication of Kirin's new book series, *Undiscovered Materials*.

The first volume was scheduled to appear in late May.

It was *Sources of Surrealism,* an overview of the history and philosophy of surrealism.

Preliminary copies had been prepared for those who attended the party.

Subsequently, a volume would appear every other month, *Visions of Surrealism* in late July, *Forms of Surrealism* in late September, *Languages of Surrealism* in late November, and so forth.

In any case—in accordance with Sakakibara's original plan, the first three volumes would be on time for the Seito department store exhibition.

Preparations for the exhibition were also well under way.

The editorial work on various brochures was about 60 percent completed, and it was now the responsibility of the Hakuden Agency to follow through with the photography and printing. Since the conception and design work for the collection had been established, publication of the subsequent volumes should proceed quite smoothly.

On the day of the party, the Seito Group sent a large bouquet of flowers. President Tsujimi's personal secretary made an appearance to read his message of congratulations.

To cap the event, the Kirin staff hoisted Sakakibara high into the air.

Among the staff were three new employees whom Sakakibara had hired after Kasadera's death: Kuwamura Yasuichirō; a recent graduate, Hōjō Masashi; and Wakabayashi Kyōko.

The following day, Sakakibara and Keiko were to embark on a nine-day honeymoon in Paris. Their departure was early the next morning, and so they would stay at a hotel overnight.

They did their best to leave the party early, but everyone teased them, saying, "We know it's not the first night for you two!" They went to an after-party and an after-after-party.

Sakakibara had asked Kuwamura to take care of things in his absence. Because the nine-day vacation included two weekends, Sakakibara would only miss one week of work. And at this point there shouldn't be any problems.

Kuwamura and Sakakibara had graduated from the same French department in the same university, but Kuwamura had been two years behind him. Kuwamura had worked in an import-export firm for about three years and then resigned to pursue a career as a freelance translator.

He'd been on good terms with Sakakibara since college.

"By the way, Sakakibara, about the *Languages of Surrealism* volume—"

The fourth volume in the *Undiscovered Materials* series, *Languages of Surrealism,* would center on poetry.

"Who should I ask to do the translation of the three texts?"

He was referring to Who May's three texts, "Another World," "Mirror," and "The Gold of Time."

After his encounter with the ghost of Kasadera that night, Sakakibara had honestly vowed never to touch those manuscripts again.

He had, in fact, buried them deep in the office file cabinets and had never taken another glance at them.

He couldn't work up any enthusiasm for it.

Yet again . . . if, yet again, Kasadera's ghost were to appear from the lines of the poems, he would lose all confidence in his sanity.

Nonetheless, those three works were far too important for him to abandon them for personal reasons.

Regardless of who had actually signed the name Who May, and regardless of who had actually written the three manuscripts, the Who May manuscripts provided a hypothetical connection between Artaud, Breton, and Dalí.

It might even be that . . . Who May was not an actual person but a character used by some group or secret association as a collective name. If that were the case, it was even more interesting. It had deeper implications.

He couldn't let them be buried away.

Even if they couldn't determine their identity right now, the mere suggestion of an enigma would have a powerful impact.

And so—

Sakakibara had nonetheless included the three works with the name Who May on the list of materials for the proposed volume on *Languages of Surrealism,* with an asterisk beside each title.

The asterisk indicated that these were very important works.

In any event, the time had come to find a translator for them right away. And once they are translated into Japanese, he might be able to look at them with a fresh mind.

In that case—there would be no question of Kasadera's ghost making an appearance. It just wouldn't be possible.

There would be no longer any connection between Kasadera and Who May. Kasadera's ghost had dwelled in the copy of the manuscript clutched in his hand at the time of his death. That was one way of making sense of it.

Even then . . . nonetheless Sakakibara had wavered.

Until today he had found reasons to put off the decision on an appropriate translator.

On the one hand, he rather wanted to hand them over to someone he didn't know, and yet, on the other hand, he felt exceedingly uneasy about handing them over to a stranger.

This was a perfect opportunity.

"It is already May, and these are fairly long works, you know—"

Sakakibara poured some whiskey for Kuwamura, who was looking concerned.

"As a matter of fact, I had forgotten about it. I hate to drop it on you, but could you find someone while I am gone?"

"It's really no trouble, but who do you think would be good for this? If necessary, I can try to do it myself."

"Absolutely not!" Sakakibara said loudly and then fell silent in confusion. But even in his confusion, he resolutely shook his head side to side. "I'd like to send this one outside. There was the incident with Kasadera and . . ."

His voice trailed off.

"You think that it's a bad omen? That's not like you."

Kuwamura laughed. But he didn't look particularly pleased. He probably thought that Sakakibara doubted his abilities.

"No, that's not it at all . . . if you get wrapped up in it, you won't be able to attend to other matters. That's what worries me."

Sakakibara gave the obvious excuse.

"It will chew up a lot of time, you know. I wonder how much it will take, for all three manuscripts—?"

"Let's see—" Kuwamura thought for a while and then replied. "One manuscript is about ten thousand words, or about thirty pages. For all three, we're talking about a hundred pages."

"We'll need someone who can translate quickly. Let's ask for a draft, and you can check over the work that way."

"That should work . . ."

In a happier tone, Kuwamura mentioned the names of several young translators.

"I'll leave it to you."

"How about Fujisawa?"

"You mean Fujisawa Satoru?"

Sakakibara knew the name well. He had even met him a few times. He had a reputation for a quick turnaround on translations. His translations were literal and rather stilted but highly accurate.

Still—something bothered Sakakibara. He knew that Kasadera had been fairly good friends with Fujisawa.

Ironically, Kuwamura had probably thought of Fujisawa for the same reason. And sure enough—he went on to add, "Fujisawa would be thrilled to do it. If we let him know that this is work left behind by Kasadera, he'll jump at the chance."

" . . ."

There was nothing but for him to agree.

He couldn't shake the disquieting thought that Fujisawa, as a friend of Kasadera, might conjure up his ghost once again. But then it occurred to him that Fujisawa would surely console and ease the dead spirit, precisely because he had been his friend.

"What do you think? Shall we go with him—"

Noticing the expression of deep concern with which Kuwamura was looking at him, Sakakibara drained his whiskey and water in a single gulp. He then answered, "Okay. Let's go with him."

Sakakibara and Keiko left for Paris the next day.

The nine days flew by.

It was Monday night in Japan when they returned. By the time they cleared customs and boarded the limousine bus from Narita airport into town it was past ten.

From the bus terminal they took a taxi, and when they reached the new apartment they were renting in Nishi-Waseda, it was nearly eleven.

After more than twenty hours on the plane, the two of them were dead tired.

Still, Sakakibara was worried about things at the office.

Kuwamura picked up when he called. Kojima was also there working late.

"Just go to bed before me. I'm going to take a quick look."

With these words to Keiko, he stuffed some souvenirs in his bag and left the apartment.

In the corner of the garage, under a sheet, his beloved CBX 650 stood waiting for him.

He removed the sheet and started the engine.

Their new apartment was closer to the Takada-no-baba offices than his old one. It took less than five minutes to get there on the bike.

Thrilling to the familiar roar of the bike after his absence, he arrived at Kirin Publishers. He looked up and saw that only the lights of the third floor offices were on. The fifth floor was dark.

Now that they had finished sorting through the materials, there was no need to work as intensely as before.

He took the elevator to the third floor.

Kuwamura and Kojima were waiting for him, ready to joke and give him a hard time.

He bought some peace by pulling out some souvenirs from France for them and then went to his desk.

A pile of messages lay there.

"Anything new?"

"Well, starting today, *Undiscovered Materials* is on the shelves in the stores," Kuwamura replied.

"Oh, and there's this—"

Kuwamura handed Sakakibara a stack of papers.

"These came in from Fujisawa today. I just glanced through them, but they look really interesting."

He felt shocked for an instant.

They were standard manuscript pages. In bold letters on the title page was "Another World." Beneath it were the characters *sakka fumei* or "author unknown." Which could also be read, "Author: Hu Mei"—probably his idea of a joke.

"Fujisawa also translated the title as 'Another World,' didn't he?"

With this rhetorical question, Sakakibara leafed through the pages. There were seventy-three pages in all. In published form that would be about thirty-seven pages. It would be the length of a short story.

But that was it for now. Fujisawa must have begun with this work.

Sakakibara felt somehow relieved.

If the title "The Gold of Time" had appeared first, it would have rekindled his nightmares.

"That's right. We gave him all of Kasadera's notes—he probably used them," Kuwamura answered.

"The other two—?"

"He's working on them now. I called him, and he said he'd have the next one done in about a week."

Nodding, Sakakibara turned to the first page.

"A fish. Dobaded. Its eyeball sliced down the middle. Sections quivering. Images reflected on the split lens are stained with blood. Dobaded. The city of people mirrored there is dyed madder red. Reversal of pressure, dobaded, and there you go! It's taking you there. . . ."

(Dobaded, huh . . . ?)

"Anyway, we'll have to dispense with 'author unknown.' I will write an account of Who May."

Even as he said this, he knew that the account would be based largely on supposition and imagination.

Nevertheless—this would have to do for Who May.

He looked around the room and spoke again.

"All right. If you can bear to drop things for a moment, let's go out for a drink. I'll treat you to something Japanese called *sake*."

4

Exactly one week later as Fujisawa had promised, the translation of another manuscript arrived by post.

It was "Mirror."

"The Gold of Time" would turn up last, after all.

Sakakibara felt genuinely relieved.

The memories of that night had nearly faded away. But even though they had already begun to fade, he did not feel like reading "The Gold of Time" again, not yet.

Sakakibara would proofread the translation of "Mirror."

When "The Gold of Time" did come in, he would entrust the proofreading to Kuwamura.

He placed a copy of the original text alongside the translation and began to read Fujisawa's translation, comparing it line by line with the original.

The first half showed a constant refrain.

Variations on "gaze upon yourself" appeared again and again.

The refrain then gradually and subtly changed, undergoing

various permutations and combinations until it reached a state of verbal chaos and then ended.

It was that sort of work.

He found it quite fascinating . . . but, quite frankly, incomprehensible.

He couldn't grasp its logic.

It seemed to entail a sort of automatism.

He tried to work through it in those terms.

Automatism was one of the surrealists' favorite experimental techniques, in which they wrote down words as rapidly as they popped into the head or flowed from the mouth.

In this way, writing so rapidly, they strove to shake off the rational constraints associated with common sense, grammar, and rhetoric, recording the very movement of thought in the domain of the unconscious, and Breton championed this technique as one "proposing a key capable of opening indefinitely that box of many bottoms called man."

As early as 1919, in collaboration with Philippe Soupault, Breton himself published a work based on automatism titled "The Magnetic Fields."

It was possible that this "Mirror" also entailed a sort of automatism.

In other words, he may have used the "mirror" as a means to liberate the unconscious mind by talking to himself in the mirror, which gradually allowed him to break with rational language, and the result had been this sort of work—

It was one possible explanation for it anyway.

It could be explained but—something inexplicable still remained.

Something else . . . something . . . just seemed to be there.

If he only had some kind of clue, he was sure to get it— it would appear clearly before him. Even though he couldn't escape this feeling, there was not a clue to be found.

It was exasperating.

Was it a problem with the translation? No, it wasn't as simple as that. The translation was on the mark. Besides, Sakakibara had been reading the translation alongside the original text.

Was it his reading ability? Maybe for the native speaker of French there was a very obvious clue.

In any event, "Mirror" was entirely different in effect from "Another World."

"Another World" was a sort of imaginary sketch. Although the ambiguity of the word *dobaded* posed a certain obstacle, the overall vision was clear enough. That's what made it a pleasure to read.

But "Mirror" was different.

Sakakibara couldn't make out anything amid the verbal chaos of the second half.

(Nothing we can do about that . . .)

Sakakibara decided to stop agonizing over it and began marking his edits in red.

It was a work that had from the outset been chosen not for its inherent qualities but for its topicality. And it was the general lot of poetry to lose impact in translation. It would just have to be presented as an experiment from the era of surrealism.

Sakakibara called Kuwamura and handed over the edited manuscript.

It looked like *Languages of Surrealism,* the fourth volume of *Unexplored Materials,* would also make it into print within the year.

Nearly all the manuscripts had been assembled.

"So, what do you think about this one?" Kuwamura asked while leafing through the pages.

"I don't see anything amiss. He did a great job. It was a good idea to ask Fujisawa. And no matter what, he always gets things done on time."

"He is really reliable. Unless there is some kind of emergency, he never fails to get things in."

Having recommended Fujisawa, Kuwamura felt reassured and beamed as if his own work had been praised.

And then—

Twenty days passed.

Checking through the list of materials for *Languages of*

Surrealism, Sakakibara noticed that the pages for "The Gold of Time" were missing.

He checked with Kuwamura, who said that the manuscript hadn't come in.

He made a call. No one answered.

Although he was somewhat concerned, he was busy with other matters, and a week slipped by.

Still, the manuscript had not arrived. And they hadn't heard anything from Fujisawa.

"What's the matter with him?"

Sakakibara was now getting impatient.

It was already July. The volume was 80 percent complete. It was pretty much only "The Gold of Time" that remained. They kept calling Fujisawa two or three times a day.

One afternoon past five someone finally picked up on the other end.

". . . yes?"

"Yes, this is Sakakibara at Kirin Publishers. Is Mr. Fujisawa there?"

" . . . y . . . e . . . s . . . it . . . is . . . I . . ."

His words of his reply were oddly stretched out.

Making every effort to restrain his anger, Sakakibara repeated his question.

"Is this Fujisawa? Fujisawa Satoru?"

". . . that . . . is . . . right . . ."

"This is Sakakibara of Kirin Publishers—"

". . . yes . . ."

"That translation we asked you to do, we haven't received it yet."

". . . y . . . e . . . s . . ."

Clearly, there was something wrong.

"Fujisawa, are you still in bed?"

". . . no . . . I've been up . . . for awhile . . ."

In that case maybe he'd been drinking? Anyhow—

"So, about that translation, when can we expect it?"

Sakakibara's tone was clipped, which didn't do much to conceal his anger.

". . . the manuscript . . . ah . . . not yet . . . not yet . . . I haven't sent it . . ."

"You haven't sent it? We're in a bind here. It's very close to the deadline. If you'd prefer, we can pick it up—"

". . . not yet . . . complete . . ."

Sakakibara bit his lip.

"We have to have those pages. The other pieces are all in place. The only thing we need now is your translation of 'The Gold of Time.'"

". . . the gold . . . of time . . . light, its shadow, and its shadow . . . in the depth of the depths . . . of light . . ."

It was unmistakable. He was whispering the first lines of "The Gold of Time."

Feeling somewhat dizzy, Sakakibara sharply cut in.

"That's right. That's 'The Gold of Time,' and when will you get it to us? And it would be a great help if you could let us know about how many pages—"

". . . yes . . ."

Obviously, there was something wrong with him.

"Fujisawa, have you been drinking?"

". . . no . . . not drinking at all . . ."

"Well, then, what's going on? Can you be straight with me, and let me know when we'll get your pages?"

". . . yes . . . any time . . . it's finished . . ."

"What! But you just said that it wasn't—"

". . . yes . . . I just haven't written it down yet . . ."

"You haven't written it?"

". . . but . . . if I write it . . . that's the end . . . it's all . . . over . . ."

"May I send someone over tonight?"

Sakakibara's voice was taut with stress.

Fujisawa lived in the mountains near Machida. Even if he sent someone, it would be an overnight trip. Still, things had come to a point where it was necessary to take hold of the situation.

". . . yes . . . no . . . I understand . . ."

None of it made any sense.

"If I come out your way, could you find me a hotel some-where or someplace for a layover?"

". . . yes . . . uh huh . . . I'll do it . . . I understand . . . right away."

Fujisawa hung up abruptly.

Sakakibara considered calling back but felt too angry for that.

The following day Sakakibara made the journey to Ma-chida with Fujisawa's address to guide him.

After about an hour's walk up a steep slope, he found Fuji-sawa's house on the corner in a new residential area.

No matter how much he rang the bell or pounded on the door, no one answered. He went to take a look around back, but the door and windows were shuttered tight.

But he spied a trickle of light between the cracks.

"Fujisawa! It's Sakakibara!"

He pounded on the shutters.

There was nothing more that he could do.

He dragged himself all the way back to the office. The sun had already set.

There was no time to find another translator at this stage of the game. It looked like one of them was going to have to do it. Resolving to take up the matter with Kuwamura tomorrow, Sakakibara returned home.

After their marriage, Keiko had resigned from Kirin, work-ing out of the home, doing freelance translation and teaching French.

It wasn't entirely out of the question to ask her. But he wished to avoid that if at all possible.

That night he got drunk before climbing into bed.

The following day, close to noon, head pounding with a hangover as he went into work—

And the manuscript from Fujisawa had arrived.

It was "The Gold of Time." It was sixty-four pages on typ-ing paper. There were almost no corrections or erasures. Ap-parently, he had produced a clean copy in one go.

He hadn't been lying when he said, "I'll do it."

Because the manuscript was so neatly done, Sakakibara could readily determine how many pages it would be in print. There was no time for any further checking. He decided to leave corrections for the galleys and had Kojima take it to the printers as it was.

It occurred to him, as he was breathing a sigh of relief, to call Fujisawa. But no one answered.

Maybe he was now angry about how Sakakibara treated him. Or maybe he was curled up in bed, exhausted.

Well, whatever—nothing he could do about it.

A call came in from the Hakuden Agency. The color proofs for the *Undiscovered Century* exhibition brochures were ready.

Sakakibara left things to Kuwamura and took Miyagami with him to the Hakuden Agency production facilities located in Yotsuya.

Work on the proofs took till midnight.

He called Fujisawa again the following day.

And again the next day—

The weekend arrived.

Saturday morning and afternoon he called repeatedly, but still no one answered.

Maybe he had gone somewhere on vacation?

The following week a thick pile of galleys came in from the printer.

The initial proof for "The Gold of Time" was there as well.

Kuwamura assumed responsibility for it.

Because he ran out of time at work, however, he took it home with him for a look-through.

Sakakibara had a bad feeling about it. But he swept the thought from his mind.

He should forget about it. He had to stop letting Kasadera's ghost creep into his thoughts all the time.

The following day Sakakibara came into work earlier than usual.

Kuwamura hadn't come in yet.

Wakabayashi Kyōko, their accounts manager, brought an expense report for manuscript work to Sakakibara for approval.

Kirin Publishers usually made payments by direct deposit.

Unable to get through to Fujisawa Satoru, however, she had been unable to confirm his bank and account number. She had decided to send him cash by registered mail.

What on earth had happened to Fujisawa—?

He tried calling a publisher in Kanda that specialized in foreign literature, for whom Fujisawa often worked.

His editor came to the phone and explained that they too were trying to determine his whereabouts. Apparently, they were facing some difficulties because he had completed only half of his translation of a novel.

They each agreed to contact the other right away if they learned where he was.

Sakakibara tried calling a couple of other places but gleaned nothing new about him.

About noon Kuwamura finally showed up.

His eyes were swollen with fatigue. He said he'd worked through the night on the galleys. That explained his lack of energy.

Kojima gathered all the corrected galleys and took them to the printer.

That afternoon a call came from Sano, the secretary at Seito department stores. Tsujimi wanted to know if Sakakibara was available for lunch the following Monday to bring him up to date on things.

Sakakibara agreed.

All the preparations for the *Undiscovered Century* exhibition were largely complete on the Kirin side.

Everything was on schedule. He felt proud to be giving that kind of report.

At this stage the principal task would be coordinating with the Hakuden Agency to follow through on the finishing touches to assure the overall quality of the exhibition.

After the fifth volume of *Undiscovered Materials,* it would then be about time to begin the initial preparations for the following year's publications.

Come September, the *Undiscovered Century* exhibition would finally open. It wasn't limited to Tokyo. It was scheduled to make the rounds of the country, showing in ten locations. Several employees from Kirin Publishers would be required to accompany it.

They thus needed to accomplish as much as possible before then.

At about three, he told Kuwamura, who was nodding off at his desk, to go home early.

Just past five he called Fujisawa again, just to make sure. Still no one answered.

5

On Friday of that week—

Late in the afternoon they received the second round of galleys for "The Gold of Time."

Sakakibara quickly looked through them, and everything looked right; there were no obvious errors.

He called Kuwamura to have him do a more detailed check.

Kuwamura's reaction was rather strange.

As if angry about something, he snatched the galleys from Sakakibara's hands in a rage and then, without a word, stormed out of the office.

(What's wrong with him—?)

While he was still looking toward the door where Kuwamura had disappeared, Wakabayashi Kyōko appeared.

"Excuse me, but this was returned for some reason—"

It was the money that she had sent registered mail to Fujisawa Satoru.

Since he had translated well over a hundred pages, it was quite a chunk of cash. The envelope was thick with bills.

"Let me think . . ."

Upon reflection, he took the envelope himself.

"I will keep it for now. I'll take it to him myself later."

That day—

Kuwamura never returned to the office.

A party to celebrate the completion of the second volume of *Undiscovered Materials* had already been planned. They had reserved a table at a nearly restaurant. There was no way to cancel it now.

They went without Kuwamura. Maybe that was why the party seemed to lack enthusiasm and broke up early. The younger staff members said they were going to a disco with Wakabayashi Kyōko.

Sakakibara left them and headed home.

The following morning—

Sakakibara woke at an early hour. It was a beautiful day, an early summer Saturday. When he opened the windows, a pleasant breeze swept into the room.

"Keiko! Hey, Keiko, let's go out somewhere!"

He dragged her out of bed and had her get ready for a bike ride.

After a light breakfast of coffee and toast, they both got on the motorcycle.

Their immediate destination was Machida.

From Shinjuku they took the Kōshū highway all the way to Shitaishihara, where they veered left onto the Tsugawa highway.

As the hour advanced, the day grew gradually hotter. But with the rush of wind on the motorcycle, they barely felt the heat. Their helmets were another matter. They could both feel the sweat dripping from their hair.

The Tsugawa highway ended at a T-intersection where they took a right, through Ookura and toward Kanai . . . and then went up a long, winding road.

They arrived at Fujisawa Satoru's house just before noon.

Sakakibara had Keiko wait by the bike while he climbed the narrow stone steps up to the entrance.

He pressed the buzzer not expecting an answer, yet to his surprise someone was at home, and he heard a key turning in the lock on the inside. But it wasn't Fujisawa.

It was a young woman. She had very straight, shoulder-length hair. Without makeup, freckles showed on her face.

Her outfit was simple, just jeans and a T-shirt.

She looked beautiful nonetheless.

"Yes?"

She looked at Sakakibara with a puzzled expression.

"Um, this is me here. This is Fujisawa Satoru's residence, isn't it?"

He took a business card from his wallet and handed it to her.

She looked down at the card, frowning, and then shook her head slightly.

"Satoru isn't here. I kept calling and . . . I was worried and came out to check on him."

"Are you his sister?"

"No . . . no, I'm not."

She blushed as she replied.

It wasn't hard to figure out. After all, she had an extra set of keys to his house.

"So, he isn't in . . . do you think he went on a trip or something?"

Sakakibara's question was mumbled, half to himself, but the woman shook her head firmly.

"He left the house in a complete mess . . . and if he were going on a trip, he would have said something to me."

She now asked him a question.

"Do you have any idea? Before I lost contact with him, there was something strange about him. And so maybe . . . he started taking some kind of drugs . . . and was getting addicted or something?"

Her tone was pleading.

"Drugs? Had he been using anything like that?"

"No, but I don't know. It's just that lately he kept saying that he was busy, so busy, and I started to wonder . . ."

"There's no way," Sakakibara declared firmly. "He wasn't that kind of person—"

"I know . . . I really didn't think so either but . . ."

"In any case . . . there's this . . ."

Wiping the sweat from his forehead, Sakakibara explained why he had come.

". . . and so I've been having trouble getting this payment to him."

"I see, well, in that case . . ."

She disappeared inside.

She returned and handed him a slip of paper.

"Here's the information for his bank account—"

"Thanks. That really helps."

"I was just cleaning up his room, and he'd left everything in a drawer, his bank book, his cards, all of it. Don't you think it odd?"

"Well . . ."

He didn't really have any answers to her questions. He asked for her phone number in case he learned where he'd gone or heard from him. Her number began with 045, which meant she lived in Yokohama.

"Well, then . . ."

As he was leaving, she called out after him.

"I am so worried, I was thinking of filing a missing person report with the police . . . what do you think?"

If she was that worried, that was probably a good idea—and with those words he left her.

They spent the afternoon in Yokohama, where Keiko did some shopping, and after dinner in Chinatown, they checked into a Holiday Inn. They had had a bit too much to drink.

And of course they were exhausted. As soon as they slipped into bed, they realized just how tired they were.

At the same time, maybe because he was tired, he continued to think about what the woman at Fujisawa's house had said about "drugs."

(Drugs . . . ?)

It was possible . . . it was surprising, but surely that was the secret reason for his disappearance.

He had been very reliable. And so, it wasn't unlikely that,

in struggling to meet his deadlines for work, he had started to depend on drugs of some kind.

And that explained it—that was the reason that he seemed so out of it when he had last talked with him on the phone.

He seemed whacked out on something at the time.

He fell asleep with his mind still going in circles around Fujisawa.

The next day they made a leisurely return to Tokyo on Route 1. Riding double on motorcycles was not permitted on the main highways.

On Monday, when he arrived at the office, a large envelope was sitting on his desk.

It turned out to be the galleys. It was the second set of "The Gold of Time," proofed by Kuwamura.

But Kuwamura himself hadn't come in yet.

Apparently, he had come in to work on Saturday or Sunday, had left this, and returned home.

But why would he do that?

And there was no good reason for his storming out on Friday. What was going on with him? Was he upset about something at work? Or he was having some personal difficulties?

Sakakibara gave the galleys to Kojima who returned them to the printers.

It was now eleven o'clock.

He had a lunch appointment with Tsujimi, the head of Seito today.

About the time he was thinking of going home to change into a suit for his meeting, Kuwamura finally showed up.

His eyes were dilated. He was unsteady on his feet.

He approached Sakakibara's desk before he could call him over.

"What's going on, what—?"

In response Kuwamura beamed rapturously, mouth twisted into a grin. Then he drew his face close to Sakakibara's, whispering.

"Did you read it?"

"Read what?"

"'The Gold of Time.'"

"Well . . . not exactly. I sent it off to the printers right away."

"I see."

Kuwamura's eyelids fluttered, as if in disappointment.

"But you will look at it sometime, won't you?"

What a strange thing to say.

Was he drunk?

(Drunk–!?) (Of course not!) (But . . .)

"Sakakibara, you probably know all about it anyway. Isn't that why you gave the galleys to me, as an experiment?"

A shock ran through Sakakibara.

(As an experiment?)

What does he mean? (Is it possible–?) Had he too seen *it*?

Kuwamura drew his face even closer.

"It's all right, Sakakibara, it's all right . . . even if you didn't know, you'll understand soon enough. Until then, I'll be going . . ."

As his words trailed off, Kuwamura broke into a rapturous grin.

His breath didn't smell of alcohol.

If he were high on something else, however . . . and if the reason that he couldn't help losing himself was . . . was the ghost of Kasadera . . .

Beads of sweat broke out on Sakakibara's face.

"Kuwamura, what the hell are you talking about–!? I have no idea what you're trying to get at–"

Kuwamura cut him off sharply, smiling all the while.

"It's all right, all right . . ."

"What's all right?"

"I kept a copy of it. So, now, I'm free."

"Free?"

"Right . . . I'm going to travel . . . far . . . very far away . . ."

"And what are you going to do about work while you're traveling!?"

None of it made sense. Before he knew it, Sakakibara had started shouting at him.

"Work . . . my work is done. As of today, I am resigning."

Kuwamura said it so casually. And then he added, "Just a little bit more, and I'll catch up to Fujisawa . . . I can feel it . . ."

"Fujisawa? You mean Fujisawa Satoru!?"

Staring off into space, his eyes those of a man dreaming, Kuwamura nodded slightly.

"You know where Fujisawa is?"

"No . . . I don't. But, it won't be long, I'll be with him."

With these words, Kuwamura stood up abruptly.

"Well, then, farewell."

"Wait! Where are you going?"

Kuwamura smiled.

"I haven't much time. Or, rather, I do. But you tend to get lost when you have too much time. I have to go before I get lost . . ."

"What are you talking about!? I just don't—"

"I understand . . . really I do. I already . . . well, maybe not quite yet . . . but I am beginning to understand . . . very soon . . . very . . . soon!"

"Wait!"

But Kuwamura had already left.

And he wouldn't come back again.

6

In the month of September, *Undiscovered Century: A National Exhibition on the Age of Surrealism* had a resplendent opening at the main branch of the Seito department store chain in Ikebukuro.

The symbol chosen to promote the opening, Breton's trunk, became an overnight sensation, turning up in every medium all at once—television, newspapers, magazines, posters.

André Breton and surrealism weren't the sort of thing to draw a large crowd.

And so, not surprisingly, the large ad campaign had been mounted in an entirely entrepreneurial spirit with no concern for artistic merit.

The exhibition became the "autumn theme" for the Seito stores.

The twenty-first century was almost at hand.

As such, the twentieth century had become a thing of the past or, more precisely, a figure of nostalgia.

It was in this sense truly "undiscovered" and "unfinished."

The basic idea of Seito's campaign was to draw on the vitality of these previously unknown materials, tapping into them as a new source for fashions and lifestyles.

In more concrete terms, this meant renewing an older vogue for Paris and for the cultivated French lifestyle, which had gradually been forgotten in Japan.

Seito's strategy could also be seen as an attempt to revive the high modern style by building on American-style commercialization while tapping into a latent demand.

In the overall scheme of things, the exhibition was the initial sally of their commercial strategy.

It was supposed to serve as the impetus for a new consumer trend.

These initiatives were to culminate in a massive year-end sale that Seito would style as a sort of "thank-you celebration."

And so the exhibition opening had been calculated to make a big splash.

In Seito's view of things, while Breton's trunk functioned as a symbol of the days gone by, it could also be seen as a magic box full of things unknown. It was nothing more or less than that.

Surrealism and its avant-garde spirit were considered somewhat passé, empty, and eccentric pursuits.

Yet due to the massive campaign, the exhibition itself had met with great success.

After spending early September in Ikebukuro, it moved to Shibuya for the rest of the month before moving on to Kichijōji in October, after which its countrywide tour of major cities began.

Responsibility for supervising the entire exhibition fell to Kirin.

At least two Kirin employees had to be on site at each venue.

But they were responsible for more than simply managing and supervising.

They were also in charge of selling a variety of pamphlets and the *Undiscovered Materials* books they had edited.

After all, even if it was a cultural event, the sponsor was a department store. They had to make a return on the money they had laid out.

The exhibition moved on a weekly basis, to Chiba, Yokohama, Osaka, and Fukuoka, and then Sendai, Niigata, and Sapporo, until it came successfully to an end in mid-December.

During this time Kirin Publishers hired new employees, for there was an increase of close to 80 percent in the actual number of working hours.

Sakakibara even pulled Keiko into things, and they flew around the country, to Chiba, Osaka, Fukuoka, Sapporo.

But there was an end to it.

With the publication of *Languages of Surrealism* just in time for the last exhibition at the end of November, four volumes of *Undiscovered Materials* had appeared in print, with a total sale of sixty thousand volumes.

It helped that they had reduced the price with each new volume, but even so the sale figures were quite surprising for such serious materials.

As they had expected, the biggest seller was the second volume, *Images of Surrealism,* with its wealth of color illustrations, while the fourth volume, *Languages of Surrealism,* had sold only about fifteen hundred copies, since it consisted only of texts and had been on sale for a shorter period.

All in all, however, it was not a bad start. If one included the sales in bookstores, they had sold more than five thousand copies within the first two weeks after the release.

It was all surely due to the power of mass media, of television and newspapers.

The Seito department store campaign, based thematically on twentieth-century avant-gardism and surrealism, entered into the general consciousness of fashion, attracting readers to the *Undiscovered Materials* series who would not normally have had anything to do with Kirin publications.

How many of them actually opened the book and read any of it was an entirely different question.

In any event, having poured its energies into Seito's massive campaign, Kirin Publishers had been amply rewarded.

On the day that *Languages of Surrealism,* with its carefully edited poetry, stories, and other literary materials, appeared in print, Sakakibara was in Fukuoka with Keiko.

It was Friday, and for the following day and day after, Saturday and Sunday, the exhibition was to move north to Sendai. Miyagami and Hōjō were scheduled to take over for them there.

Kojima called them in Fukuoka.

"The fourth volume is out. You should receive fifty copies by special delivery tomorrow. How are things there?"

"Pretty good, actually, pretty good. How did the book turn out?"

"It's really beautiful. It's the best cover so far."

Breton's trunk also served as an emblem for the *Undiscovered Materials* series.

An image of the trunk figured on the lower half of the cover, while the upper half featured artwork by a Japanese artist on the theme of surrealism. The images were supposed to vie for attention.

A new woman artist had done the artwork for the cover of the fourth volume.

Sakakibara had only caught a glimpse of the image before the book went to press.

He was really looking forward to seeing how it looked on the actual book.

The next day past noon a package arrived, special delivery.

The cover really did catch the eye. That's surely why they

sold twenty books in no time. And they were sold out by the time the exhibit closed on Sunday.

As a consequence, Sakakibara returned to Tokyo without having an opportunity to peruse the fourth volume.

The following weekend, two suicides happened in quick succession in Fukuoka. Both were female students attending a local high school who threw themselves off a building.

One of them thought she was a bird: she jumped off the roof of a building flapping her arms, crashed to the ground, and died.

Neither one of them left behind any sort of note.

In Tokyo, one of the proofreaders at the printing offices vanished without a trace.

Sakakibara had been away from Tokyo quite awhile.

After his efforts for the exhibition in Osaka and Fukuoka, he was physically and mentally exhausted.

Keiko, who had accompanied him, felt even more drained.

When they flew back from Fukuoka, Sakakibara had Keiko go home ahead of him and went to check on things at the office.

Miyagami and Hōjō had left for Sendai that morning.

Kojima hadn't come in. Wakabayashi Kyōko had no idea why. He was probably just skipping.

It looked like all hell had broken loose in the office during the twenty days he had been gone.

Probably he was just feeling tired.

Tsujimi had called him.

It was another invitation for lunch, no doubt.

He had really wanted to take the next day off and rest, but it hardly seemed possible.

A heap of mail covered his desk.

At the bottom of the large heap was a copy of the new book, *Languages of Surrealism*.

He took everything and stuffed it into a large vinyl bag.

In any event—he was spending today at home. He needed some sleep.

He'd take care of all this tomorrow.

He left Wakabayashi Kyōko in charge and left the office.

He walked home at a leisurely pace, looking in the windows of bookstores in the neighborhood.

Some of them had copies of *Undiscovered Materials* on display, and some had none at all.

It was a limited run of books, and so it made sense that they were concentrated in certain locations.

Languages of Surrealism was not yet on display anywhere.

They had rushed advance copies of the book to Fukuoka to make it for the exhibition, but the distribution to bookstores that had asked to carry them would start this weekend.

And he was eager to see what impression it would make.

It couldn't be expected to sell anywhere near as much as the second and third volumes with their illustrations.

But the fourth volume was truly remarkable for the scope and depth of its materials.

He felt confident of that . . . but then Sakakibara himself hadn't actually read through the entire volume.

It had gone to press without him reading about a third of it.

That third . . . included . . . Who May's "The Gold of Time."

Who May . . . in the end no one knew exactly who he was.

Even his connection to Breton, Artaud, and Dalí had its basis largely in speculation.

That was a matter for scholars to study and assess later.

But he felt a tinge of regret nevertheless.

(Okay!)

Sakakibara came to a decision.

As he walked, he made up his mind.

(Today is the day . . . today is the day I read it.)

5

VOYAGERS

1

Konami Shichirō, a translator, received a phone call from Harado Zenji in Osaka.

Harado taught English literature at a university in Kyoto. In his early thirties, he was very active as a scholar.

Fond of science fiction and fantasy literature, he also contributed reviews and essays on these topics to scholarly journals.

SF was Konami Shichirō's principal line of work. In addition to translations, he wrote essays and occasionally published novels under a pen name.

For two years, he had been writing a column in a monthly journal in collaboration with Harado.

Each month they would make a selection of important new books, writing a dialogue in which each discussed what he liked.

That's why Harado had called.

He and Konami had entirely different interests. Konami gravitated toward classic SF, while Harado preferred more marginal SF, some of it quite bizarre.

"Konami, have you read *Undiscovered Materials*?" Harado asked.

"*Undiscovered Materials*? Well, no. I haven't heard of it."

"It was put out by a very small publisher, Kirin, and it's a series on surrealism, with Breton's trunk on the cover."

"Oh, yeah, you mean the one from the art exhibit at some department store?"

"Did you go to it?"

"No, I didn't get to it. Not really my sort of thing. I don't even dream when I'm sleeping. So all that stuff on the unconscious leaves me cold," Konami answered.

It sounded like Harado had latched on to something weird again. (Fine, okay—) He'd just leave all that kinky stuff to him.

"Well, the fourth volume of the series, the one on *Languages of Surrealism* that came out late last year, is quite interesting."

"Languages?"

"Actually the first character of *language* is usually written with the character for *word,* but they've used the character for *phantom* instead. You know, as a play on words."

"Is it mostly criticism?"

"No. It's an anthology of experimental work, with poems, short fiction . . . and even some fairly long works, too."

"Experimental work, huh?"

"Just now I was reading something called 'The Gold of Time,' by a writer called Who May, a kind of, well, prose poem, and it's quite good, with a true sense of the marvelous. And there's another work by Who May, "Another World," which is definitely SF."

"Who May? Never heard of him."

Konami's reply was indifferent.

When Harado used the term *SF,* it sounded somewhat condescending to Konami and always ended up rubbing him the wrong way.

"So, are you thinking of using this surrealist whatchamacallit for this month's review?" Konami asked.

"Yeah, that's the idea. But even more than that, I'd like to get you to read it, too. At least 'Another World.' I think you'll like it."

"All right, all right. As soon as I have time, I'll take a look at it. It's Kirin Publishers, right?"

"Yeah. It's the fourth volume of *Undiscovered Materials,* ¥1800. You'll probably find it in the art books section—"

Konami listened but didn't bother to jot it down. He had almost no interest in reading it.

They then exchanged information about other new publications for awhile, and once they had settled on what each would do for the review, they hung up.

Near the end of every month Harado would send the manuscript of his review to Konami. Konami would use the remainder of their allotted pages for his half of it.

That was the pattern that they had gradually settled on.

Konami would collate their manuscripts and deliver them to the magazine publisher.

However—

That month the manuscript from Harado, who always kept strictly to deadlines, was already well past its due date. Konami called, but there was no answer.

Konami had no choice but to extend his portion of the review to complete the manuscript for the publisher.

This had never happened before.

Although he was worried, he still felt more anger than concern.

There was no excuse for Harado not even to have called—

The day after he turned in the manuscript, however, it was in the newspapers, and friends were calling him, and he learned what had happened to Harado.

He couldn't have contacted him. He had died.

His body was found on a bench in the park at Osaka Castle.

He was sitting there, slumped over as if dozing, dead.

The cause of death was said to be a heart attack.

His body had sat there on the bench for three days, and somehow no one had noticed.

Someone who passed by the park during their lunch break had noticed him sitting in the same position two days in a row and, thinking it odd, reported it to the police.

He was holding a book tightly with both hands on his knees.

Konami later learned from some friends of Harado that the book had been *Undiscovered Materials*.

That came as a shock.

That day, on his way home from work, Konami went into a bookstore in the train station.

Just as Harado had said, *Undiscovered Materials* was in the section of art books.

The fourth volume was thin compared to volumes two and three. Konami picked it up. He found the name Who May in the table of contents.

It read "Poet of the Fourth Dimension, Who May." Three of his works appeared.

Konami opened to those pages. He recalled the title "The Gold of Time."

He started into it:

"The shade of the shadow of light. The depth of the depths of light. Equinox of light. Around behind light, at the time it arrives here. Time is gold. Gold itself has the same aspect as time. Time is gold, and its shadow too is gold. . . ."

He felt drawn into it despite himself.

At some point his soul started drifting away.

It was a strange . . . eerie feeling. Pulled into the lines of words, he then passed through them, and the poem itself grew ever more distant . . . (Am I simply exhausted?) . . . (I'm starting to lose consciousness.) Such thoughts echoed from the corners of his mind.

Yet he continued to be carried away.

(Where am I going . . . ?)

He didn't know. Harado's countenance appeared before his eyes. He was smiling. He was smiling so very happily.

Opening his mouth, he whispers something . . . but the voice is not audible . . . a vortex appears . . . and disappears. It is a celestial body. The motion of the celestial body becomes visible as if a singular concept.

There is a wheel. There are spokes within the wheel. It is the vortex once again. Slowly . . . and gradually faster . . . he is going to be sucked into it.

As he gets closer, each and every one of the points forming the wheel turn out to be human faces. Next to him—immediately next to him, is Harado. He can sense it.

For an instant—he sees himself.

There he is, walking along the street. But he is not in present time. That part of the city also looks quite different. His head is covered in white hair.

(The future!)

He felt it clearly. He was seeing the future. But the scene immediately began to melt and fade away. And unfamiliar cities flitted past his eyes.

Once again it is the vortex . . . the vortex spiraling, sucking him into somewhere else. He is watching it all from afar.

Suddenly, he sensed that Harado had vanished.

He had left. He had left for some distant place.

Konami was alone. And he was free.

An instant—! An instant—! An instant—!

Countless instants bounded by.

And then he saw it. Or, rather, he knew it. He thought he knew it. It was the vortex. The vortex was spiraling down into infinite depth. On the edge of the abyss was Konami.

On and on, entirely different consciousnesses flowed past him, affording glimpses of a series of scenes and places unfamiliar to him.

The sun rose, and the sun set. Again it rose, again it set. Again it rose and again set.

"Sir!"

A voice suddenly rang in his ears.

It all vanished in an instant. It was ripped away before his eyes.

He had dropped something without noticing.

It was the book. It had fallen open to the page bearing the title "The Gold of Time."

"The store is closing—"

Startled, he looked at his watch. It was past seven.

It had been barely five when he entered the bookstore.

But he had had no consciousness of time passing.

(What the . . . ?)

Konami hastily bent over and picked up the book.

"Do you wish to buy that?"

The shop clerk sounded exasperated.

"No, no—"

He returned the book to its place on the shelf with trembling hands.

"I don't need it. Really, I don't need it."

And he ran out of the store.

2

It was a day full of frustration.

She had finished her final exams today. But she still felt as prickly as she had the day before.

For one, her period had started during exams, and she hated it. Still, it was better to have it than not.

Once she'd been two weeks late and had been a nervous wreck.

She hadn't seen Yoshio since.

That was how it had to be. It only took one slip to make a heap of trouble. She would spend spring break in bed, alone. She didn't feel at all like going out anyway.

Still, today was special. She didn't want to go right home.

Exams had been as hellish as she'd anticipated, especially Japanese history. She wondered if she'd managed twenty out of a hundred. She blamed Makiko for that. She refused to show her crib sheet to her.

She didn't want to go home right now and have her mother see how distraught she was.

Some classmates had invited her out. But she'd turned them down. She wasn't feeling much like tromping around with them.

And so she had come to Shinjuku by herself.

She changed out of her school uniform in the restroom of a department store and put on as much makeup as a drag queen.

And then, with her uniform stuffed in a shopping bag, she wandered aimlessly. She had no money. So she couldn't even see a movie. The wind was terribly cold. She had to keep walking.

If some old guy tried to pick her up, she figured she'd go with him. How much was a high school girl getting these days? Maybe twenty or thirty thousand yen. Anyway, if you did ten guys, you'd come out with about two to three hundred thousand yen. It was hard to believe. She knew a girl who paid for a trip to Hawaii that way.

(If I were a man, I wouldn't pay two thousand yen for the likes of me . . .)

With such thoughts flitting through her mind, Eguchi Misa went into a large bookstore in some building.

(I'll just steal something.)

The idea popped into her head. It wasn't her first time shoplifting. She'd known the thrill of it from junior high.

She worried about getting hooked on it and so usually restrained herself. But today was different. If she didn't do something, she'd never clear her head.

The store was crowded. Especially around the magazines and new books corner, there were throngs of people.

She avoided those areas, heading to the back of the store. There were security mirrors hung along the ceiling. Shifting her position bit by bit, she found the blind spot. There was nobody around.

(Now!)

It was the art section. The fat oversized books would be impossible to do.

She glanced around. On the middle shelf were some fairly small books with attractive covers.

She stuffed two or three into her shopping bag, without even checking the contents. And then a few more—

Now her spirits soared. The stress vanished like smoke.

She removed her scarf and slung it over the bag to hide the books. She then hurried out of the store.

A feeling of elation coursed through her.

(I did it!)

Bursting with pride in herself, Misa nearly ran all the way back to the train station.

Her home was in Suginami, the eighth stop on the local train.

Taking a seat on the train, she pulled out one of her prizes. One thousand eight hundred yen. And there were five more. That made a total of about ten thousand yen.

She looked at the title. *Undiscovered Materials*—

(What the hell is this . . . ?)

She cursed inwardly. This wasn't something she could sell to her friends. Maybe she could take them to a used bookstore. But she'd hardly make anything at all on them.

Oh, well. It hadn't been for the money.

She cracked open the book nonetheless. The pages were full of fine print:

". . . if Artaud's so-called "surgical" and "purgative" plays are placed alongside those of Jarry and the pataphysicians as pointedly concrete manifestations of their deconstructive tendencies, which runs counter to the slanderous criticism that attended them . . . ."

(. . . "surgical" . . . "purgative" . . . "pataphysician" . . . "deconstructive" . . .)

Misa snorted.

If everything were an instance of something, then anything could surely be anything. Then there wasn't anything that couldn't be explained.

(What nonsense!)

No wonder there was no one in that part of the store.

Misa flipped through the pages: "Special Feature: Who May, Poet of the Fourth Dimension."

Poet—! (Huh!) Come to think of it, there had been a poem by Hagiwara somebody or other on the test today. She just couldn't remember the rest of his name. I was pretty sure it was Hagiwara Kōtarō. That is what she had written. Now she wasn't so sure.

A title appeared, "The Gold of Time."

It looked like a story. If so, it might be worth reading.

"The shade of the shadow of light. The depth of the depths of light. Equinox of light." She'd been wrong, very wrong. It wasn't a story. (But . . . what exactly was it?) It was like a poem, but it had lines like prose. Were there poems like that?

Despite herself Misa continued to follow the words: "Extending the gold. Spreading it. The light is withholding. Going around behind the shadow of the withholding light. . . ."

(What the hell is this . . . ?)

Still, there was something pleasant about it.

Maybe it was the heat of the train . . . a feeling of drowsiness, the warm sponginess of fresh bread . . . soft and fluffy . . . why was that? . . . "Like one swimming, you scoop through the light . . . like one flying, you flap upon the wave-like layers of time . . . ." You . . . you? . . . (does that mean me?) . . . you're truly flying . . . the feeling . . . is a good feeling . . . everything in your head starts gradually to go numb . . . what . . . what—

The train jerked to a halt.

She looked up out of habit. The platform looked familiar. It was the station where she was supposed to get off.

Misa hurried to her feet.

With the book tucked under one arm and the shopping bag in the other, she scrambled out of the train.

The sensation stayed with her, even after passing through the turnstile. Her heart raced with excitement, it was not unlike falling . . . in love.

As she walked, she was conscious of a heavy unwelcome wetness because of her period. But she didn't feel it all that much. Her spirits were soaring.

Misa skipped about half of her ten-minute walk back home. She entered the house.

"Mi-chan? Is that you, Mi-chan?"

It was her mother's voice. Without answering, she hurried upstairs to her room. She sat at the desk and opened the book.

Once more, from the beginning: "The shade of the shadow of light. The depth of the depths of light. Equinox of light. Going around behind the light." She hadn't been imagining things. She hadn't been mistaken. Why had she never realized that poetry could be so marvelous.

Probably it was only this poem. Probably only this poem could work such magic.

Why weren't they teaching this at school? If they put this in a textbook, everyone would develop a love of poetry.

"Mi-chan, how did exams go?"

She heard her mother's voice again.

Misa just ignored it and went on reading.

"Mi-chan, hey, where did that book come from?"

"Bought it."

She had no choice but to answer. But she didn't take her eyes off the page. What a nice feeling . . .

"You bought it? But why do you have so many copies of it—"

(Crap!) Everything had spilled out of her bag when she tossed it on the chair.

"Just leave me alone! Can't you see I'm studying?!"

"Studying? But wasn't today the end of exams?"

"What's so wrong about studying after exams?"

"Look here . . . Mi-chan, don't give your mother—"

"Stop it! This is my room! If you don't need anything, get out!"

Misa snapped the book closed, stood, and started to wriggle out of her skirt.

"Oh dear! Mi-chan, just look at that stain!"

When she noticed the large stain on her underwear, her mother's voice became shrill with disgust.

"Look, I'm already changing! See! Now get out!"

"Mi-chan, I don't know what's going on with these books,

but you'd better not let your dad see them. You should put them away somewhere."

"What! Why can't I let Dad see them?"

Her mother left the room without another word.

Not wanting to fuss, she changed the sanitary pad in her room. And then, in nothing but her underwear, she sprawled on the bed.

She opened the book again.

Her spirits rose at once, clearing and brightening. (. . . Ah . . .) A sigh escaped her. (. . . what a feeling . . .)

She didn't go down for dinner when called, saying she didn't feel well.

All through the night . . . time and time again . . . Misa re-read the poem . . . until she finally fell asleep from sheer exhaustion just before dawn.

Who May . . . that was the author's name.

But she couldn't grasp anything of the other two poems in his name.

This poem alone was special, after all. Only "The Gold of Time" contained within it this special magical power.

And then Misa had such dreams.

In a foreign city she met a beautiful young man with large dark brown eyes.

Somehow she felt it was France.

The language spoken by the beautiful young man sounded like French.

Although she didn't understand the exact meaning, she grasped something of what he was trying to say. "You're looking for Who May, aren't you, young lady? That would be me."

He spoke again. "Let's go."

"Where?" Misa asked in return.

"Where, anywhere—" he replied. "Anywhere, and at any time, you can go. You'll have the ability to go. But . . ."

He smiled.

It was a beautiful smile. But there was something sad about it, too.

Suddenly, the scene vanished before her eyes.

Vast endless space appeared. She didn't know what it was. It was physically too vast for her to grasp. She couldn't see anything. She couldn't breathe.

Instinctively, she began screaming.

Her screams woke her.

It was now morning.

"Mi-chan, wake up! Mi-chan!—"

Her mother was out there yelling.

Misa jumped out of bed.

She had a lot to do today.

She simply had to tell somebody about this poem.

3

(What the hell!? What is this . . . ?)

Kiuchi Yoshiaki shook his head violently from side to side.

His glasses nearly slipped off his nose. Pushing them back on, Kiuchi looked around the teachers' office with frightened eyes.

The sixth period had already begun. More than half the teachers had already left the teachers' office.

All was still.

The remaining teachers were grading papers or preparing for classes, heads bent over their desks.

No one noticed Kiuchi's unusual behavior.

As he looked around, the vice-principal raised his head. Their eyes met.

With a slight shrug, Kiuchi returned his gaze to the book in front of him.

It was a hardcover volume. It had a beautifully illustrated jacket. But apparently it had seen some rough treatment, since it was quite tattered.

With the book closed, one section appeared grimy with use. It was easy to see that that part had been read over and over again.

Kiuchi heaved a large sigh.

He had taken the book from a student in the previous

period. He had called the student's name repeatedly during roll call, but the student hadn't answered. Thinking the student asleep, he went over to find him absorbed in a book lying open on the desk.

He rapped him on the head and confiscated the book.

He told him he could pick it up after school and returned to teaching.

The student's name was Takehashi. He was a fairly good student. He was a shy boy who belonged to the astronomy club.

The book that Takehashi had been reading so attentively that he missed roll call bore the title *Languages of Surrealism*.

It wasn't at all what he had expected. He'd first thought that he was reading some sort of pornography. But then he opened the book to the well-worn section and started to read . . .

(And after all that . . . utter nonsense!)

Kiuchi considered reading it again. But it frightened him.

Surely, it's an illusion, he thought. Yet if it wasn't an illusion—it must be a drug.

Still, that wasn't possible. This was a serious, solid work of art historical research. And it was in translation. Letters . . . words can't possibly act like drugs.

Critics sometimes referred to works as "intoxicating," but that was rhetoric. But a prose poem that actually exerted a narcotic effect on its readers . . . (Ridiculous!) . . . there was no such thing as spells or enchantments . . . it defied reason.

(It's an illusion.) (I must be tired . . .) (That has to be it.) (. . . and yet . . .) (But . . .)

As the same thoughts churned in his head, the bell rang, announcing the end of sixth period.

"Mr. Kiuchi."

He turned his head at the sound, and Takehashi was standing there. And it wasn't just Takehashi. Misaki, student council president, and Shizimu Reiko, the vice president, were with him.

Shizimu Reiko spoke in a low, measured tone. "You read it, didn't you, Mr. Kiuchi?"

"What are you talking about?" Kiuchi asked in return.

Shizimu Reiko glared at him, eyes aflame.

Misaki stepped forward, and without asking, snatched the book from his hands. Only then did Misaki speak: "You'd better keep quiet about this. Reading such material in the teachers' office won't be permitted again."

"What are you talking about, you—!"

Without realizing it, Kiuchi was shouting.

He felt entirely at a loss faced with such behavior.

"If you like, Mr. Kiuchi, we will give you a copy. In return, you'll keep quiet about this with the other teachers. That's our only request."

Misaki finally adopted the behavior befitting a student and bowed deeply. Takehashi and Shizimu Reiko followed his example.

"In your class, then, this . . ."

It finally dawned on him. If that were so . . . then—!

Misaki's mouth twisted into a smile.

"This is our class secret. It is one of our few pleasures. Please don't take it away from us. Ever since we began to pass *this* around, we've really come together as a class. And our scores have gone up, too. So please do this for us."

Indeed, their class average on the standardized tests was now at the top.

Some of the teachers had suspected the entire class of cheating together.

He could see how the class might come together, but why had their scores gone up—? What was it exactly, this book—?

"All right. That will do. You may go now."

"Can we count on you?"

Misaki was not about to let it go.

Kiuchi didn't see any better solution.

". . . sure, I'll keep quiet about it this time. You may go."

The three bowed again and silently left the room.

"Did they do something wrong?"

Their class monitor approached him with a worried look.

"No, it was really not a big deal."

Kiuchi shook his head.

"I caught a student reading something during my class, and so I gave him a warning. It wasn't anything frivolous; in fact, it was pretty lofty stuff . . . I was rather surprised."

"What sort of stuff?"

Kiuchi made up something to satisfy the curious monitor and then left the teachers' office to supervise some extracurricular activities.

That day—

On the way home Kiuchi dropped by a large bookstore near the school.

"Do you have a copy of *Languages of Surrealism* from Kirin Publishers?"

One of the usual clerks knew the title.

"Oh, that one. That came out at the end of last year. It was part of a series of four, and we used to have all four."

"It is sold out? If so, I would like to order it."

The clerk shook his head.

"Unfortunately, Kirin Publishers went out of business. Apparently, several employees just vanished. Business was going well, and so some people said that it was some kind of planned bankruptcy. If you look around the used bookstores, you can probably find some remaindered copies—"

That night—after thinking it over and over, Kiuchi finally decided to call Misaki.

"Misaki, about that book . . ."

"You want a copy, right?" Misaki answered immediately. "I was certain that you'd want one after all."

In July of that year, a three-man rock-and-roll band called PLO made its debut. This PLO had nothing to do with the Palestine Liberation Organization. *PLO* stood for Private Love Orchestra.

Their debut song was "Who May Letter." They became a sensation with their performance of a translated poem set to music that went on for hours.

Needless to say, it wasn't easy to record it, and so they got their start with live performances for small audiences, but they soon had a fanatical following.

At a concert held in Shinjuku, one third of the audience, that is, about one hundred people, blacked out during the performance, which made PLO a household name.

Still, fearing another incident, the concert hall in Tokyo was hesitant to have them perform, and so they began a nationwide tour.

The number of PLO fans increased with every stop on the tour.

A cassette tape of one of their performances, recorded live, copied, and sold for almost nothing, began to circulate among fans.

Finally, a record company got into the act.

A certain company was about to release a highly unusual four-disk recording of their live performance.

But the collection was never released.

All three members of the PLO died in a terrible car accident.

Nevertheless, there were plans to make a record from the tape circulating among avid fans. Yet that too was abandoned.

Rumors circulated that the recording had been deliberately suppressed.

There were even rumors that the deaths of the PLO members had not been an accident.

None of these rumors was proved, however, and by the end of the year, they had faded away.

For the PLO fans themselves also vanished without a trace.

Scholars initially called it "fatal autism."

But investigations into its causes made no progress. In the meantime, the situation continued to advance.

At the start of the new school year, one in eight seats was empty in the classroom, and two in ten students had died over the vacation—yet, despite such alarming statistics, the existence of the name Who May and the work "The Gold of Time" remained unknown to those who had lost their children.

Well, there was one among them who knew.

An official in the Ministry of Welfare, Ueno Katsuhiko, had been aware of it from the very start.

He had lost his only son to the PLO.

His son has been one of the earliest victims, at the time when the newspapers and media had just begun raising the cry about "fatal autism."

He then discovered that the PLO song "Who May Letter" was based on a work called "The Gold of Time" by the poet Who May.

In the drawer of his dead son's desk, he found a copy of the work.

With the copy in hand, he soon found out that it had been published in translation in a book series that was now out of print.

Although no longer for sale, the entire series was in the National Library.

Ueno was aware at the time of the symptoms of addiction. And so he kept careful notes on the progress of his symptoms.

At the meetings held within the Ministry of Education, however, his report was ignored. No one in that Ministry appeared willing to push his claims forward.

And then—Ueno died.

I am not going to die. I am just going. I am joining up. And then I won't be returning anymore. Just wait and see.

His final note ended with those words.

The Committee for the Prevention of Fatal Autism changed its name to the Committee for the Control of Spells. The facts of the matter were not openly presented.

A special operations police force for the control of spells was created within the Ministry of Education. Responsibility fell to the offices of the Ministry of Education due to the way in which events had unfolded, and to avoid administrative confusion with the Bureau of Drug Control within the Ministry of Welfare.

But facts of the situation were not made public knowledge,

nor the existence of the regulatory bureau, nor the reasons for establishing it.

Directives and regulations were all implemented in the name of countering fatal autism.

Public announcements were made about the existence of a book hazardous to persons with autistic tendencies—and thus to assure the well-being of youth, possession, reproduction, exchange, purchase, and sale of it were forbidden.

But, because they did not specify exactly what was hazardous about the book, there were immediate outcries that the measures violated freedom of speech.

Nevertheless, the government completely ignored such issues.

To counter such criticism, they began to clamp down on public discussion of the matter.

Before long, there were no opportunities for voicing opposition.

Society had largely eroded away and was on the verge of utter collapse.

Yet the majority of citizens remained unaware of the facts.

It was better not to let them know.

It seemed preferable to eradicate the disease without their being aware of it.

And yet no one had found a way to figure out what was going on—to determine how the very cause of the disease, the "spells," produced their effect on the human body, on the mind and body.

The primary source of clues was "Ueno's Notes."

The terms used in his notebooks, such as *soul travel, time split, fourth-dimensional sense,* and *slip-away,* became key terms for specialists.

But the time for investigation had passed.

Eradication of the disease was the top priority.

To that end, the special police had free reign to do what they saw fit.

Whatever they saw fit—

4

A look of relief showed in her eyes when he pulled his cock out.

Seeing that look, Kuroda pulled up his pants and fastened the belt.

"That okay, honey? Okay if I leave now?"

The woman spoke in a husky voice.

Actually, she was not quite a woman but still a girl.

Kuroda grinned slyly and nodded.

"It's okay. Of course."

Suddenly the woman's eyes bugged out. She screamed.

"That's a lie! You're here to kill me!"

Kuroda frowned.

Those in the advanced stages were tough to dispose of. Some of them could see five to ten minutes into the future.

"You tricked me! You promised you'd let me go if I let you do me—"

She sat up, looking at him expectantly, her legs still spread wide, wet from their sex.

"You're going to shoot me with a pistol."

She was absolutely right.

That's what he had been about to do.

A smile of embarrassment flitting across his face, Kuroda pulled a small automatic from his shoulder holster. He pulled a silencer from his pocket and screwed it on to the muzzle.

"Sorry about that. But don't hold it against me. I've got a shitty job, and if I can't get a bit of something on the side, it's just total shit—"

"Wait!"

She screeched at him.

"What's that?" Kuroda's lips twisted. "Too bad but no time for another go. Busy day for me."

She glared back at him. But her anger quickly vanished, and she snorted a laugh through her nose.

"One minute . . . no, thirty seconds is enough. Just give me that. Then I don't care if you shoot me—"

Kuroda glanced suspiciously around the room.

Would something happen in the next thirty seconds? Would someone be coming to her rescue? But—there was no chance of that. Cops were all over the entrance to the house. They had taken her parents in for questioning.

There was no fear of her getting away.

"Why?"

Kuroda asked her anyway.

"To pray."

Her voice was almost inaudible.

Kuroda nodded slowly.

"All right."

Before the words died on his lips, her eyes lost focus. And then her face went blank.

A second, two seconds, three . . . her body suddenly started shaking. And she collapsed, flat on her back.

Her eyes remained wide open. She was clearly breathing. Yet it was clear that, in that instant, she had completely lost consciousness.

"Kuroda!"

The door opened behind him.

"You! Are you at it again—"

It was the chief, Sakamoto.

Kuroda pursed his lips and shrugged.

"It's not how it looks, you see . . . she was coming on to me, and . . ."

"Shit!"

"But I found it, the PLO tape. That stuff is still making the rounds."

Kuroda pulled out the cassette tape he'd recovered and handed it to Sakamoto.

Sakamoto took it and then crouched next to the girl.

Cursing and clucking, he pulled the girl's skirt back down over her legs and then looked up at Kuroda.

"So what happened, then, with the girl?"

"Well, it looked like she made her 'slip-away'. . . "

"While you were doing her?"

"No. Come on. That would have been 'heavens-away.'"

"Cut the jokes. I'm serious here."

"All right, it was—after that. She asked me for a couple of seconds before I shot her, and that's when—"

Sakamoto stood up.

The girl's eyes were still open wide.

But there was absolutely no sign of life in them.

She had gone away. But where—? Where had she gone?

(I think I know . . .)

A feeling of dread passed through Sakamoto.

He was starting to understand . . .

Three times—

Finally, unable to resist the temptation, he had read it, three times.

The first time nothing had happened. Or maybe he had simply told himself it was nothing.

For, within three hours after he first finished reading it, he found himself wanting to read it again.

And then the following morning, he woke up while it was still dark out, went into the toilet, and secretly read it once again.

The third time he fell totally under its spell.

His soul left his body, and he even felt himself being cut off from time.

When he tried to move . . . he found he could.

By simply bending his thoughts, he soared away from his house and soon was gazing down on his street, now under the midday sun.

"It's an illusion!"

But it was such a vivid illusion.

He had the impression that he could travel to any time and any place simply by bending his thoughts again.

The premonition of such absolute freedom terrified him.

He quickly bent his thoughts in reverse. He went too far, and there was no one in the toilet in the dark. He retraced his path again.

Repeating the process, he eventually regained consciousness in his body.

At that moment—sweat was flowing from every pore in his body. (I will not read it ever again.) He made a vow to himself. (Not ever!)

When he went back to his bedroom, he put away the book with its yellow jacket in a drawer of his desk. He even locked it.

(Throw it away! Burn it!)

One part of him was issuing such commands.

But another part of him (But it's for work. It's important for you as a policeman responsible for regulating hallucinatory words.) was desperately making excuses.

He was so torn between the two impulses that he could not even close his eyes to sleep.

It was still dark out.

It was only two hours until the alarm clock would go off, but it felt like ten years.

He worried that if he let his mind slip even for an instant his spirit might drift away.

Bathed in a cold sweat, he shivered incessantly.

"Something wrong?" His wife mumbled sleepily from alongside him.

"No, it's nothing. Just a chill."

"Catching a cold?"

With these words, his wife fell asleep again.

"Mr. Sakamoto."

Kuroda's voice sounded close, right in his ear.

"What's the matter? You don't look so good."

He must have been zoning out.

"Um . . ." The words caught in his throat. He forced them out. "Coming down with a cold or something. I'm not feeling so good."

Voice barely above a mumble, he looked around.

"Where's the rest of it? There's got to be more than just a tape."

"Yes, sir, right away. Right to it—"

"Great. But dress her properly first. You're way out of line, you know . . ."

"Yes, sir, I'm really sorry about that."

Sakamoto left the room.

Kuroda was a classic case of delinquent-turned-cop.

The spells were spreading like wildfire.

And there was an increase in the number of cops like Kuroda, cops with flexible morals who took pleasure in degraded acts.

Shouldn't there be a lot more complaints about the situation?

"Shit . . ."

Clucking his tongue again, Sakamoto started down the stairs.

It looked like the girl's parents were also users. But their symptoms were not so apparent, and they were kicking up a fuss.

In any event, there would be a thorough search of the house.

They couldn't let a single page, no, not even a single word, escape them.

At that very moment, mid-thought—

A shock coursed through him. His thoughts veered away on their own.

Nearly plummeting headlong down the stairs, Sakamoto struggled to keep his footing.

"Sir, are you okay?"

An officer had seen him from the bottom of the stairs and reached out to stop his fall.

"No . . . just a bit dizzy . . . started coming down with a cold yesterday."

Sakamoto repeated the same excuses.

"You're just worn-out, chief. Just head home and leave this here to us, okay?"

The officer looked quite concerned. But you never knew what they were really thinking. Who knew what they'd do with Sakamoto off the scene?

Still Sakamoto nodded in agreement.

"I'll do that. I'm not feeling good. Might even see the doctor. Take care of things."

On that note, he headed out.

Neighborhood housewives were loitering outside in the street. No doubt they knew the police were there.

As he came out, they all looked the other way.

Even though the general public had been kept in the dark, the term *word police* was already widespread and meant no good. They were as feared and despised as the special-force police in the prewar era.

He quickened his pace to reach the main street.

Just as earlier that morning, his entire body was drenched with sweat.

He wondered if he would make it.

It wasn't so unpleasant. On the contrary. He was struggling to repress the feeling of euphoria bubbling up within him. It was rather like trying to withhold an orgasm.

He hailed a cab. He gave his home address.

He arrived home within twenty minutes.

His wife greeted him with a look of surprise.

"You caught a cold after all, didn't you?"

She had him take cold medicine despite his protests. She sent him to bed.

Sakamoto slid under the covers.

After a while his wife went out on errands.

Sakamoto was shaking. His entire body was trembling like a leaf.

He sneaked out of bed. He unlocked the desk drawer.

The yellow cover appeared. He had confiscated a bunch of stuff from Miura Sachiko, one of the cases he had disposed of. And he had ended up slipping just this one copy into his pocket.

He slipped back into bed. And with trembling hands, he opened the pages.

"The Gold of Time . . ."

He spoke the title aloud as he began reading. And then he continued.

"The shade of the shadow of light . . . the depth of the depths of light . . . at the equinox of light . . . around behind the light."

He was suddenly thrown aloft.

Or, rather, to be exact, his consciousness was sucked out by some powerful force.

It was being carried off, just like that.

Soon darkness enveloped him. The darkness was spinning, turning round and round. Everything was turning around.

Countless threads of light appeared amid the darkness.

Scorching heat and intense cold ruled the darkness. It entered his comprehension as a concept.

The spinning became faster still.

Something was approaching from in front. It was a red circle. A circle . . . no, it wasn't that. It was a sphere!

A giant whirling sphere was approaching at an incredible speed.

The darkness faded, and then the threads of light. Before he realized it, the sphere had completely filled his conceptual field of vision.

(I'm falling!)

For some reason he felt he was. In the instant that he felt it, he understood that it wasn't the sphere that was spinning around, it was his consciousness.

In that case—

What was the world of darkness through which he had passed? The threads of light—and this enormous, red sphere—

Before he knew it, the surface of the sphere was before his eyes.

It's Earth—! Red Earth was there before him. And it was spinning.

And there was—

He was pulled into it. And then it stopped.

(What place is this!?)

This body, of which he was conscious, was moving independently of his intentions.

"Move out!"

He heard the voice. It took some time before he realized that it was coming from him—it was issuing from the mouth of this body that he now felt as his own.

His body started walking.

He looked at his hands. They were rough hairy hands. The hands gripped a long pole of a sort that he had never seen before. It looked like a weapon.

Ahead flames were whirling out of something that looked like a house. It was a house . . . probably a house.

Corpses lay scattered across the reddish earth like so many rags.

(This place—where is it!?)

It wasn't him. That much was clear to him. This body was not his body.

And the *place* and the *time*—neither was his.

This very world was not at all like the one he knew, Japan of the late twentieth century.

His face turned skyward.

The sky bore a tint of pale pink. And there was not a cloud in it. Directly overhead the sun was shining. But—it was so small. Compared to the sun he knew, it looked so very small.

(. . . !)

Astonishment ripped through his mind.

Ripped open, his mind gushed thoughts that touched other consciousnesses. And then they overlapped and merged. It all came to him in that instant.

This was neither his place nor his time. Nor was this body his.

It was 2131—he could read the year from the minds that had merged.

He had been flown away. Or, rather, he had been sucked up.

And he had been sucked into an unfamiliar body belonging to an unfamiliar world in this unfamiliar time.

Anything else was unthinkable. Or maybe the notion was simply easy to believe.

This man—the name of the man marching across this desolate red earth with Sakamoto housed within him was Schmitt, Carl Schmitt.

5

"Move out!"

He gave the order to move and advanced two, three steps.

At that moment—he felt something.

He turned quickly, finger on the trigger of his assault weapon. He swung the muzzle left and right, seeking his prey.

It must have been his imagination after all.

Not even so much as a shadow was moving.

Nothing but corpses as far as the eye could see.

Housing complexes in the residential area were ablaze with fire. It was only a matter of time before they burned to the ground. It didn't seem possible that there would be anyone left alive.

Nonetheless, something was amiss.

He could definitely feel something. And very close to him—

With the sleeve of his combat suit, Schmitt wiped away the fine Martian dust that had accumulated on his goggles.

He no longer felt the presence. Yet he couldn't shake the unpleasant feeling that something was watching him.

It wasn't possible.

Schmitt inspected the entire perimeter once more, looking down the muzzle, and then advanced.

The hell on earth right before him seemed unreal.

Everything around him suddenly went silent.

Tat tat tat . . . . Tat tat tat . . .

The popping of assault weapons sounded far off as in a dream.

Then it stopped.

This operation was quickly coming to an end. The Golgi settlement had been eradicated.

Schmitt's squad alone had killed some three hundred people.

It had been an easy mission.

With such defenseless targets, it was easy to shoot them down and advance; the only obstacle was a sense of conscience. With Schmitt's troop, that hadn't been an issue.

The soldiers operated as one on the battlefield. They turned into a single weapon for military deployment. That's how they were trained.

Even upon slaughtering hundreds and burning down entire settlements, their faces remained cool, impassive.

This squad had eight soldiers. Usually they combined with a second squad to form a sixteen-man attack force, but their partner squad hadn't joined them today. There had been too many rookies in their number.

The eight under Schmitt's command were seasoned in combat.

Which is to say, they were all men without any other career options open to them.

The job attracted anyone who wanted to make a clean break with his past.

And they were no longer required to think for themselves. They went wherever commanded. They embarked on missions as ordered. That was the beauty of it. It wasn't a bad bargain at all.

In particular, for a man who had witnessed his beloved wife trampled to death in the midst of a riot less than five meters away, there was no better place to find some peace of mind than the barracks of one of the military units of the Martian Guard.

Mars was also a good option for the various nations of Earth that needed to deal with the global population explosion, the depletion of resources, and economic collapse, affording a New World for the destitute and rejected.

Even before the overnight transformation of the planet through terraforming had been put into orbit, massive fleets of refugees from every nation had already built settlements across the surface of Mars, gaining a foothold on the planet through anticipated but nonetheless massive sacrifices, and finally establishing a planetary federation, and now one century later—

A population of nearly eighty million thronged the planet,

comprising both recent immigrants as well as the descendents of the first generation of settlers.

Riots and insurrections continued to break out on an almost daily basis in every location. That was why Schmitt's line of business never suffered from a lack of clientele.

The Martian Guard was a corporate enterprise. It was all about profit. And so they involved themselves in all manner of situations.

The military complement of the Martian Guard comprised a total of about twelve hundred soldiers, three thousand armored vehicles, and two hundred warplanes.

Of course, they were not as large in actual numbers as the Martian Federal Army. But in actual skill, they far surpassed it.

On a planet that had not officially established any national armies, the actual role of the army was somewhat unclear. There were some obvious limits to enforcement. If they intervened into labor disputes unilaterally, they not only met with resistance from Martian citizens but also were subject to criticism from Earth.

Still, the riots and insurrections couldn't be left alone. Ultimately, even the disputes of a single organization could have fatal repercussions for society as a whole.

That was when headquarters received a request for mobilizing the Martian Guard. Their clients were primarily private enterprises, but demands for the Martian Guard rather than the Federal Army also came from local and provincial governments.

The Martian Guard bore the brunt of any criticism. But then the Martian Guard was largely deaf to any criticism.

Earth was still brimming with people to be sent off to Mars. And given the severe conditions of life on Mars, there was always a demand for fresh young labor.

Ultimately, the raison d'être of the Martian Guard lay in maintaining this felicitous relation between supply and demand, and, if possible, enhancing it. In a word, it was a matter of population adjustment through extermination.

With the tacit approval of this principle, the ranks of the Martian Guard were swelling.

Naturally, there were voices strongly opposing this rampant militarization.

But in fact, insofar as Mars was perceived as a world for Earth's human detritus, armed forces were deemed "inevitable," their interventions simply had to be "justified."

Thus the squad under Schmitt's command saw a lot of action. They went wherever ordered and conducted whatever interventions were ordered.

In most instances the orders were simple and direct.

Immediately eliminate anyone who resists or who shows signs of resistance.

Needless to say, to eliminate someone meant to wipe them off the face of the planet.

This time, however, the guidelines were somewhat different from what they were usually.

The client was an organization they had never heard of, called Earth Alliance for the Prevention of Epidemics.

And that wasn't all. The Alliance had conducted an orientation session for the troops, to explain the special conditions.

Instructions were presented in excruciating detail.

Rookies were excluded from this operation; only very experienced soldiers were included.

Above all, the mission assigned to them by this client was unusually rigorous and physically demanding.

"The Mars environment is harsh. We realize that it can prove intolerable—"

The representative for the Alliance had begun the briefing on this note.

"That is why we generally turn a blind eye to the use of certain intoxicants and hallucinogens to some extent. In fact, in some cases, we're even in favor of them."

There was a burst of laughter from the troops.

"Exactly. I expect that many of you have no particular problem with this situation either. But—"

The man paused and looked slowly around the room before continuing.

"This situation is entirely different. I want you to be fully aware of how very different the situation is from anything before. Now—"

The locks on his briefcase snapped loudly as he opened it.

And then, as gingerly as if handling explosives, he pulled out a small booklet with a worn and faded cover.

"I believe you've all heard of a settlement by the name of Camp Golgi. It is an agricultural cooperative of about thirty thousand settlers located on the south slope of the highest peak on Mars, Nix Olympica. A very dangerous habit has become widespread there, not related to a specific drug or narcotic agent, but something that produces narcotic and addictive symptoms. To repeat, it is fundamentally different from the usual narcotic or hallucinatory substances. It constitutes a threat unlike anything we've ever seen. And not just for the inhabitants of Golgi but for all the people of Mars, and even those of Earth, it poses the gravest of dangers. And this here— is it."

He waved aloft the booklet that he'd taken from the briefcase.

"For almost two years it escaped our notice. The Martian government is largely responsible for that. But we were clearly careless as well. And so, we were looking in the wrong place for the causes of the sudden decline in productivity at Golgi. The signs were already all there, clear enough. But we thought it nothing more than a harmless and inconsequential trend, merely self-indulgent and somewhat peculiar. The truth is . . . the habit of reading the *poem* had begun in Golgi some two years previously."

The man's face twisted in disgust.

"This is it. This is the original. There are copies of it everywhere. They come in so many formats that you can't always pick them out. This is it, though. I want you to remember the color, shape, and title of this booklet. Under no conditions, however, are you to read it. Do I make myself clear? Within the Federation, anyone who so much as looks at the contents, whether in the original or a reproduction, will be considered guilty of an act of treason. No doubt my discussion has also stimulated your curiosity. But not only is reading it an act punishable by death: it can only bring you profound unhappiness. I hope that I am getting that much through to you."

With a gesture of resolute determination, the man held the book even higher.

The cover bore these words: *Manifestos of Surrealism 200th Anniversary Edition: Unknown Luminaries II*. Translated by Leonore Buñuel. 2124. University of Utah Press.

"Buñuel, the scholar whose name is written here, edited this booklet. While working through the posthumous texts left behind by artists of the previous century, he gathered the works of unknown poets, translated them into English, and published a series of five booklets, with purely academic intentions. But! Who would want to read it? Huh? Exactly. No one read it. On Earth, at least, it was thrown away, buried like rubbish, and except for the University of Utah Library, not a copy remained. Still, somebody brought it to Mars. Just like that—! Now it turns out that people can't wait to get their hands on it."

His tone of voice was severe.

But the reasons for such severity were lost on Schmitt and company.

What was so dangerous about it? Thoughts jotted in a book? Philosophy? Or maybe religious teachings?

Schmitt recalled a thinker who had referred to religion as a drug.

Was it that sort of thing? Yet on Mars, where anyone could get their hands on drugs, religion wasn't much of a draw. There were of course those who believed. But very few were serious about it. It was unimaginable for an entire settlement to go for it.

"I am not in a position to tell you what is actually written in here. I don't know myself. To know means that you've already fallen into the trap set by words as powerful as any drug. That's why I keep warning you. Don't read so much as a sentence when you're in the Golgi area. There is one thing I can tell you. The author of this damned poem is Who May. The title is 'The Gold of Time.' Look out for those words. If you come across them, burn them at once. Of course, it will be more than a mere set of words that you're destroying. That goes without saying–"

Biting his lip, the man placed the booklet on the table.

He had more to say.

"The good news is that Golgi is remote and secluded. It has little contact with other areas. And we're currently looking into those few contacts. This leaves you free to concentrate your forces fully on Golgi. There's still time to contain it. You can take out the area. This is the decision that we've arrived at."

He gazed into space.

"Tomorrow is it. Tomorrow all the inhabitants of Golgi will be utterly wiped off the face of the planet, and with them the malignant spells that have been festering among them. Your historical role is that of rubbing them out like an eraser."

(Spells? Did he say spells?)

Whispers ran through the room, but the man broke them off by raising his voice.

"Not a single page, not a single line can remain. And anyone who knows so much as a word of the poem will be burned alive. The Golgi area is to be swept from the face of Mars without a trace."

6

(It's over . . .)

Schmitt raised his hand, commanding his troops to halt.

They did a final round of the perimeter.

He glanced at his watch. They were right on schedule.

Now they had only to return to their assigned rendezvous point.

"All right, everyone, change your tube."

The projectile power of this new assault weapon came from

magnetic pulses. It didn't require cartridges. In principle, as long as you fed it bullets, you could keep blasting, for almost forty hours at a stretch.

A single tube held about eight hundred bullets.

They'd all pretty much emptied their tubes in the massacre.

They hadn't met with any real resistance.

The people of Golgi had greeted the death squad with resignation.

It had defied belief.

The bulk of them hadn't even made the effort to run.

Maybe the massacre hadn't been necessary. Their complete lack of energy gave the impression that if they had been left as they were, they would have perished on their own accord.

The troops finally had some inkling of what the epidemics officer had meant by "the gravest of dangers."

Whether it was a spell or not, if such apathy spread to society as a whole, the world would indeed come to an end.

(Who May, was it . . . ?)

As Schmitt gave a short blast on his whistle, he recalled the name, his lips mouthing it silently.

Whatever it was, they were still on the battlefield and couldn't let down their guard.

Once the tubes were changed, they checked the charge on the magnetic pulse emitters.

They still had juice. They could wipe out another town or two. And they still had five of the twelve hand missiles that they'd brought.

Schmitt regrouped his freshly reloaded squad.

The massive housing complex that they'd torched collapsed with thunderous sound, sending a fiery bloom of sparks skyward.

"Shall we move out?"

A Mars-born soldier of East Asian descent, Hank Kawasaki, turned to Schmitt, the smile on his lips indefatigable.

"Right you are . . ."

Schmitt slowly examined the perimeter again.

He still felt uneasy. He couldn't shake the feeling of some-one watching them.

It was an intuitive sense honed on the battlefield. His sur-vival depended on that intuition. It wasn't something he could afford to ignore.

"Hank, do me a favor and make one more round. Some-thing doesn't feel right."

"Yes, sir."

Hank snapped to attention, formed a squad with three other soldiers, and soon disappeared behind the blazing fires of the town.

Hanson, Coolidge, and Guan remained behind.

Ten minutes went by. Hank hadn't returned.

Another five minutes passed. And another five—

"Commander—"

Coolidge sounded uneasy.

". . ."

Biting his lip, Schmitt kept his eyes glued on the site where Hank and the others had vanished.

It was very strange.

He had asked them to make one round. It shouldn't have taken this long.

What had they found—? Or had something else . . .

There was a thunderous explosion.

Startled, they dropped to the ground, weapons aimed to-ward the explosion. They saw white ribbons of smoke swirling into the sky. The last of the housing complex had burned away to the point where it finally collapsed of its own weight. That's all it had been. That was all.

"Commander, permission to reconnoiter."

Guan was poised as if to leap into action, but Schmitt stopped him cold.

"Nothing doing! We stay together. We move as a group. Stand down!"

It was the basic rule of war. If they scattered, they were easier to take out one by one. Schmitt now regretted that he had unwittingly broken the rule by sending Hank and the others on patrol. Still, it was really hard to believe that there was anyone left out there who presented a threat to them. But in any event . . .

Something was—not right.

They were being watched by someone—he was more and more convinced of it. He couldn't tell from what direction, however. He had the impression of being watched from very close range.

Schmitt shifted his grip on the assault weapon and once again scrutinized their surroundings. But, as far as he could see at least, the four of them were the only humans alive. Other than within the fire itself, there was no place else for anyone to conceal themselves.

"All right. Let's move out. And stick together."

Use of the wireless was restricted to emergencies. Using it for no good reason was cause for an official write-up. A write-up meant embarrassment. It would be seen as a problem with the team.

The four slowly began their advance as a unit. The scattered piles of corpses slowed their progress, as they had to step over them. On either side, flames still leapt skyward from the remains of the housing complex. It was too hot to approach. They had to keep to the middle of the road.

"Hank!"

He risked calling out his name.

An indistinct echo or a response reached their ears.

The street widened. The stench of burnt flesh wafted to them on the wind. The smoke swirled about them. Their visibility was severely restricted.

Then it happened.

"Commander!"

Shouting out, Hanson aimed his assault rifle. He was aiming at something, there, just beyond the smoke—

Something was coming their way. There were four shadows. They were moving very slowly.

Schmitt ripped the goggles clouded with dust from his face.

The smoke immediately stung his eyes, and tears streamed down his cheeks.

Still he strained to see. It really was them. It was Hank's group.

A gust of wind swept by them. The smoke streamed away, and their view cleared.

"Hank! Jasper!"

Hanson ran toward them, calling their names. Then suddenly he stopped in his tracks, nearly falling forward.

"What the hell—!?"

It made no sense. And because it made no sense, they couldn't grasp at first why it made no sense.

The four in Hank's group were running headlong at them. The look of exertion on their faces showed they were giving their all.

But . . . and yet . . . they were not moving forward at all.

Their feet kicked at the ground. Sand was circling skyward, slowly, gently. They were floating on air. Their feet kicked out trying to find purchase, but in slow motion. Their bodies were still floating.

They were shouting something. Their mouths were open wide. Finally, one foot touched ground. But again the next step took them gradually into air.

It was just like a film in slow motion. Yet this wasn't on film or tape. It was actually happening before their eyes.

It wasn't possible. Such motion clearly defied the laws of physics. Physically, of course, they could deliberately move slowly. But a person could not kick off the ground and physically float in air for such a long period of time, ignoring the laws of gravity.

Of course—it was possible with film to stretch the intervals of time and produce slow motion. But that wasn't how time usually flowed—

(Time—!?)

It suddenly came to him. Time—! It had to be that. The flow of time had been altered. The four men in Hank's squad were caught in a different time stream, cut off from Schmitt's.

In other words, it was a gap in time that had come between them—!?

(Ridiculous!)

His very thought shocked him.

It was an illusion. His eyes were playing a trick. Toxic gases released in the area were affecting his nerves. Things would soon return to normal.

Schmitt shook his head violently from side to side.

He then started to run.

Hank and the others hadn't advanced more than two or three steps toward them. And so he'd have to go to them.

Weapon high, he ran toward them.

Then—he was bounced back. Something, invisible to the eye, had yielded like rubber stretching and then had bounced him back.

(. . . !)

He tried going forward again. But there was no way.

"What is going on here? What the . . . ?!"

Hanson thumped into it, too, and was thrown on his ass.

(A wall . . . of time!)

Or it might be a cage. And Hank's team had been trapped in it.

(No, wait!)

Schmitt turned in a circle, scrutinizing everything around him.

He saw the houses in flames. But—but—the leaping of the flames and the rising of the smoke were odd. Everything was moving lazily, languidly, somehow taking its time.

Was it a wall—? Or a cage—? In either case, it seemed that Schmitt's group was now trapped. It wasn't Hank's group but Schmitt's whose time had been stretched. Which meant that one second beyond the barrier was like ten seconds, twenty seconds, or maybe even minutes in here.

"Aarrrh!"

Someone screamed. It was Guan.

He turned. Guan was on the ground, flat on his back, and was frantically scrabbling backward.

His eyes, crazy with fear, were fixed on a point in space.

At that point—something ominous was there.

Something . . . like smoke . . . or a shadow . . .

Wavering and wriggling, something was taking shape.

(Eyes!)

He first noticed its eyes. From the shadowy entity, what looked like two eyes emerged.

Without stopping to think, he took aim at it. His finger squeezed the trigger.

Pa, pa . . . pa pa pa . . .

The motor whirred, and the monitor blinked. Magnetic pulses propelled superspeed bullets.

The bullets, however, passed right through the shadowy shape, ricocheted off the invisible barrier, and came directly back at them.

"Drop!"

Before his command rang out, Coolidge had fallen, clutching his shoulder. His cries of agony echoed.

The shadow wavered.

All of a sudden a figure materialized, coming into focus like a holographic projection.

The figure was human. It was looking down at Schmitt. Its eyes were enormous.

(A specter!?)

The part of its face where the mouth would be had not yet come clearly into focus but could be seen slowly moving.

Then they heard its voice. It sounded distant. It sounded like it was coming from someplace far away.

"Did you see them?"

The words came from the specter.

"This took place on Mars in 2131 AD."

It spoke English. But then—was it really English? It sounded rather like English to Schmitt. This was probably because it was the only language he knew. In any case, he understood it. And so it felt like English. But . . . nonetheless . . . was it really English?

He felt as if . . . as if thoughts were being communicated directly to his mind.

In any event—it was his first encounter with a specter. Actually, he'd never had any sort of encounter with the supernatural, specters or otherwise. He didn't believe in it. And so he felt no impulse to flee, his body remained immobilized.

(I have killed too many . . .) He thought. (Without mercy . . . defenseless people . . . and I've been cursed.)

"You! Who are you?"

His voice had finally returned. But it sounded rather pathetic.

"I've been waiting for you. I have something to show you."

The face blurred. And then it cleared again. It was the face of a youth. He looked Asian. His countenance was beautiful. Yet his eyes looked overly large.

The lower half of his body was shrouded in mist. His legs weren't at all visible.

His torso alone appeared, as if poking through the mist.

"Surely you know my name? It is Who May. I am Who May."

"It is Who May!?"

Schmitt repeated his words in a stunned voice.

"You mean the Who May that—"

"It is exactly as you saw. The same thing is happening here. And the same thing will continue to happen . . ."

The specter did not take his eyes from Schmitt's face as he spoke.

"And then, in the end, something truly unexpected will happen. That's right. . . . All will be lost. . . . There won't be anything left behind . . ."

His voice trailed sadly.

"What are you talking about—? So you're Who May? What the hell are you trying to say—!?"

Schmitt was shouting now.

"I didn't intend . . . I didn't mean at all for this to happen . . . I can only talk to you here, like this . . . I'll soon vanish . . . I have seen it all . . . I have seen it all disappear, because of me . . . And yet I too will just vanish with it . . . That is why

I had to tell you. And I have a request of you. You can change things. You can return time to its course. I . . . well, it's too late . . . I knew too much . . . I can't come back . . . The best I can do is to project myself into the vortex like this."

Schmitt—it dawned on him.

The eyes of the specter were staring at him from directly in front. And it was speaking.

But . . . but then . . . (it's not looking at or speaking to me!)

As soon as he realized this, his entire body began to shudder.

(There really is someone!)

Someone was watching him. He had felt it all along—someone gazing on him.

Now at last he knew who it was.

That had to be it. That's why he hadn't been able to find the seer.

(Someone—is inside me!)

OBLIVION

"...Another universe...inconceivable...with words I
would fashion it...or so I thought. But words proved too
imperfect for the task. And so I used a little trick where their
imperfection caused distortion...Dobaded...Exactly...
The word was a sort of adhesive..."

Sakamoto listened. He listened through the ears of the man
named Schmitt, mercenary leader of the Massacre of 2131 on
Mars.

Through his ears...? Well, that wasn't it exactly. The
words came to him as sounds he did not understand. And yet
he did understand. He grasped their meaning.

"...from the continuum that is the universe, words have
been cut out, crudely segmented. However you put them together, you won't return to the original universe. I tried to fill
that interval with the word *dobaded*. It was a pluripotentiated
word.... Or, rather, one might equally well say that it was a
word that was not yet a word..."

He didn't understand. (Did he say *dobaded*?) Who was this
Who May? Naturally, he knew him as the one who had writ-

ten the spell titled "The Gold of Time." But . . . but . . . what was this Who May trying to communicate to him in spectral form?

By showing him the tragic events on Mars, was he trying to make clear the futility of efforts to contain the spell?

(It must be a dream.)

That was the quickest way to explain things. Under the power of the spell, he was dreaming.

"But through my experiments I eventually discovered the secret affinity obtaining between words and things. First was 'Mirror.' With 'Mirror,' what I tried to make was . . . even if I could not make actual substances, with the spectral figures engendered with 'Mirror,' I could re-create the universe as a spectral existence amid their reflections . . . . Once convinced of this, I transformed them into works . . ."

The specter chattered on.

Specter . . . ? In Schmitt's mind, there was no other way to refer to it, except specter. But, then again . . . was it really a specter? If so, I too must be some sort of specter—such were Sakamoto's thoughts.

"And so, on that fateful night . . . 'time' popped into my head. Time . . . time stream . . . just as I had used words to project substance, I could now express time. I realized that . . . I had the power to stretch or shrink time as I liked, to soar on it, to spin or distort it . . ."

(Time . . . ?) Did he mean "The Gold of Time"?

"Exactly . . . that was when I felt something enticing me. 'Write time. Tell what time is . . .' And then immediately after—inspiration came to me. 'The shade of the shadow of light . . .' Precisely! Light itself is, in fact, the shadow of time . . . and if one poked through to the other side of the shadow, would you not attain a vision of time itself—!?"

(I knew it!)

"Light . . . a shining! Such connections brought to me the magical power possessed by gold. Gold! Truly, gold itself was the substance that contained the key to unlocking the secret of time. When time congeals . . . a chunk of forgotten time, greedily hoarded . . . at that time I caught a glimpse of the dream of alchemists, which was to control time!"

Time . . . truly was sedimented there. Time had been stretched almost without limits in that place that held Schmitt's team, while moving restlessly.

Sakamoto could feel it. He had an awareness of it.

"I then began writing. The rendezvous with Monsieur Breton, the next day at three . . . by then everything was supposed to become clear. Yes, indeed . . . in every word . . . in every letter . . . I felt the keys to the secret unfolding before me one after another . . ."

Schmitt was shaking.

The intrepid soldier was trembling head to toe like a patient with malarial fever. His will was clearly becoming weaker and weaker.

"As I wrote on . . . I felt myself beginning to float away . . . a moment of pure rapture! But it was not yet—not yet complete. I returned to myself and continued to write. Again I let myself go with the flow of time . . . drifting . . . returning . . . . After repeating this a few times, I finally finished writing. I had already broken with everything that might anchor me . . ."

Maybe not a specter . . . Who May's oversized eyes were bright with tears.

"I am here right now. With every ounce of strength I am holding on to this still point of time—this here. And you can see my form, can't you? And you can hear my voice? But those are not me. They are but shadows of me. Please try to imagine. A being living in a two-dimensional world is one day carried off to a three-dimensional world. Imagine what would happen if that being who had taken on a three-dimensional existence tried to transmit a message to the two-dimensional world."

(Two-dimensional being . . . ? Three-dimensional existence . . . ?)

What next? Four-dimensional . . . five-dimensional . . . six-dimensional . . . ?

Sakamoto tried to stretch his imagination. But he wasn't sure which way to stretch it.

"When I first drifted off . . . it occurred to me. Human existence is just like driving a car in reverse. It's like a driver who can only see what lies behind him, in the past. He sees nothing of what lies ahead—"

With this analogy Sakamoto got the picture.

"—for instance, you drive merrily along not knowing that a dead end lies directly ahead . . . . the road so far has been perfectly straight and so you step on the gas, even though a bend in the road is coming . . . or, even though you reach a wide open place, you advance fearfully . . . human beings are such dangerous drivers. You look over the scenery that has gone past as a point of reference to try to 'foretell' what 'must' happen next . . . but ultimately you fail, lose your cool, and rush headlong into disaster . . . . that's what history is."

Who May's voice varied in intensity, wavering like an echo. Where exactly was the voice coming from? Were his words coming from an extradimensional world—?

"Have you understood me? You simply have to turn around. If you turn around, you'll see. You can see what lies ahead, just as you see what you left behind. And once you do that—! There is nothing to fear, nothing to confuse you. You see exactly what is coming and can choose the path that suits you—that is what I believed. And that is why I absolutely had to write it down. With 'The Gold of Time,' I believed that an entirely new world would open before us. And yet—"

The image of Who May wavered. It faded, nearly vanished, and then once again flickered back into view.

"I wrote it down . . . I drifted out of myself . . . and then it dawned on me. It wasn't only me . . . countless others appeared, cut off from time . . . but none of them could get back . . . . Imagine people from the flat two-dimensional world who have taken on three-dimensional form. From the heights of the three-dimensional, they can see all of the two-dimensional world. But . . . although they can see all of it . . . they can never go back to it. Which means that we cannot change a single thing in it!"

Sakamoto was confused.

If this were true, what did it mean? If spells, that is, "The Gold of Time," were at some point forgotten, people would have no choice but to rush headlong into the last moments of time, seeing only what lay behind? Is that what Who May was trying to tell him?

"You—I don't know anything about who you are. But it was I who had the power to bring you here."

Who May's gaze passed through Schmitt's body, staring at Sakamoto within it.

"You are about to drift away . . . but not yet. You are not yet completely cut off from time. And so you haven't lost the power to affect substances, the shadow images of time. Right here and now, the force that has sucked you into this man's body is also your power of affinity. Such force no longer adheres in me. I can just barely project my image into this world by stopping the flow of time. I beg you . . . beg . . . you . . ."

Who May's voice reverberated again and again.

"Time is like gold. Malleable, it takes on whatever form you impose. But no matter how much you shape it or change its form, it remains gold. Likewise, the substance of time remains the same. And so I implore you. Please change its shape! I cannot go back. I have lost the power to return. I can only ask someone to do it. Someone whose soul has not yet lost the power to affect substances—that is why I summoned you. I am only able to convey things to you here in this way. Innumerable companion consciousnesses are spinning here in the vortex, ineluctably shorn of substance. As a result of the massacre. The vortex has created this still point. I was wrong. I was entirely mistaken—!"

The shadow image of Who May flickered uncertainly, as if on a flame almost immobilized, frozen solid.

"I want you to do it over. I want you to take my place and remake it—!"

Sakamoto didn't understand . . . he didn't understand anything . . . if it was a dream . . . if just a dream . . . he wanted to wake up soon. He wished.

And then, unable to hold back, he had to ask.

(What should I do?)

"Come. Come with me—I will show you. With me—"

(Where to—?)

"To Paris of 1948—, to my apartment—"

(And then?)

"And then—I want you to become me!"

All of a sudden . . . he felt himself being pulled out.

In an instant the still point had melted away.

He could see Hank running toward him with all his might.

He felt the heat of the fire and smoke again and saw them tossed about.

But, in an instant, everything spun around again. The red earth was quickly moving away from him. It turned into a sphere and then disappeared into the depths of space.

In its place a blue, brilliantly shining sphere rose out of the darkness. Sakamoto knew exactly what it was.

It was Earth. But it was not the Earth he knew.

He felt something alongside him. He could feel it right next to him.

Earth . . . it was probably Earth well before his birth. It had to be.

And then . . . and then . . . he was pulled into the globe.

In the Chaillot district of Paris lives an old man who speaks excellent Japanese.

He looks to be of Asian descent. Yet he says he is Parisian to the core, born and bred.

He is about sixty years old.

He has been running a small souvenir shop for some twenty years.

Whenever he sees Japanese tourists, he chats with them, asking about what is happening in Japan.

As a consequence, he knows a great deal about Japan.

When Sakakibara Kōji and his wife Keiko (née Mishima) visited Paris on their honeymoon, they happened to stop at his shop.

Sakakibara runs a small publishing business in Tokyo. Keiko once worked there as well.

The old man began to speak with them.

As they talked about various things, the topic of work arose.

Sakakibara explained that he published many French works. At present, he had just begun publishing a series of books on surrealism—when the old man heard this, the color drained from his face. He spoke up.

"In that case, you probably . . . well, it is unlikely but . . . you may have heard of a poet named Who May?"

Sakakibara was surprised.

"I know of him. But—well, this is quite incredible. We found two manuscripts attributed to Who May in André Breton's trunk. I was planning on including them in the fourth volume of the series, *Languages of Surrealism*. And yet—"

"Languages, is it . . . ?" The old man looked rather displeased for some reason. But then he smiled again and asked, "You wouldn't by chance be using the character for *phantom* to write the word *languages,* would you?"

Sakakibara's eyes opened wide.

"Yes, we are! That's exactly it. But, how is it—?! How is it that you know about Who May?!"

"Just a lucky guess, really. But there's something I would like to say . . ."

The old man looked down for a moment and then raised his head.

"Who May . . . I thought it might be he. Yes . . . it must be. A poet by that name once lived here in this district. . . . It was some time . . . ago."

"So, you knew him—!"

The old man shook his head vaguely and then nodded as if left with no other choice.

"Yes . . . I was acquainted with him. We met by chance . . . and not for very long . . . our encounter was quite brief."

"Really?!"

Sakakibara looked into the old man's eyes.

His eyes were large with a youthful gleam at odds with his age.

"May I ask your name—?"

"Me? My name? Of course . . . my name is . . . Carron. I use my stepfather's name."

Upon answering, the old man questioned Sakakibara in return.

"So, you found manuscripts by Who May? You only found two of them?"

"Yes—that's right—but—" Sakakibara asked excitedly, "then, are there others? Are there other works by Who May?"

"Others . . . hmmm . . . in fact, as I recall, there was another . . . one more."

"Really—where is it now? And who exactly was Who May? Was he a real person?"

"Who May . . . of course he was a real person. He really existed. As a young man."

"You mean . . . ?"

The old man gazed off into space without answering.

"You're familiar with it, aren't you? The other work that he wrote—"

Sakakibara's questions became insistent.

"Yes . . . I know something of it, of course . . ." The old man's voice sounded deeper than before. "But I threw it away. As he had asked me to do—I tore it up and threw it out."

"You threw it away? But why?!"

"The work was a complete failure . . . that's the best way to think about it. In any case, it was the sort of work that couldn't be shown to people—or so he believed. He came to that realization . . ."

"Even if the work was a failure . . . what a waste . . ."

"Not at all!"

The old man shook his head vigorously.

"It was—better that way."

How much did the old man actually know about Who May?

Had he really made his acquaintance?

Sakakibara put more questions to the old man, still uncertain of him.

"What happened to him later—Who May? Apparently, he was in contact with André Breton. Do you know anything about that?"

The old man's expression softened. But instead of answering the question, he asked one of his own.

"André Breton . . . that's right . . . you must be an expert on him. Do you recall what was written as his epitaph?"

His Japanese was impeccable.

Sakakibara was becoming more and more uncertain about the old man's identity. His pronunciation was so perfect that he had to be Japanese.

In any event—he supplied an answer. "Yes, I do . . . it was, I think—'I seek the gold of time.' Breton was very taken with alchemy. Some say that he belonged to a secret society—"

The old man smiled faintly as he said this.

"Alchemy, is it? . . . that's right . . . it is not unrelated to alchemy. It is closely related . . . closely . . ."

He continued as if talking to himself, shaking his head slowly.

"There is indeed a relationship . . . I too know about it . . . after all, I have studied a great deal since then . . . André Breton . . . surrealism . . ."

With these words, the old man heaved a sigh.

"I also went astray . . . I alone . . . that's right . . . I was alone . . . Breton dead . . . when I think about it once again . . . I think I should return right away . . ."

"Return?" Sakakibara asked. "Where to?"

"Yes . . . to see my wife and children . . . that is, to where I should be . . . but . . . if I did, what would happen then . . . were I to do it, what would happen . . . ?"

" . . . "

Keiko gave Sakakibara a poke in the ribs.

The old man was beginning to sound sad and forlorn.

Clearly, something was wrong. They could feel it.

"But . . . in the end, I gave it up . . . everything, I gave it up . . . I decided to forget it all. Now I hardly remember any of it at all . . ."

What had the old man resolved to give up, abandon, forget–? Could it be . . . he himself is the one known as Who May . . . ? The thought came suddenly to Sakakibara.

And then the old man began to smile again. Looking at the two of them, he asked, "Incidentally, how old do you two think I look?"

Sakakibara and Keiko looked at one another.

Tilting her head as if considering it carefully, Keiko answered, "Well, fifty . . . or thereabouts?"

"I see . . . hmmm . . . just as you say. Or maybe a bit older, wouldn't you say? I was born on June 3, 1951, or by the Japanese calendar, Shōwa 26. That is my birthday."

Sakakibara and Keiko looked at each other again.

That wasn't possible.

If he had been born in 1951–that would make him the same age as Sakakibara.

But the old man standing before them with the vague smile was sixty if a day.

"Dear, don't you think it's about time . . ." Keiko suddenly looked at her watch in agitation.

There was a slight tinge of fear in her voice.

The old man was . . . unsettling. Or maybe it was a joke, and they just weren't getting it.

Anyway, there was something off about him.

". . . uh huh . . ."

Sakakibara looked at his watch, too.

He was still trying to make up his mind.

After all–this old guy had known the name Who May.

"You're right. And we still have to pack . . ."

With these trivial words, Sakakibara looked once more at the old man's large eyes.

"Before we go, I mean, before we go back to Japan, could I talk with you again? Could you tell me more about Who May?–"

Smiling all the while, the old man shook his head resolutely.

"That's all there is. That's it. I have forgotten. I have forgotten everything. Please don't make me remember any more. Or else . . ."

The old man shook his head firmly two or three times.

"Or else I would be overcome with loneliness. I would be unable to sustain my job as a watchman of time . . ."

With these enigmatic words, the old man closed his mouth.

And then he looked away.

An expression of sadness played across his face, and a trace of satisfaction.

AFTERWORD
Vortex Time

Thomas Lamarre

Like Kawamata Chiaki's other novels, *Death Sentences* moves quickly, reads rapidly. Nearly every sentence is set off as a paragraph, and sentences are short, simple, and on the whole, regular and complete, which imparts a great deal of energy to the sentence, visually and verbally. Exceptions to the rule—paragraphs of two or three or (rarely) four compact sentences—confirm the overall sense of the power and simplicity of the standard sentence. But such simplicity is not that of, say, Gustave Flaubert, where limpidness is tortuously wrung from language with endless revision, resulting in awkward yet striking rhythms. Nor do these sentences strive for imagistic effects, such as those commonly associated with haiku poetics, in which carefully turned and juxtaposed images and terms are designed to afford snapshots of an uncertain reality. Largely eschewing lyricism and incongruity, Kawamata's style is to some extent a familiar one for readers of Japanese popular fiction or "light novels." In such works, the approximation of sentences to paragraphs is often calculated for its punch, either comedic or action packed. Unable to hold on to a phrase, the reader is compelled forward.

Yet Kawamata's style introduces a wrinkle into the headlong movement of sentences, an idiosyncratic gesture, almost a stylistic tick that begins in previous novels such as *Hanzaishi no kagami* (Mirror of an antiexistent soldier, 1979) and *Kaseijin senshi* (A prehistory of Martians, 1981) but is first fully realized in *Death Sentences*: precisely because the regular, almost generic sentences are unremarkable, they highlight and release the force of punctuation, which is initially most palpable in the rote gesture of a full-paragraph stop at the end of each sentence. The sentence as diction and image recedes; punctuation comes to the fore but without providing imagistic, lyrical, or poetic orientations. Punctuation is activated, not only in the use of periods and quotation marks but also in the form of parentheses, ellipses, dashes, and paragraph breaks. While the rhythms of punctuation soon feel normal and unobtrusive, they nonetheless set the stage for some truly interesting temporal and conceptual effects.

On the one hand, while the thoughts of characters are often clearly delineated with parentheses and easily translated in the first person, Kawamata makes frequent use of the free indirect style: following a sentence or a group of sentences presenting an action with a clearly designated actor, there is a shift toward the thoughts, reflections, or perceptions of the actor, which could as easily be rendered in the first person or the third person. For instance:

> Yet he continued to be carried away.
> (Where am I going . . . ?)
> . . . he didn't know. Harado's countenance appeared before his eyes.

It makes sense to use "I" for the thoughts in parentheses, but the next sentences ". . . he didn't know. Harado's countenance appeared before his eyes" might equally be rendered ". . . *I* didn't know. Harado's countenance appeared before *my* eyes."

Sometimes literary critics hastily attribute this overlap or confusion between first person and third person to the structures of the Japanese language, to its tendency to omit pronoun and other subject markers when the subject is already sufficiently obvious. In this instance, however, this stylistic gesture is not reducible to the linguistic effects of a national language—and indeed, one of the themes of the novel is that literary effects are not confined to language narrowly conceived in national terms: the magic poem or phantom poem in *Death Sentences* exerts its effects across languages and media. While Kawamata is deploying certain features of the Japanese language, he is drawing on the stylistics of free indirect discourse, which has literary life that extends from (at least) Flaubert to Anne Rice. Take Flaubert's famous turn of phrase in *Madame Bovary*: "She no longer played the piano: Why play? Who would hear her?" It is impossible to attribute these sentiments entirely to the character or to the narrator.

Kawamata does something analogous when presenting perceptions, recollections, and ruminations, especially of his principal characters—André Breton, Sakakibara, Sakamoto, and Carl Schmitt. Yet by using parentheses primarily to convey thoughts in the first person, he forcibly drives a wedge between first person and third person, which tends to create a divide between thought and action. But then he makes thoughts and actions feel indiscernible in another register—that of perceptions, impressions, recollections, and experiences, which slide away from their attributed subjects, creating a space in which the concrete subjects of action, whose goals may initially feel unambiguous, dissolve into a singular (but not unitary) subjective trajectory.

And so, if we accept, for instance, that special operations cop Sakamoto enters into the body of Martian soldier Carl Schmitt and later into the young poet Hu Mei or Who May, it is not in small part because these subjects already share perceptual experiences and memories at the level of literary style: they enter into an enlarged version of "Who May," of that anonymous "And who may you be?" Indeed, even though André Breton and Sakakibara serve as interlocutors for the character Who May and thus remain distinct from him, they are already part of this larger "Who May?" It is in this manner that Kawamata's use of punctuation in conjunction with the free indirect style, in contrast with the laboriously wrought objectivist *bêtise* that characterizes the omniscient style of Flaubert, leads to a different sort of objectivism—of subconscious perceptions, experiences, and recollections. And it is here that Kawamata offers his take on the mission of surrealism—to afford an exact, objective, practically clinical approach to the workings of the unconscious mind—which he fulfills in an admirably offhand, casually demotic style.

Readers quickly reach the end of the book. Nonetheless, while *Death Sentences* is written to encourage you to rush forward sentence by sentence, ultimately, you do not reach the end; rather, the entire book turns beneath you. It folds back on itself, taking its readers with it. Its prose verges on poetry or verse in Maurice Blanchot's sense: "Prose, a continuous line; verse, an interrupted line that turns about in a coming and going. . . . The first turn, the original structure of turning (which later slackens into a back and forth linear movement) is poetry."[1]

What is truly remarkable about Kawamata's novel, however, is that it deploys this simple yet powerful style to offer a vision of the history and politics of French surrealism; a surrealist genealogy of science fiction; a reflection on media networks and interpretive communities; an exploration of the power of words and sentences, of translation and transmission; and an entirely original and timely meditation on questions of sovereignty that pits surrealism against fascism, evoking André Breton against the political theorist of German fascism, Carl Schmitt, who appears as a mercenary in a future war on Mars. These dimensions of the novel all hinge on an experience of time, on a global yet multipronged transformation of received ways of articulating relations between space and time.

For instance, in addition to its twist on free indirect discourse, in which the magnification of punctuation allows for a subjective merging of characters that turns the headlong race to the end of the story back on itself, there are larger, more overt disturbances of the straightforward linear movement of time. The prologue begins near the end of the story, with Sakamoto, head of a special operations squad, tracking and killing a woman who is "afflicted" by a text titled "The Gold of Time." This is not an unfamiliar temporal disturbance. It is redolent of the generic unities of detective or suspense fiction in which the story begins with the crime and then returns to the events leading up to it. Indeed, the prologue of *Death Sentences* appears to introduce readers to the genre milieu of undercover drug enforcement, only to introduce a twist near the end: the dangerous "stuff" is not a narcotic, at least not of the usual sort. The narcotic stuff is a text, and for some reason the cop can't keep his nose out of it. The prologue, then, does not simply begin the story out of order in accordance with the dictates of the genre. It evokes and breaks genre expectations: instead of some familiar variation on drug wars, with a casually recursive gesture it offers us an enigmatic text, apparently more addictive and powerful than any drug. And now the leap to André Breton in Paris 1948 is not merely a matter of relating events out of sequence. It is not simply a matter of a scrambling of chronology or a shift in genre, say, jumping from a detective story to literary history. In a sense we are still in a detective story, but the killer that must be tracked down turns out to be a phantom poem, an incantatory verse. The text thus begins to turn around another text, spiraling into it, and anticipating the figure that dominates *Death Sentences*—the vortex.

The figure of vortex occurs in so many registers. Not only are the effects of the poem itself described as a vortex, but also the narrative structure and style inscribe vortices: the seemingly straightforward, rigidly structured lines of intrigue and expression gradually curve beneath us, folding back. Again, this is not primarily a matter of sudden plot twists. The straight line turns out in retrospect to have been curving all along. While the jump to Mars in the final chapter may seem to come out of the blue in narrative terms, not only has the text consistently foreshadowed the red skies of Mars, but the flight from Earth, like that of the soul from the body, also describes a trajectory that folds back on itself. What initially feels like a resolute departure or radical break brings us back to the body and to the earth. Our world is no longer described by the physical confines of a globe, of a sphere suspended in empty space around which we orbit. Our world is a space-time vortex.

Space travel, then, is a matter of neither instantaneous teleportation nor carefully engineered vehicles and trajectories. Souls lift from bodies only to be sucked into the gravity of other bodies, other worlds.

Still, it is one thing for a novel to insist on a figure such as a vortex. It is entirely another matter to afford an experience of our world as a vortex. This is the challenge of *Death Sentences*: beyond showing a vortex, beyond telling of a vortex, it strives for a "vortical experience." The novel thus introduces vortical effects at so many registers of the text—that of style (its take on free indirect discourse), of representation (the space-time vortex), of plot (a nonchronological presentation of events that allows the story to begin again), of pacing or timing (long stretches of waiting that do not advance the plot followed by rapid developments and omitted actions), of words (the use of puns or rebus-like words), and of the use of rebus-like characters (most obviously, Who May). By inscribing vortical effects in so many different registers, Kawamata's text takes on a kind of poetic force, which is not without risks. For, if we can evoke Blanchot's notion of poetry as an "original structure of turning," we might also recall Mikhail Bakhtin's critique of the "centripetal force" of poetry, whose monologism he contrasts to the centrifugal dialogism of the novel.[2] In other words, by using the same kinds of effects in different registers of the text, *Death Sentences* verges on pure isomorphism, making the prose feel somehow figural and poetic, yet by the same token (in Bakhtin's view), running the risk of eliminating a sense of dialogue, of engagement with otherness, and thus opportunities for dissent.

The novel ultimately doesn't eliminate dialogism and alterity but, as we will see, resituates it in relation to the military-industrial complex. Nonetheless, acknowledging the dangers implicit in the figural emphasis of the novel forces us to ask: What is the point of an experience of the vortex? Is it just a thrill, or a distraction? Or does it afford a new critical edge in fiction? Such questions lead directly to Kawamata's engagement with the politics of surrealism.

It is particularly in the use of rebus-like words that the novel engages surrealism. The largest instance is the name Who May, which not only appears to voice a query or permission in English but also works as a Chinese name (Hu Mei) and is subsequently complicated by a Japanese pun on the name as *fumei,* that is, unknown or anonymous (rendered *hu mei* in the translation to underscore the double entendre). The novel redoubles the oscillation implicit in the name Who May in broad and sometimes tendentious ways, describing the character, born of a Vietnamese mother and a French father, as poised between West and East, and even between feminine and masculine. Who May or Hu Mei comes to function as a verbal and visual cipher, and as a sexual and geographical enigma. In addition, when the editor Sakakibara, an expert on surrealism, launches his series of books on surrealism, each of the titles adopts a relatively common two-character term beginning with the sound *gen* and uses the character *gen* meaning illusion or phantom. Terms such as source (*genryū*), form (*genkei*), language (*gengo*), principle (*genron*), reality (*genjitsu*), present (*genzai*), and limit (*genkai*) are written with the character for illusion or phantom, resulting in a series of visual-verbal puns that resist smooth translation, for they implicate connotations of the illusory into each of these ordinary terms. English translation can only qualify the terms, for example, phantasmatic source, illusory form, visionary languages, hallucinatory principles, and so forth.

While such rebuses are evocative and resistant to translation, they are more clever than profound, and like André Breton in the novel, some readers may find it difficult to suppress a groan when Hu Mei writes his name in the air as Who May. It feels too clever, almost precious. But then such puns or rebuses are not intended of themselves to afford an experience of the vortex. In fact, it is their resistance to translation that in some sense disqualifies them. After all, the novel insists that the effects of the "death sentences," the lines of the prose poem that "kill" the reader (her earthly body at least), are eminently translatable. One exemplary instance of such effects, the word "dobaded" (*doubado*)—which is said to function as a noun, verb, or adjective—appears in the first poem by Who May, "Another World."

"Dobaded" is said to accomplish in the dimension of space what "The Gold of Time" produces in the dimension of time. Again, what is important is that such effects lend themselves to translation from the original French into Japanese or English. The novel does not gravitate toward a paradigm of the untranslatable, a paradigm that tends to confine the power of words to national languages, reducing literature to the parlor games of national sensibilities. The power of words, of poetry, of this novel, lies in the figural. We can give this figural force a name and a shape—vortex—but it is in fact a force that comes prior to words and images, arising in their interactions and in the gaps between them. Thus, as magical and phantasmatic as such a force might seem, it is entirely translatable. It is not entirely beyond our grasp. This is where *Death Sentences* takes up the mission of surrealism much as Peter Sloterdijk describes it, "to demonstrate a precise method to make it possible to master access to the 'unconscious.'"[3]

Sloterdijk stresses the objective and operative goals of surrealism, underscoring that "the point was to render the content of dreams and deliriums objective with the precisions of an old master."[4] This is a point worth emphasizing. We have become accustomed to thinking of surrealism in terms of a delirious stream of enigmatic words, unfiltered gestures, and incongruous images that somehow result in "convulsive beauty."[5] Naturally, characterizations of surrealist art often do confront the question of its objectivism, as in Michael Greenberg's formulation of "concentrated exactitude: faithfulness to reality turns reality into a dream of itself,"[6] and yet we generally approach surrealism in narrowly aesthetic terms, lingering on its dreamlike qualities, largely ignoring its operative, objective claims on reality. As such, Sloterdijk's shift in emphasis is welcome: "Surrealism ranks as a manifestation of the operativist 'revolution' which aimed at continually forging advancements in modernization."[7] And we begin to see how surrealism can be taken as a precursor of science fiction, as it is in *Death Sentences*.

If we gauge surrealism entirely in terms of an avant-garde resistance to, or critique of, modern mass culture, we miss its engagement with modernization, its willingness to work on the same ground, to occupy the same site as what might loosely be dubbed technoscientific modernity. While the idea of a poem with the power to kill, to detach the human soul from its body, might appear mawkish and predictable in some respects, it unequivocally establishes the stakes of the surrealist method: to produce an aesthetic object with the power to forge an advancement in modernization. This is precisely why the poems of Who May prove so dangerous, and why the paragons of surrealism in Kawamata's novel—Breton, Duchamp, Gorky—are at once fascinated and terrified by them. Although the poems are not exactly surrealist in a narrowly aesthetic sense, they are precisely surrealist in an operative sense. It is above all the operative dimension of surrealism that *Death Sentences* brings to the fore with its vortical experience of the phantasmatic poem.

In a review essay written on the occasion of the 2002 exhibition of surrealist art at the New York Metropolitan Museum of Art, James Fenton succinctly outlines the impasses of surrealist aesthetics.[8] He cites at length from "The 1934 Dialogue" between André Breton and Marcelle Ferry:

FERRY: What is beauty?
BRETON: It is an ethereal cry.
FERRY: What is mystery?
BRETON: It is the proud wind through a suburb.
FERRY: What is solitude?
BRETON: It is the queen sitting at the base of the throne.
FERRY: What is jealousy?
BRETON: It is a bugle on a laid table.
FERRY: What is debauchery?
BRETON: It is the place in the meadow where the grass suddenly becomes thicker. It can be seen from a long way off.[9]

As Fenton points out, for all the genuine poetic value that potentially emerges through this surrealist "trick" or "game," ultimately, the bugle on the laid table "could equally well stand for solitude, or mystery, or indeed beauty."[10] Likewise, the proud wind through a suburb could stand for jealousy, or debauchery, or even solitude. Kawamata places a similar critique in the mind of a university student, his character Misa in chapter 5, leafing through surrealist literature and scholarly work on it: "If everything were an instance of something, then anything could surely be anything. Then there wasn't anything that couldn't be explained." She concludes that it is all nonsense.

It is not surprising then that in *Death Sentences* Kawamata largely avoids the received, narrowly aesthetic gestures of surrealism. It has become painfully evident that many such aesthetic tricks and devices are so rote in popular culture that they may appear silly and shopworn. When the novel does play with "classic" surrealism, the moments are brief and generic, as in this citation from Who May's "Another World":

A fish. Dobaded. Its eyeball sliced down the middle. Sections quivering. Images reflected on the split lens are stained with blood. Dobaded. The city of people mirrored there is dyed madder red. Reversal of pressure, dobaded, and there you go! It's taking you there. . . .

What is more, we learn that the effect of this prose poem lies not in its generically surrealist incongruity and delirious images, but in the rhythmic qualities of the word "dobaded." In fact, Breton and Duchamp conclude that the poem's effects are a gimmick, a trick, and not really literature, not really art at all. But then isn't that precisely what surrealism in its operative dimension strove for?

Needless to say, these two dimensions of surrealist procedures—the operative and the aesthetic—are inseparable. They are more like tendencies. And what I have for the sake of simplicity called the (narrowly) aesthetic is really an emphasis on procedures of representation. If we approach surrealism primarily in terms of its style of representation, we will probably find that what once passed for gut-wrenching imagery, absurd juxtapositions, and deft verbiage today feel familiar and even hackneyed. This is no doubt why such procedures of representation largely drop out of *Death Sentences* in favor of the operative tendency of surrealism. Indeed, the readers of Who May's poems remain indifferent to the niceties of poetry, to avant-garde procedures of representation and depiction. Rather, they read for the rush, for the high—the vortical experience. In this respect, Kawamata's work also presents a significant departure from the strands of surrealist aesthetics that Japanese avant-garde artists unraveled and entwined in so many different ways across the twentieth century.[11] If the familiar aesthetic procedures of surrealism are nearly eliminated, it is surely because Kawamata, like the editor Sakakibara in this novel, studied surrealism in college, and he is well aware of the critiques and impasses of it. Indeed, in his exploration of André Breton's responses to other surrealist artists, and in his treatment of Sakakibara's concerns about the commercial renewal of surrealism in Japan, Kawamata touches on the very points that Fenton enumerates:

> Surrealism . . . gave a multitude of artists (painters, poets, photographers, and so forth) the opportunity to be part of something larger than themselves. It handed out badges that were gleefully worn. It also tore the stripes off its perceived renegades, for it was clamorously factional, politicized in the worst sense. Of all movements, it should have been most free (it was antibourgeois, it dealt with an unruly subconscious), but it had phases of willed instrumentality. It wanted, in such moments, to be good for society. It should have stuck with wanting to be bad for society.[12]

Fenton's recap brings us to the essential question: what would it take for surrealism to be bad for society today? This is the challenge to which *Death Sentences* responds, with an unusual hypothesis. What if there were a tendency, within surrealism or on its fringes, not entirely recognizable or acceptable to it, that in fact fulfilled its aims better than the surrealist movement itself? What if it were the "instrumentality" (the operative tendency) of surrealism and not its resistance to instrumentality that posed a challenge or even a danger to society?

Now, however, another challenge arises. If surrealism is to be bad for society, for what society, and in what historical context? After all, it is not possible or particularly productive to speak of society in general. And it is here that the preoccupation with French surrealism in the context of the German occupation of France during World War II in *Death Sentences* takes on new urgency. The novel lingers on the exile of Breton and fellow surrealists in New York during the war, posing questions about resistance to war, militarism, and fascism, which are extended into the postwar experience:

March 1946—
Breton returned to Paris.

The terrible reality of the postwar world immediately fell on him, swallowing him up.

The birth of the atomic bomb cast a cloud over humanity, darkening the end of the Great War.

His former comrades had split into various factions, some hostile and some friendly. Thus began the days that severely taxed Breton—battling for an applied surrealism while fighting against social realism, and then critically confronting a situation in which the return to power of those authorities who had collaborated with the Vichy government was simply ignored.

As such a passage attests, *Death Sentences* is highly specific in its vision of modern society. It is a dark vision of unrelenting and ever-expanding military destruction, in which the collaboration of political authorities and the complicity of artists with fascist regimes force Breton into a state of melancholy and despair. And, in keeping with the Japanese experience, the postwar era does not herald a luminous new world but a sense of deeper complicity with militarism. What can art do under such circumstances? Is it doomed to be simply inconsequential, or fated to be complicit in the mobilization of the masses and the destruction of the world?

In a sense, the last line of the novel provides a solution, adding the resolve of Sakamoto to the melancholia of Breton and the anguish of Who May, and arriving at a compound subject that looks back on the role of twentieth-century art not only with "an expression of sadness" but also with "a trace of satisfaction." Such a mixture of sadness and satisfaction seems to hinge on a paradox: the operative tendency of surrealism must be at once fully experienced and erased. The compound protagonist (Who May and Sakamoto) stops the "death sentences" by returning to the past and assuring that they are never written. In this respect, the novel may invite a Heideggerian or Derridean reading, as an instance of "surrealism under erasure," and with SF as the renewed yet eternally deferred promise of surrealist poetics. Still, it is the virtue of *Death Sentences,* as literature rather than political or literary treatise, that it prefers to stage these questions instead of providing a definitive answer, not even settling for a deconstructive answer such as "surrealism under erasure." In fact, the novel's staging of the politics of art in the era of global militarization runs counter to a reading centered on the play of presence/absence of the magic poem, in which the real experience of the poem never arrives. The novel appears determined to stage the real experience of that poem, to translate the vortical experience fully, even as it explores the poem's "condition of (im)possibility," to evoke a deconstructive turn of phrase. It strives for the reality and objectivity of surrealism, beyond its possibility or impossibility. And this is precisely how surrealism proves "bad for society."

The society in question is initially that of the surrealist group centered on André Breton, especially during the wartime years of exile in New York. Through Breton's eyes, we see a society of artists, writers, and intellectuals that entails both jealous rivalries and genuine friendships. To its credit, *Death Sentences* doesn't fall back on a spurious opposition between surrealism and militarism in terms of "art community" versus "military society." The surrealist group does not afford a model of community without alienation but presents a society with actual conflicts and discontents. And interesting enough, Who May and his poem certainly prove bad for this surrealist society. But how can a poem be bad for the militarized and mobilized society of total war?

Death Sentences presents an unusual take on questions about art and resistance. While the novel stresses Breton's resistance to the war, it does not entertain a vision of a social alternative to militarized society, and so it actually deepens the sense of the futility of resistance, and despair over the future of art. Even as the novel dwells on French resistance to Nazism or fascism, it avoids any idealization of resistance. In this unwillingness to idealize resistance, the novel seems to respond to Japanese legacies of understanding French resistance.

In the mid-to-late-nineteenth century, in Japan as elsewhere in the world, the French Revolution was naturally an important point of reference for democratic aspirations and political institutions. But it was especially in the wake of Japan's Fifteen-Year Asia-Pacific War (1941–45) and in the context of Japan's defeat and the American occupation (1945–52) that the political experiences of France took on new resonance. In the early postwar years, Doug Slaymaker remarks, "That France had 'won' and Japan had lost did not change the fact that both countries shared both hope and despair in the specters of defeat and occupation, shortages of food and housing, rationing, black markets, complicity, resentment, victimization, and defiance."[13]

Because of the sense of sharing with France an experience of defeat and occupation, the ideal of French wartime resistance proved compelling in postwar Japan. Take the example of the *Matinée poétique,* a group of Japanese scholars of French literature. During the war years, as Nishikawa Nagao tells us, its members "were able to maintain a sensibility and a manner of thinking which was opposed to militarism."[14] Yet if Nishikawa also stresses the general antipathy toward this group, it is because their opposition to militarism largely took the form of an elitist and culturalist sentimentality that avoided dealing directly with the realities of the war. As one of the *Matinée poétique* group's more renowned members, Katō Shūichi, later remarked, "those of us who had lived through the war were very much surprised, indeed shocked, when we learned of the existence of the French *litterature de la résistance,* even during France's occupation by the Nazis."[15] In this way, the idea of French wartime resistance, so strategically promoted by de Gaulle and meticulously explored in postwar French literature and thought, became something of an ideal in postwar Japan, and Japanese writers and thinkers began to gauge their wartime experience in terms of that ideal, asking why there had been no literature of resistance in Japan. There were even efforts to produce such a literature retroactively. But such literature has subsequently met with harsh criticism, as with Nishikawa's assessment of Katō Shūichi's novel, *Aru hareta hi ni* (One fine day, serialized in 1949): "To write a 'Resistance novel' after the war is already over is a pathetic joke."[16]

Nonetheless, the ideal of French resistance encouraged an ideal of antiestablishment individualism in Japan, which afforded a critical alternative to the hegemonic model of U.S. democracy. The American model lost considerable credibility during the "reverse course" of the American occupation in the early 1950s as capitalism came to take precedence over democratic aspirations, quite brutally. Thus the ideal of French resistance in postwar Japan served to open questions about the political role of artists and intellectuals, not only in the past under the Japanese empire, but also in the present in the context of Japanese collaboration with American imperial aspirations in East Asia.

While *Death Sentences* shares this legacy of engagement with French wartime resistance, it does not hold it up as an ideal to be emulated. Instead, it imbues resistance with a sense of impotence and failure, dealing with artists who experience the war as if at a great distance, who struggle yet doubt their very efforts. This is partly because the novel's point of reference is surrealism not existentialism, and artists who found refuge in New York rather than those who remained in France. But more important, by the time *Death Sentences* appeared in the mid-1980s, the combination of the Japanese economic miracle and the ascendency of the United States in East Asia made for a situation in which the nature of resistance had to be seriously reconsidered. There was widespread dissatisfaction with the maintenance of American military bases in Japan, the political stranglehold of the Liberal Democratic Party (initially leveraged into power by the United States), and the continual undermining and compromising of national sovereignty, and yet it seemed impossible to argue with prosperity, regardless of its hidden costs. This is what Takayuki Tatsumi refers to in his foreword as "Pax Japonica."

The resistance of the editor Sakakibara exemplifies this new situation of Pax Japonica that propped itself up on Pax Americana: where Breton strives to challenge fascism by working with the Voice of America and sustaining the surrealist movement in exile and after the war, Sakakibara resists the inroads of corporate capital by founding a publishing house devoted to publishing high-quality works, especially literature in translation, and eschewing large runs and profits. Significantly, however, like Breton's, Sakakibara's resistance may be said to fail, or at least to meet with serious compromise. Offered the windfall of working with recently discovered surrealist materials and mounting a major retrospective exhibition with a massive budget, Sakakibara ends up working within the very circuits that he has previously resisted.

If the novel avoids making Breton or Sakakibara into heroic agents of resistance, however, it is in order to work through resistance and historical transformation at another level. In keeping with the surrealist interest in the unconscious, the novel shows something at work behind the conscious efforts of these characters. For instance, although Sakakibara would surely never publish the "death sentences" of the phantom poem if he had looked at them rationally and consciously, everything conspires to make him an unwitting collaborator in the mass dissemination of these poems. Similarly, by locking away Who May's poems, Breton actually transmits them to future generations, instead of taking them out of circulation. The novel invites us to consider these actions on two levels. On the one hand, we may read them in terms of the subconscious desires of individuals: Breton and Sakakibara covertly want to put the poem in circulation. On the other hand, the novel also insists on metaphors of contagion and epidemic and stresses the materiality of different modes of distribution and circulation of texts. The poem spreads by way of a kind of media contagion. In sum, the poem entails an unconscious agency, one that does not belong to anyone in particular, and that operates at a very fine level of materiality—a sort of media unconscious.

Interestingly enough, it is not the newest mode of media distribution that proves effective in getting the poem to people. In the surrealist era, it is handwritten copies rather than typewritten pages that circulate it most effectively. Years later, as police crack down on photocopy machines, mimeographs become an effective means of distribution. Similarly, it is fan-recorded cassette tapes of concerts rather than studio-recorded albums that reach the largest audience. In other words, it is not the fastest, latest, or even dominant modes of media distribution that prove operative, but residual modes or nonmainstream circuits. The residual or outmoded continually eludes control and slips through the cracks.

Moreover, these residual circuits are frequently associated with what today might be dubbed subcultures or fan cultures: Who May's poem makes the rounds of rock fans, SF fans, and school clubs, which invite us retrospectively to look at literary societies or art circles as precursors of contemporary fan cultures. And *Death Sentences* seems especially prescient in its portrayal of educators and bureaucrats referring to the effects of the poem on the young in terms of "fatal autism." In contemporary Japan, fans whose consumption is deemed excessive are frequently pathologized as suffering from social withdrawal syndrome, multiple personality disorder, or autism. Those who read the poem experience a vortex, but those who witness the affliction see a fatal shutting down of the self within itself. To the uninitiated, the vortex looks like autism.

Although *Death Sentences* does not necessarily provide a sympathetic portrait of such fans, it makes clear that small, informal, residual networks of distribution and interpretation are genuinely a force to be reckoned with. And it is their residual materiality that affords resistance to those authorities who strive to control the force of the poem's spell, the operative unconscious itself. Such residual materiality plays a crucial role in reversing the effects of the poem as well: Who May cannot return to the past because he has become completely disembodied, while Sakamoto's soul still feels the pull of physical bodies, gravitating toward them. Resistance, then, lies in the lingering materiality of the soul that continues to feel the gravity of bodies, remembering their attraction.

Ultimately, then, resistance in *Death Sentences* is not the property of individuals but is an unconscious material force. As with the disease vector of the poem, it cannot be grasped or contained. Yet it is precisely what must be stopped, for it threatens to destroy the world, to bring about the apocalypse. There are, however, very different kinds of relation to the end of time in *Death Sentences,* and the novel explores different ways of "stopping" the poem, which are at once different relations to the unconscious and different political responses. This is where the politics of surrealism truly come into play. Although the resistance of individual characters does not present a political solution (alternative societies are too easily swept away by totalitarian formations), their resistance does set up a political orientation. In the first context of surrealism (Breton), militarism comes to the fore as the enemy (Nazism, fascism), and in the second (Sakakibara), the emphasis falls on resistance to corporate capitalism (Pax Japonica, Pax Americana). But as foreshadowed in the prologue to the novel, militarism and corporate capitalism turn out to be two faces of the same foe. And on Mars in 2131, this foe—militarized capitalism or corporate militarism—has reached its peak.

While the leap of the story to Mars may feel abrupt, it follows directly, even logically, from the prior political orientations, making them explicit. The story follows the Martian Guard as it exterminates the population of a settlement—provocatively called the Golgi Camp—where an English translation of the Japanese version of Who May's French poem has already contaminated the inhabitants. The Martian Guard is a corporate enterprise, an extralegal militia, all about profit, doing whatever it takes to keep the peace. But the peace here is the peace of commerce, of diminishing obstacles to flows of capital: "Ultimately, the raison d'être of the Martian Guard lay in maintaining this felicitous relation between supply and demand, and, if possible, enhancing it. In a word, it was a matter of population adjustment through extermination."

Thus the underlying political contrast of the novel comes into focus: not just Breton's resistance to fascism and militarization, not just Sakakibara's resistance to the rise of postwar corporate capital, but the two folded together against a compound enemy, corporate militarism on Mars. A compound (French-Japanese surrealism) faces the military-industrial complex. And consonant with the Japanese reception of French resistance in the postwar era, the situation on Mars can be seen as the continuation of a tendency within postwar Pax Americana. Mars, the New World, pushes the American combination of multiculturalism, militarism, and corporate hegemony to its limits. Still, the novel is not anti-American. Rather, it is deeply concerned with articulating resistance to a political tendency within modern societies that becomes pronounced in the American political model. As the appearance of Carl Schmitt indicates, *Death Sentences* is ultimately concerned with the subordination of politics and thus war to the dictates of commerce.

A German Catholic political and legal theorist whose theories served as an ideological foundation for dictatorship and the totalitarian state, especially for the Nazi Führer, Carl

Schmitt and his theorization of the "state of emergency" or "state of exception" have received greater attention in recent years, not of course for the endorsement of totalitarianism, but for the potential critique of the permanent state of crisis in the contemporary world. The rediscovery or renewed interest in the dialogue between Walter Benjamin and Schmitt has been particularly important. While some recent discussions may be accused of intensifying and even exaggerating the connection between Benjamin and Schmitt,[17] Giorgio Agamben (among others) has shown that the two men were clearly familiar with each other's work and has argued persuasively that they share a theorization of the modern state, even if their political responses to it are almost diametrically opposed.[18]

What, then, is the basis for Schmitt's theorization of the state of exception? Udi Greenberg writes:

> In his famous critique of liberalism and the parliamentary system, Schmitt argued that the two confused politics with the logic of commerce, and sought to subordinate the former to the latter. . . . The central position occupied in the liberal system by free and open discussion represented its naïve aspiration to transcend the political grouping of friend and enemy, which to Schmitt's eyes was the basic principle of human organization.[19]

As a consequence of its unwillingness to take seriously the distinction between ally and opponent, the liberal system, in Schmitt's opinion, had lost the ability to put a limit on conflicts, resulting in the rise of generalized, unlimited military conflicts, a sort of war of all against all, which Schmitt also saw as an end of the world, the end of time, apocalypse: "As a result of British dominance in the world, the possibility of conducting a limited, organized political conflict would be destroyed, to be replaced by chaos and fear of total, never-ending war."[20]

In addition, Schmitt argued that as the logic of commerce (open and free exchange) assumed dominance over and dictated the logic of politics (friend versus enemy), conflict would no longer depend on rationally identifying one's opponents but on irrational and generalized criminalization. The result is rather like the blurring of peace and war that occurs in George Orwell's *1984*, another source for *Death Sentences*, in which the object of conflict perpetually shifts: "We're at war with Eurasia. We've always been at war with Eastasia." Or is it in fact Africa? The target of Orwell's critique is, of course, socialism rather than liberalism, but if we wish to take seriously the challenge of Orwell, Schmitt, Benjamin, and Kawamata, we should avoid the fashion for criminalizing particular social or political formations and think instead in terms of a political tendency within modern social formations. Both Schmitt and Benjamin thought of this tendency in terms of a permanent state of emergency, or state of exception, in which conflicts were continually posed as a crisis of the law, or outside the law. It fell to Benjamin to stress that under such conditions, instead of a limited, rationally limitable conflict between allies and enemies, conflict now settled on an unlimited conflict between the police and the criminal. Thus, as Agamben in particular has emphasized in recent years, sovereignty, constituted to operate outside the law, then comes to reside in a new agency—the sovereign police, which is not the police in the limited sense of the local police force but police in the sense of special police operations and extralegal military forces. In sum, the generalization of the state of exception results in the globalization of a "law" of commerce that operates primarily through the perpetuation of unlimited conflict between military forces unconstrained by law and criminalized others who are also placed outside the law and thus subject to unchecked exploitation and extermination.

This is precisely the political tendency that *Death Sentences* pushes to an extreme on Mars, as the Japanese policeman Sakamoto (head of a special operations force likened to Japan's wartime *tokkō*, or Special Higher Police, so named by how it operates outside the law) enters into the body of the leader of a unit of the Martian Guard, Carl Schmitt. Those afflicted by the poem fall outside the law. The disease of the poem spreads too quickly to deal with them politically, medically, or legally, that is, rationally. The afflicted are to be exterminated as quickly and efficiently as possible but are in the meantime available for exploitation. They have become what Agamben glosses as "bare life" or "naked life." Thus sovereignty comes to operate outside the law in a new way, not through the agency or in the figure of the monarch, but through that of the sovereign police—as with the renewed special police in Japan or the Martian Guard.

From the point of view of the sovereign police, then, the poem appears as a windfall, for it will always escape control, thus ceaselessly opening new opportunities for exploitation and extermination. The poem promises to keep them in business, strengthening the partnership of free trade and war. This is because even though the poem threatens an apocalypse, corporate militarism acts to defer the end of time for as long as possible. The political relation, then, is one of perpetual crisis on the edge of apocalypse, expanding the sovereignty of special operations while stripping humans of all qualities, rendering them nothing but bare life. Agamben argues that this is the contemporary truth of both liberalism and fascism, the truth that Schmitt's theory exposed yet avoided: where Schmitt felt that a dictator or totalitarian state might stand against this tendency, such a bid for sovereignty only reinforced the tendency that Schmitt detected within the empire of commerce—the tendency toward the sovereign police, the German Gestapo, or the Japanese *tokkō,* eking out the apocalypse.

In *Death Sentences* Kawamata does not rest content with staging the sovereignty of the police, however. He offers another relation to the poem and to the end of time. This relation does not stand in opposition to the sovereign police in the sense of presenting a different political condition or alternative society. It accepts or at least seems to agree that this is indeed the contemporary condition. Yet it tries to seize the temporal and historical implications of this modernity differently. Clearly, the poem's operation must be stopped rather than endlessly deferred, but that stopping must not be an ending, in the sense of an end of days, or apocalypse. A different relation to time is in order, neither endless expansion in space (what Benjamin called "empty homogeneous time") nor the end of time (apocalypse). If Walter Benjamin's account of modern time comes to mind here, it is not only because it stands as a response to Schmitt, but also because, like Kawamata Chiaki, Benjamin grapples with surrealism. As Michael Lowry writes, " 'Fascination' is the only term that does justice to the intensity of the feelings Walter Benjamin experienced when he discovered surrealism in 1926–27. His very efforts to escape the spell of the movement founded by André Breton and his friends are an expression of the same fascination. As we know, it was this discovery that gave birth to the 'Paris Arcades' project."[21] By way of surrealism and Marxism, Benjamin arrived at the notion of a "revolutionary spell" that might be found in the everyday life of the city.

Like Benjamin's Arcades project, Kawamata's *Death Sentences* strives to grasp spells, dreams, and magic from their revolutionary side, to find a spell that would be truly bad for society, that is, bad for the modern tendency toward an apocalyptic, "free and open" commerce of endless expansion and empty time. Significantly, in Kawamata's book it is the compound character of Sakamoto and Who May who discovers another relation to the poem's fatal magic spell. Rather than stop the poem's force, Sakamoto/Who May uses it to return to the past and create a time line in which Who May does not write the poem. In fact, Who May is no longer simply Who May. Thus the novel produces a vortex of the poetic vortex, which folds the apocalyptic force of its temporality back on itself. The novel then consists of two time lines, vortically entwined. Such a move recalls Benjamin's notion of weak Messianic force. Rather than embrace the strong or grand Messianic event (apocalypse) or try to prevent it (endless empty deferral), the goal is to find a weak version of Messianic time in the everyday, in the profane. In the compound rebus-like character of Who May (too weak) and Sakamoto (too strong), *Death Sentences* arrives at a vortical force of perfect weakness.

As Susan Buck-Morss writes, "Benjamin was at least convinced of one thing: what was needed was a visual, not a linear logic: The concepts were to be imagistically constructed, according to the cognitive principles of montage. Nineteenth-century objects were to be made visible as the origin of the present, at the same time that every assumption of progress was to be scrupulously rejected."[22] Is this not precisely the logic of the "undiscovered century" in *Death Sentences*? Twentieth-century surrealist objects become visible as the origin of the present, without any assumption of progress, of linearity. Yet this twentieth-century concept is not that of montage but that of the vortex. And within the accelerated linearity of that everyday literary form, popular genre fiction, Kawamata Chiaki finds a source of disruption, apparently weak, but just disruptive enough to make us discover the total historical event of our modernity, turning around a lost and maybe never written poem. It is the force of the dialectical image or revolutionary spell. It is the time of the vortex.

NOTES

Foreword

1. Philip K. Dick, *Martian Time-Slip,* trans. Obi Fusa (Tokyo: Hayakawa, 1980), 341. Originally translated into Japanese in 1966.

2. Ibid., chapter 10.

3. *Death Sentences,* chapter 1, "Another World," emphasis mine.

4. Nishiwaki Junzaburō, "Surrealist Poetics," trans. Hosea Hirata, reprinted in *The Poetry and Poetics of Nishiwaki Junzaburō: Modernism in Translation* (Princeton, N.J.: Princeton University Press, 1993), 9, 27, 39.

5. Gene Van Troyer and Grania Davis, *Speculative Japan: Outstanding Tales of Japanese Science Fiction and Fantasy* (Fukuoka: Kurodahan Press, 2007).

6. Kawamata, "Yume no kotoba, kotoba no yume" (Dream words, word dreams) (Tokyo: Kiso-Tengai Publishing, 1981), later reprinted as a paperback in 1983 by Hayakawa Publishing.

7. Ibid., 163.

8. Tony Tanner, *City of Words: American Fiction, 1950–70* (New York: Harper and Row, 1971); Susan Stewart, *Nonsense: Aspects of Intertextuality in Folklore and Literature* (Baltimore: Johns Hopkins University Press, 1979).

9. Kawamata, "Jushō no kotaba" (Acceptance speech), *Tokuma's SF Adventure* (January 1985): 13.

10. Aritsune Toyota, "Daigokai Nihon SF Taishō senkō hōkoku" (Selection report on the winner of the 5th Japan SF Grand Prize), *Tokuma's SF Adventure* (January 1985): 14–15.

11. Takayuki Tatsumi, "Kaisetsu," in Kawamata's *Genshi-gari* (Tokyo: Chūō kōron, 1985), 383–92.

12. Ezra F. Vogel, *Japan as Number One: Lessons for America* (Cambridge, Mass.: Harvard University Press, 1979).

13. Marilyn Ivy, "Critical Texts, Mass Artifacts: The Consumption of Knowledge in Postmodern Japan," in *Postmodernism and Japan,* ed. Masao Miyoshi and H. D. Harootunian (Durham, N.C.: Duke University Press, 1989), 26.

14. Ibid., 33.

Afterword

Special thanks to Brian Bergstrom, Adrienne Hurley, Christine LaMarre, and J. Keith Vincent for their detailed corrections, suggestions, and enthusiasm.

1. Maurice Blanchot, *The Infinite Conversation,* trans. Susan Hanson (Minneapolis: University of Minnesota Press, 1993), 30.

2. Mikhail Bakhtin, *The Dialogic Imagination,* trans. Caryl Emerson and Michael Holquist (Austin: University of Texas Press, 1981), 270–73.

3. Peter Sloterdijk, *Terror from the Air,* trans. Amy Patton and Steve Corcoran (Los Angeles: Semiotexte, 2009), 76.

4. Ibid.

5. André Breton, *Nadja* (Paris: Gallimard, 1928): "Beauty will be convulsive or will not be at all."

6. Michael Greenberg, "The Novelist Who Can't Be Stopped," *New York Review of Books,* 13 January 2011, www.nybooks.com/articles/archives/2011/jan/13/novelist-who-cant-be-stopped/. Accessed May 2011.

7. Sloterdijk, *Terror,* 77.

8. James Fenton, "Shock Absorbed," *New York Review of Books,* 23 May 2002, www.nybooks.com/articles/archives/2002/may/23/shock-absorbed/. Accessed May 2011.

9. "The 1934 Dialogue" between André Breton and Marcelle Ferry is quoted from Jennifer Mundy, *Surrealism: Desire Unbound* (Princeton, N.J.: Princeton University Press, 2001), 21. Because I am working with Fenton's point here, I follow him in omitting some examples between these latter two.

10. Fenton, "Shock Absorbed."

11. For an account in English of prewar and postwar surrealism in Japan, see Miryam Sas, *Fault Lines: Cultural Memory and Japanese Surrealism* (Stanford, Calif.: Stanford University Press, 1999); and Sas, *Experimental Arts in Postwar Japan* (Cambridge, Mass.: Harvard University Asia Center, 2011).

12. Fenton, "Shock Absorbed."

13. Doug Slaymaker, "Confluences: An Introduction," in *Confluences: Postwar Japan and France,* ed. Doug Slaymaker (Ann Arbor: Center for Japanese Studies, University of Michigan, 2002), 5.

14. Nishikawa Nagao, "France in Japan: An Essay on the *Matinée poétique* Group," in *Confluences: Postwar Japan and France,* 71.

15. Katō Shūichi, "Thinking beyond Parallel Traditions: Literature and Thought in Postwar Japan and France," in *Confluences: Postwar Japan and France,* 54.

16. Nishikawa, "France in Japan," 82.

17. Udi E. Greenberg, "Criminalization: Carl Schmitt and Walter Benjamin's Concept of Criminal Politics," *Journal of European Studies* 39, no. 3 (2009): 306–307.

18. Giorgio Agamben, *State of Exception,* trans. Kevin Attel (Chicago: University of Chicago Press, 2005), 53–54.

19. Greenberg, "Criminalization," 308.

20. Ibid., 310.

21. Michael Lowry, "Walter Benjamin and Surrealism: The Story of a Revolutionary Spell," *Radical Philosophy* (November/December 1996): 1.

22. Susan Buck-Morss, *The Dialectics of Seeing: Walter Benjamin and the Arcades Project* (Cambridge, Mass.: MIT Press, 1989), 218.

KAWAMATA CHIAKI has written many critically and popularly acclaimed science fiction novels, including *Hanzaishi no kagami* (Mirror of an antiexistent soldier); *Kaseijin senshi* (A prehistory of Martians); and *Kasei kōkakudan* (Martian armored-suit army) and its sequel *Wairudo mashin* (Wild machine). *Death Sentences,* originally published in Japanese as *Genshi-gari,* received the Japanese SF Grand Prize in 1985.

THOMAS LAMARRE is professor of East Asian studies and communication studies at McGill University. His books include *The Anime Machine: A Media Theory of Animation* (Minnesota, 2009) and *Uncovering Heian Japan: An Archaeology of Sensation and Inscription.* He is on the editorial board of *Mechademia.*

KAZUKO Y. BEHRENS is assistant professor of developmental psychology at Texas Tech University.

TAKAYUKI TATSUMI is professor of English at Keio University and the author of several books, including, most recently, *Full Metal Apache: Transactions between Cyberpunk Japan and Avant-Pop America.*